Da

MW00901621

To all those who know that a battle
will leave scars,
but do it anyway — with love.

Dedicated to Frank
who rides the "crazy train"
with me every day.

Thank you to Shawn
for the spectacular cover.

Cover Photo by Shawn Adair
http://shawnadair.com

A percentage of all sales from this book will go towards
programming for adults with autism.
www.theartswithgrace.org

1

Joan
God Bless
Melissa Camphill Rowe

Dance of Joy

Published by Melissa Campbell Rowe

Copyright 2015 Clark Campbell Company

Chapter 1

Meredith Howard's eye was almost swollen shut. She held a baggy filled with ice to her eye as she hurried into the emergency room pulling her young son behind her. She signed in and plopped down in a chair near the nurse's station. The boy didn't sit by her, but instead walked down the long line of chairs, stopping to look out of the corner of his eye at each chair. He finally positioned himself at the other end of the waiting area in a burnt orange corner chair.

A man rushed into the waiting room and marched straight to Meredith. "Where is he?" he asked breathlessly as he raked his brown hair back with both hands. He needed to see the boy.

Meredith motioned to the chair across the room. Ten-year-old Tucker sat playing a Nintendo DS game. The boy didn't look up.

Jeff cupped his hands over his mouth and inhaled deeply and exhaled slowly. He felt his heart slow to a regular beat. He sat down near Meredith on one of the orange plastic chairs that lined the waiting room. He smiled slightly as he looked at the boy enjoying the handheld video game. Jeff looked back at his wife. Worry lines returned to his forehead."Let me see your eye."

Meredith winced as she removed the bloodied dish towel and cold baggy half-filled with ice and half-filled with water. Jeff squinted his eyes and held his mouth slightly opened as he took a wary look at the cut. "It's not too bad. It definitely needs a stitch or two."

She eased the ice bag back onto her eye. Jeff's face still held a grimace. He was about to speak when the nurse called Meredith's name. Meredith stood, but Jeff remained seated as he watched the nurse swipe her badge in front of a black panel and Meredith followed, disappearing behind the double doors. Jeff yelled to Meredith as the doors were closing, "I'll stay here with Tuck." He went down and sat by Tucker. "How are you, Tuck?" Jeff asked.

No answer.

Meredith's head pounded as she took each step. The papered exam table looked like an oasis for a needed nap. She laid back and relaxed as her head sank into the pillow on the exam table. She closed her good eye. The other one was swollen shut. Her body begged her to sleep. The doctor's voice startled her when he spoke, but Meredith kept her eyes closed. She resented being woke up.

"Mrs. Howard," the doctor said, "let's see what's behind the ice bag."

Meredith wanted to respond. She willed her eyes to open.

"Mrs. Howard," the doctor said louder.

Her hands finally obeyed. She kept both her eyes closed as she removed the bag.

"I need to get a look at your eye if possible. Bear with me."

Meredith inhaled a deep breath to counteract the pressure and pain. When the light passed over her eye, she made an audible groan.

"I'm not able to get a good look at the surface of your eye. Were you able to see out of the eye before all the swelling began?"

"I think so . . . maybe. . . I don't know. It happened so fast."

"This will be cold, but I'm just going to clean it up a bit. There will be a pinch and then a slight burn."

Meredith braced for the injection pain. It was quick and then she relaxed. She could feel the tugs on her eyebrow.

"The scar will barely be visible because the cut follows the bottom of your eyebrow so closely. You're lucky. I'm going to get an X-ray and CT scan to check your eye for any damage or glass fragments. You're also lucky because for a Friday night, we're not busy at all. This shouldn't take long. The technician should be here shortly and then I'll be back and we will go over the results before you leave."

Meredith nodded and continued to lie on the table with her eyes closed, thankful that she didn't have to get up and leave. Lying still with her eyes shut eased the pounding in her head. The phone in her hand vibrated and lit up as a message from Jeff blinked onto the screen. She dutifully raised the phone to her face and squinted at the screen with her one good eye. *Call me when the doctor leaves appeared* in a balloon on the screen of her phone. She clicked Jeff's name. He answered on the first ring.

"What did the doctor say?"

"The doctor said I was lucky twice. Seemed strange. I'm all stitched up and I'm waiting for an X-ray and CT scan."

"Are you going to be okay?" Jeff asked but didn't wait for an answer. "I'm going to take Tuck home. He's getting restless and it's getting late and I can still get the bedtime routine completed and get everyone in bed at a decent hour. I guess the girls are at the house together?"

"Yeah. Isabelle was crying when I left," Meredith said. She leaned up on her elbows looking around for something to drink.

"Okay, call me when you're done and I'll come back and get you or call me if anything changes."

She clicked end on the phone. When the nurse came into the room, she asked, "Can I get some water?"

"I'm sorry. I can't give you anything just in case they need to take you to surgery."

"Surgery?"

"After the test we'll know more and I can get you something then."

"Can you turn the light out?" Meredith asked weakly and was surprised when the nurse said sure. The nurse pulled some cords and left on an indirect light and flipped off the overhead light. Meredith immediately dosed off.

"Come on, Tuck," Jeff said and took Tucker by the hand as

5

they exited the emergency room. Tucker continued to play the DS on the ten-minute drive back to the house.

Jeff saw Myla peeking out the curtains when he pulled into the driveway. She ran and gave him a hug when he came in the house. "Is Mom okay?"

He nodded and kissed her on the top of her head. "Are you okay?"

She nodded as she bit her bottom lip.

"Where are the other girls?" he asked.

"Clare's in bed. Isabelle is here somewhere."

Tucker walked over to the couch and sat down without looking up from the DS. Jeff surveyed the house. Myla had cleaned up after the chaos. There were a couple drops of blood on the floor near the sink in the kitchen. The trash overflowed with a bloody dish towel, broken vase, and bent flowers.

Jeff went upstairs into Clare's pink bedroom. He picked up a pink and a yellow pillow from the floor and placed it on a chair draped with something that he thought must be a homemade butterfly net. It had a pillow case taped to a hanger with duct tape. The middle of the room held a circle of rocks. A pink teapot with cups and saucers balanced on a flat rock. Jeff smiled and thought, *camping in style*.

Clare was already asleep. With the precision of a father with three girls, Jeff unclipped the no-nonsense barrette holding back her blonde bangs. No decorated barrettes for this girl. He took her glasses off and placed them on the table by her bed. Her seven-year-old self was tucked up under the covers, breathing the deep breaths of peaceful sleep. Jeff kissed her forehead. She didn't stir at all. Her peaceful face held Jeff's attention. He watched her sleep until he heard a bang from downstairs. He waited. No other sound came, but he got up to go check. Just then the light from the hall came on and the room brightened. Isabelle and Myla stood in the doorway—silent—in their nightgowns, looking up at him. He whispered to the girls. "Mom is going to be fine. She will be home in a little bit. Have you brushed your teeth?"

They nodded.

"Let's get you two in bed. I need to get Tuck down."

"It's only 8 o'clock," Myla whined, "I'm not even tired. I don't have to go to bed until 10:30. Besides, it's not a school night."

Jeff groaned, "It seems much later."

"Tucker hit Mommy with the vase," Isabelle chimed in with tears in her eyes, but the tears did not spill onto her cheeks. "I just wanted to watch Beauty and the Beast, not that old video of Star Wars again."

"It's okay. It's not your fault. You did great staying here with Myla and Clare. Mommy is going to be fine. It's not that bad."

"It looked really bad. There was a lot of blood," Myla stated with the maturity of an adult.

"It's not that bad. The doctor even said she was lucky because no glass got in her eye. I need to get Tuck started on his bedtime. You two can stay up."

The girls smiled at each other at the victory.

Jeff returned to the living room where he found Tucker still sitting on the couch playing the DS. "Time for bed, Tuck. Go take your bath." Tucker got up and walked into the bathroom. "Use soap, shampoo, and then rinse yourself off," Jeff reminded Tucker. Jeff stood in the hall; he pressed his back against the wall and slid down until he was sitting on the floor just listening to Tucker singing in the tub. When the water shut off, Tucker came out, mostly dry, with his pajamas on. Jeff tucked his son into bed, kissed him on the forehead, flipped out the lights in the room, plugged the DS in for charging, and left the door opened just a little.

Then Jeff went into the kitchen, wiped up the drops of dried blood, scoured the sink, and took the trash out to the curb, effectively ridding the house of the proof of destruction. He poured himself a glass of lukewarm water—no ice—and sat down on the steps, waiting. He stared out into the dark yard at nothing in particular. He just waited and listened for any unusual noises from the house.

◆ ◆

The doctor returned to the exam room with Meredith's test results.

"You are a lucky woman, Mrs. Howard," he told Meredith. No broken occipital bone. No permanent damage to the eye. Just a prescription to manage the pain."

"Thanks," Meredith said and took the prescription and stuffed it into her jean's pocket knowing she wouldn't fill it. She had no time to be disoriented by pain medication.

"How did you happen to get the black eye and gash?"

"It was an accident."

"What kind of accident?"

"Just the ordinary kind. My son knocked over a vase. He's a boy. Accidents happen."

"This seems severe for a knocked over vase."

"He was mad, but he didn't mean for it to hit me. He's just all boy. He's ten."

"Okay. Well, try to avoid any more ordinary accidents," the doctor said and patted her leg twice.

Back in the waiting room, Meredith pulled out her phone to call Jeff. It rang, but he didn't answer. *Please answer*, she thought. She sat in the burnt orange corner chair that Tucker had been sitting in and called Jeff again. *Please, please pick up.* Realizing she was on her own, she thought, *Well, I drove myself here, I might as well drive myself home.* On the drive to the ER, she had adrenaline to get her there, but on the way home, her throbbing head screamed at each bump.

Jeff was sitting on the front porch steps in the dark when Meredith pulled up. He squinted his eyes as the headlights glared in his face. Meredith stepped onto the driveway feeling off balance and woozy. Jeff jumped up, ran to her, and put his arm around her. She leaned into him. Jeff said, "I thought you were going to call?"

"I did. But you didn't answer."

His face went blank. "Oh, my phone's in the house," he said and then scolded her. "You should have called the house phone, Myla would have answered." He started giving his report. "Clare's asleep. Myla and Isabelle are awake. And Tuck has had his bath and is in bed. I took out the trash."

"How's Tucker?"

"He's fine but not remorseful at all. He didn't make the connection. It'll be interesting to see if he says anything when he sees your eye. When I was about Tuck's age, I thumped my sister in the forehead with a golf club that I was swinging around in the yard and she has the scar to prove it. I never saw her, but I felt really bad about it. But Tuck, he didn't even ask me how you were."

"I know. After he hit me, Isabelle started screaming and I ran to the kitchen sink. He just put in the video that started the fight. I don't know. Maybe it's a boy thing?"

"No, it's not."

Chapter 2

Jeff handed Meredith a glass of water and two over-the-counter pain relievers. Then they laid down on the bed both staring at the ceiling. "What happened this time? What was the trigger?"

Meredith exhaled and gritted her teeth attempting to stop the pain in her head and then she went through the events of the night. "There was no trigger. It just happened. He is out of control. I was in the kitchen fixing dinner not ten feet away when the shouting match broke out. I got in the living room just in time to see Tucker clear the coffee table of the magazines, but then he stopped. I thought for a moment it was done. So, I bent down to retrieve the magazines, and that is when he threw the vase. I was close and he was angry. Who knew someone could get so angry over Beauty and the Beast? Anyway, Isabelle was horrified and began screaming. I made it to the kitchen sink and knew I was going to need a stitch or two. Myla came running in to help me. Then, she calmed down Isabelle and I wrestled Tucker to the car. You know the rest."

Jeff didn't reply. He just mumbled, "Hmm. Well, he did have a trigger. He wanted to watch Star Wars and Isabelle wouldn't let him."

"That's no reason — no real reason," she said enunciating every word. In her mind she kept seeing the look of horror on Isabelle's face. She saw Myla spring into the fight or flight mode to help her. No teenager should have the skills for disaster honed like Myla did. "It's getting harder to control Tucker. His outbursts have gotten worse. He's getting so big and is so physical. You realize he is almost as tall as me now. I'm not sure I'm going to be able to handle him much longer."

"And then what?" Jeff asked with an irritated edge to his voice.

"I don't know. I guess you'll have to handle him. It's just . . . when he acts so impulsively, I wish I could get him to stop and think before he does something that he . . . I mean I'm . . . going to regret later. It's hard to admit, but I think we might need professional help. This is so hard. It's too hard. I just feel like a—"

"You're not a failure," Jeff interrupted. "He is just a boy. He is just like a bull on steroids in a china shop. All boys go through an awkward phase."

They heard banging on the wall coming from Tucker's room. They quit talking and just stared, listened, and waited. Neither one moved.

"Get some rest. I'll go see." Jeff walked soundlessly on the balls of his feet downstairs to Tucker's room and listened outside of the door. There were no more noises, but he still waited in the hall. *Oh, Tuck, what are we going to do with you?* he whispered to himself. He looked across the hall to Myla and Isabelle's room. He peeked in and saw they were sleeping soundly. He felt above the girl's door frame to make sure the key to unlock their bedroom door was still in its place. It was, so he quietly turned the inside knob and locked the door from the inside so Tucker couldn't get in the girl's room. Meredith was already asleep when he went back upstairs.

In the morning, as Meredith was inspecting her swollen eye in the bathroom mirror, Clare came into the bathroom and jumped up on the countertop.

"Your eye looks scary," Clare said.

"Do you think I'll scare my kids on Monday?"

"Maybe this will help," Clare said and handed her mother some make-up.

"Thank you. But I'm not sure that will do the trick. I think I'll just wear an eye patch."

"You could be a pirate," Clare said with widened eyes. "I

want to be a pirate."

"Then pirates we shall be. Let's go find your sisters. I think they're in the basement."

Jeff was at the kitchen table when Meredith and Clare came downstairs. "Do you think it looks worse?" Meredith asked. "I think it's more swollen."

"It looks fine," he said glancing up.

Clare went on down to the basement and found Isabelle playing with two Barbie dolls planning a party. The light flooded the basement through the French doors that opened out onto the stone patio. There was not much furniture in the basement which allowed Isabelle and Clare to leave out their Barbie stuff in the open area. Tucker was jumping on a mini trampoline in the corner of the room.

Meredith picked up an orange and sat down to peel it at the table with Jeff. "Did you give any thought to what we talked about last night?"

"What . . . the counseling? You can't be serious. Our family is fine."

"Look at me. Does this look fine?"

"He's a boy. It was an accident."

"Accidents are happening a lot lately — to me. I need you to hear me. I want some help with Tucker."

"The doctor said he's high-functioning. So he has a few quirks. Who doesn't?"

"This is the second time I've been to the ER in the last three months. The next time it might be one of the girls. How would that make you feel?"

"That is not going to happen." Jeff stared at Meredith and said, "You are overreacting."

"I don't think so. I think you are under reacting."

"I just need to spend more time with him. We need to get him out in the wide open spaces. Most of the time he's the only guy cooped up with all this estrogen. He needs to do something physical— something outdoors. I should try taking him running with me again."

"And when is this going to happen?"

"Soon."

Tucker bolted into the kitchen, stopped, and looked at Meredith. He walked over to her with a concerned look on his face and gently touched her eye and said, "What happened?"

"Hey, don't forget this is our Sunday to volunteer downtown," Jeff yelled to Meredith as she headed to the basement.

"I'm not going to go this time," Meredith yelled back up the stairs.

Jeff followed her to the basement. "Oh, com'on. It's great. It's great for the kids and it's great for the community."

"I'm not going with my eye looking like this."

"No one is going to care about your eye. They're in worse shape than you."

"I'm not going," Meredith said again with force.

"Meredith, com'on. It's good for the guys to see my family every once in a while. We never do any of the other events anymore."

"I'm not going. You can still take the kids with you if you want. I'm tired and I'm not up to it. Go and have fun." Meredith rolled her shoulders back trying to relieve the tension in her neck.

Jeff turned to look at the girls. "It looks like it's going to be Dad and his girls."

"What about Tucker?" Myla asked.

13

"He can stay here and rest with Mom."

"What about some guy time?" Meredith asked.

"You know I can't watch him and serve meals."

Myla looked back and forth between her mom and dad and then said, "I'm staying home too."

"Me too," Isabelle said.

Jeff sighed and looked at the girls. He let it go. It didn't seem worth it.

Chapter 3

On Sunday morning Jeff left alone and arrived downtown wearing his Accountants for Community T-shirt. The smell of lasagna flooded out from the discarded building used to serve the homeless and those struggling. Jeff went inside and sat a stack of paper plates near a steamed ladened window. The aluminum pans holding the lasagna stood next to bags of bread. Jeff grabbed some plastic serving gloves, put on a clean apron, and took his place in the serving line to serve bread. There were three varieties: French bread, garlic bread, or Italian seasoned bread.

Jeff always made a point to look up at the people he was serving. This wasn't just an assembly line. These were people. They might be struggling or having difficulties, but they were people and deserved dignity. Jeff offered them a choice of the breads. Some had a preference, but most were indifferent. Jeff made eye contact with the next person in line. "Which bread would you like? French bread, garlic bread, or bread with Italian seasoning?" He held the eyes of the person. She was thin. Her hair was unkempt and her skin had the appearance of not bathing recently. Her clothes hung loosely off of her frame. She stared at him. There was something about her eyes that he couldn't let go. They stared at each other. Then it hit him. In a quiet voice he asked, "Kate?"

She set down the plate and took off heading for the door. Jeff abandoned his station and skirted around the serving tables and ran after her. He grabbed her by the arm and turned her around to face him. "Kate?" he questioned again. He knew it was her, but he needed some acknowledgment from her.

"Hi, Jeff," Kate said with downcast eyes. "It's me."

"Kate, what's going on? What are you doing here? What happened?"

She didn't answer. She shook her head no while keeping her eyes focused on the floor.

Jeff continued, "Are you working here?" He knew she wasn't a worker, but he was trying to make sense of the skeleton of a woman before him that he once knew as a vibrant, confident, and funny person.

"I'm not a worker," she said with her eyes still fixated on the floor and her body positioned towards the door. Jeff grabbed her arm again to keep her from bolting for the door. Kate frowned looking at his hand on her arm and then she looked up at Jeff. He let go but held both his hands up near her shoulders in a gesture of surrender hoping to calm her or block her. He wasn't sure.

"Wait here—please!" Jeff pleaded, "Please, I'll be right back." He pulled a chair out. "Please, sit here." And he placed her in the chair. He retrieved her plate and arranged some regular French bread on the plate beside the lasagna and picked up a dessert and a milk.

He slid the plate of food in front of Kate and was relieved when she started to eat. She kept her eyes on Jeff as she pinched off pieces of the bread and put them in her mouth using her dirt stained hands. He shook the milk carton and then opened it and placed the straw in the opening, situating it in front of her as if she were a child.

"Aren't you going to eat?" Kate asked as she looked up.

Jeff stared at her slender face for a moment and then said, "Sure." He popped out of his chair and poured himself a coffee and picked up a brownie. He sat down across the table from Kate and took a bite of the brownie. "They always have great desserts here. It's the only place I can get a good sugar fix." His humor fell flat.

Kate nodded and looked down at her plate, sliced off a piece of lasagna, and ate it. They ate in silence for a few minutes and then Kate asked, "How's Meredith?"

Jeff didn't know whether the truth would make Kate bolt or if she would sympathize so he chose a middle ground in his description. "She is doing well. We've been having some problems with Tuck. You know how big he's gotten and Meredith and him are butting heads and she has the stitches to prove it."

Kate's eyes locked on Jeff's and he knew he had been too truthful. He looked away first.

"She's going to be fine. She'll have a little scar from the stitches, but it will be almost invisible," Jeff explained, trying to recover and not lose Kate. "She's been trying to call you."

Kate looked away.

Jeff began again, "Well, What about you?"

"What are you doing down here?" Kate asked not bothering to answer Jeff's question.

"I volunteer with my accounting buddies. We come down here about once a month," Jeff stated and then returned to his previous question. "What about you? What are you doing down here? Jeff asked and then added, "besides enjoying lunch." He smiled.

Chapter 4

"Mrs. Howard, we need you to come to the office," the intercom blurted out interrupting the math lesson on fractions.

Oh no, Meredith thought, *not again.* This makes the third time in three weeks of school that she had been called to the office. The other 3rd-grade teacher, Mrs. Earnest, peeked through the door that connected the two classrooms and nodded and waved for Meredith to go on to the office.

"Students, open your books to page 15 and start working on the practice problems," Meredith said before she left the classroom.

When she arrived in the office, she saw Tucker sitting across from the principal. He looked up at her with a relaxed look on his face. She felt tense. Being disciplined didn't rattle him much. It was quiet in the principal's office. Meredith held her breath and waited for the principal to begin.

"Meredith, please, have a seat."

"No, I'm fine."

"Okay then," Mrs. Riley said. "Tucker had a problem today during PE. The students were playing soccer outside, and when the classes came into the lunchroom to get drinks at the water fountain, Tucker threw a chair."

"Did someone get hurt?"

"No one was hit or hurt—this time. I know you know that Tucker has been having problems this year. This is the third time he has been in my office in three weeks. We have modified as much as we are able for a school our size. I'm sorry, but I can't make a place for Tucker at Cornerstone anymore. This is truly a safety issue. I can't put the other children at risk for Tucker to attend classes. And I feel that Tucker's needs could be best met somewhere else."

Meredith knew the protocol for expulsion but had hoped as a

teacher at the school, her son would get special consideration. Meredith sat down in the chair. "I see…"

Mrs. Riley continued to speak as Meredith looked down at the floor thinking through the events of the last few weeks. She forced her thoughts back to the present, and she strained to focus on Mrs. Riley's words.

"The public setting would be a more appropriate placement for Tucker. I think he can get more support and services through a public school. A small private school like ours just doesn't have the funding for the help that Tucker needs. I know this puts you in a bad position since you are a teacher at this school. We have two days left this week. I'll arrange for you to take them off. This will give you a couple of days to get him enrolled and settled in your public school district. I have already sent his records over to Central Elementary, and they are expecting to hear from you." She paused. Her voice softened. "I'm so sorry, but I have no choice. I have to think of the safety of the other students. I hope you understand."

"Yeah, I understand," she said, but she didn't like it. She hoped the heat she was feeling in her face wasn't showing. It felt like she had been caught in a lie. The lie was to herself. She had been telling herself that Tucker wasn't that disabled and that he would outgrow his issues. But at that moment she knew she was lying to herself. Although her face appeared calm, her heart was pounding, and she deliberately focused on breathing slowly. It took all her restraint to keep from grabbing Tucker's hand and yelling, *We don't need your stupid school,* and running out of the building with him. But Meredith simply nodded to acknowledge Mrs. Riley.

Mrs. Riley continued, "We have 30 minutes left in the day and Tucker is welcome to stay in my office. You can pick him up here."

Meredith looked at Tucker. He looked up at her again. His gray blue eyes seemed transparent. When he made eye contact and locked his eyes onto hers, it seemed he could almost see into her soul. He rubbed his nose with the palm of his hand and looked back at her and smiled. She wondered if he could see her heart break. "I'll be back to get you in a few minutes."

"Okay," he said.

Meredith noticed her hands were shaking, but she calmly walked back into her classroom.

After the dismissal bell, Myla appeared at her classroom door with Isabelle. "Tucker was not in his classroom, and his teacher said he was sent to the office."

"I know why." Isabelle paused for emphasis and put her hand on her hip. "Tucker shoved a chair. He wanted a drink of water, and he didn't want to wait so he cut in line, and when the teacher scolded him, he shoved the chair. It made a huge sound like a gun going off." Isabelle spoke with widened eyes about Tucker. "He was extremely thirsty."

"Let's get Tucker and go home," Meredith said as she placed her substitute folder on the top of her desk.

As the five walked to the car, Isabelle interviewed Tucker, "What were you thinking today in the lunchroom?"

"I don't know," Tucker nonchalantly replied.

"You should have seen the way everyone got quiet when Tucker shoved the chair. It was one of those metal chairs that Mrs. Ellen sits in at lunch by the door. When he shoved it, it hit the end of one of the lunchroom tables, and it was so loud it echoed. Everyone got quiet." Isabelle paused for effect. "I saw the chair slide into the table, but I didn't know that Tucker was the one who did it. I was standing by Rachel and we were just looking around. No one said anything. Then. . ." she said with suspense, "the PE teacher turned around and started walking down the line looking at everyone. Kevin pointed at Tucker. Mrs. Guest looked at Tucker. Isabelle pretended to hold a soccer ball against her hip imitating the teacher's stance and her voice. *Tucker, did you throw that chair?* Then Tucker said, *Yes.* Then she took Tucker to the office."

Isabelle turned to Tucker. "Were you afraid? Did Mrs. Riley paddle you? What did she do to you?"

"I don't know."

They drove in an oppressed silence the rest of the way except for Isabelle deliberating over expressions to define the silence of two classes waiting in line. "It was quiet as a church mouse. So quiet you could hear a pin drop. How about so quiet you could hear a mouse drop a pin?"

Meredith thought, *How about the quiet before the storm?* When they arrived home, the kids lumbered out of the car burdened down with their backpacks. Once in the house each child dropped their burdens and went to their separate corners. Meredith went to her room, sat down on the bed, and stared at the wall already dreading the next day. She heard Jeff pull into the driveway. She sighed. She would have to think later, so she washed her face, pulled her brown hair back into a ponytail, and went into the kitchen to start dinner.

The news of the expulsion hit Jeff like a weight falling on his shoulders. Raising his voice, he blamed everyone except Tucker.

"I guess you are going to expect me to drop him off at school?" Jeff demanded.

"I can't be in two places at once— so yes. After he gets started you are going to have to help."

"You can't stand that I get an hour to myself before I go to the office."

"This is not about you," Meredith said calmly while staring with disbelief at Jeff.

Jeff glared back at Meredith. He grabbed the door to slam it on his way out, but instead he caught the door to keep it from slamming and just shut the door hard.

Meredith followed him out the door and yelled, "Just slam it!" Then she thought, *He always has to stay in control.* Jeff got into his car and recklessly pulled out onto the quiet street heading more away from than to a destination. She went back into the house and slammed the door.

Chapter 5

Meredith and Tucker arrived at Central Elementary—Tucker's new school— which was not only functional but aesthetically pleasing. The school's design had been featured in an architectural magazine and for good reason—it was beautiful. There was a mural of glass depicting a forest scene ending with three pathways on the floor to each of the three hallways. It felt kind of like beginning a journey on the yellow brick road. The nature theme continued with water fountains that looked like huge boulders and an area in the main hall with real Norfolk pines growing. The whole atmosphere had a calming effect.

The principal's office was through a brick archway. It had slate floors and granite countertops. The receptionist took Meredith and Tucker into the principal's office. There was a manila folder that had Tucker's name on it setting on the desk.

The principal, Dr. Fisher, introduced himself to Meredith and Tucker. He opened the folder and Meredith waited while he read the pages. "I see Tucker has a diagnosis of mild autism, he was mainstreamed at Cornerstone Academy, and he was expelled for behavioral issues after shoving a chair into a table in the cafeteria."

Meredith interrupted, "Would it be possible for Tucker to wait outside with the secretary while we have our discussion?" Meredith took him to the front office and said to Tucker, "Wait here." She gave him his handheld game. She turned to the secretary. "If you need to leave for any reason, let me know.

Dr. Fisher continued when Meredith returned, "His records indicate two other behavior infractions this year at Cornerstone. The first was going to the school library without permission." He looked up at Meredith. "It says here they had to do *lock-down* to search for him." He looked up at her again as if he was waiting for an explanation. She said nothing and he continued speaking. "The second was refusing to do his schoolwork and destroying school property. He tore up a reading book?" He glanced up again at

Meredith.

She nodded yes. Her legs were crossed and she was shaking her foot.

"I'm assuming there were others, but these were the most noteworthy."

Meredith finally spoke. "Yes, those things did happen." She knew about each occurrence. As a teacher herself, she was familiar with documenting in a student's files regarding misconduct. Cornerstone had a three-strikes and you're out policy, and the procedures for documentation of Tucker's misconduct were followed in each of the cases. Her signature was at the bottom of each form acknowledging that she was aware of the incidents.

"These incidents are noted as deliberate breaking of the school's code of conduct." Dr. Fisher statement was more of a question.

"I don't know about deliberate. He has autism and it's more impulsive than deliberate. I know it's a fine line."

Dr. Fisher continued, "Here, we have a resource room and a self-contained classroom. Both have strict behavior guidelines that Tucker will have to follow. At Cornerstone, he was in a resource room, and that placement was not appropriate since he failed to adapt. Is that correct?"

Meredith did not answer but just stared at him. There was something about Dr. Fisher's word choice—failed—and his tone of voice that she didn't like. She was thinking about writing him up for being a "smart aleck" in his principal file when Dr. Fisher's voice brought her back to the present.

"Mrs. Howard?"

"Yes," Meredith said shaking her thoughts away to concentrate on Dr. Fisher.

"Mrs. Howard, this is why you are here, isn't it? Tucker's placement in a resource room at Cornerstone Academy failed and he was expelled for misconduct. Correct?"

"Yes," Meredith quietly affirmed. She knew her anger at Dr. Fisher was misdirected.

Dr. Fisher continued, "Like I was saying, we have both a resource room and a self-contained classroom to serve students with disabilities." He had slowed down his speech and was speaking distinctly to her as if she was a child. "Since the resource room was ineffective, I think placing Tucker in the self-contained classroom is the optimal choice. Tucker can get behavioral support in the self-contained classroom. Do you concur?"

Meredith thought about her black eye. She agreed, but she still didn't like his word choice. After several moments of staring at Dr. Fisher, she finally said, "Yes, I agree. Tucker needs help with behavioral problems." She was impressed that Dr. Fisher didn't say anything about her black eye. Maybe it isn't that noticeable, she hoped.

Dr. Fisher plastered a smile on his face and folded his hands together and placed them on his desk. "Now . . . what else can you relate to me about Tucker to help me understand him so we can have a successful year?"

Meredith didn't like his smile either. She began to defend Tucker with the explanations of the recorded offenses. "Tucker has difficulty with change and the incidents listed were all results of a change in his routine. When he went to the school library to use the computer, he didn't ask permission to leave the room because that's when the class usually went to the library for computer time. The problem was the day had been shortened because of an assembly and that period had been eliminated just for that day."

Dr. Fisher simply said, "I understand. We have only been in school three weeks so far this year, and so he's obviously been struggling this entire school year."

"Yes and he does act out when he can't come up with the words he wants. It's just frustration." Meredith touched her eye which was now yellowish rather than black and blue and continued, "I know he has problems with students being absent. He likes everyone to be at school, and I guess he worries about his friends coming back. Sometimes," she said emphasizing the word, "he won't do his work. But overall, last year, Tucker did well in the mainstream setting. Last year, he went to morning classes independently with no modifications, and then his afternoons were spent with the special education teacher who helped him with his schoolwork, and she reviewed his lessons with him. She was very systematic and structured with him. He did all his work and made excellent grades. He never had any problems in her class. This year things have been different."

"What changed this year?"

"Well, the special education teacher did not come back, and the school decided to try and use teacher's aide for kids needing extra help. It's just not working for Tucker this year. I feel like he was set up to fail. It has been a hard three weeks so far at home and at school. He has been in the regular class more this year, and there have been more problems. The teacher's aide has been trying, but it's not the same as last year."

"He is obviously not getting the support he needs," Dr. Fisher said. "The mainstream setting is not supportive enough. Based on what you have told me, at this point I think the self-contained classroom is the appropriate setting because of the support provided. Let's get some new testing completed. But I also think the structure of the self-contained classroom would be the most appropriate considering the behavioral issues. The Individualized Education Plan (IEP) for the self-contained classroom will include behavior objectives as well as academic objectives. I see from his record that he was identified as a child with autism at age 3. Was this the last time he had a formal evaluation?"

She mumbled, "Yes."

"Before our meeting, I spoke with the school psychologist

and she will be able to do some testing after lunch today and can finish the testing tomorrow— if you're available."

"Sure," she said feeling her apprehension about the situation actually decreasing. *Knowledge is always good,* she thought.

"We are lucky we can get this done so quickly. So we should have the updated test results in a couple of weeks and at that time we will make the necessary changes. But based on the information I have, I think we need to start with the self-contained classroom and focus on behavior management. Without controlled behavior, it's impossible to grow academically."

Meredith did agree with Dr. Fisher— in principle. He obviously was an intellectual man— who loved big words. Maybe she was too quick to judge. Maybe this was the professional help for Tucker that she needed, and he would finally get the support and direction he needed. Her frustration shifted from Dr. Fisher to Mrs. Riley at Cornerstone. Her own words now haunted her, *He was set up to fail. Mrs. Riley probably wanted to get rid of him all along*, she thought to herself. *Wow, now I'm getting paranoid.*

Meredith remembered her sweet boy when he was three and back then she had wanted a label for Tucker's behaviors—an explanation for his hand flipping, his strange play, and his pronoun confusion. She had felt relieved and scared at the same time when the psychologist had labeled Tucker as autistic. A person can't deal with what they don't know. It's only through knowledge that a person can move forward. And now all she could do was move forward with what she did know—she wanted the best outcome for Tucker's life. It was the same thing she wanted for all her girls. And maybe—just maybe—this was the path. Maybe she was the one who didn't like change.

She often thought Tucker's behavior problems stemmed from their hectic lifestyle. By the time she got home from teaching, fixed dinner, helped everyone with homework, got baths, and read to the kids — there was never enough time to give Tucker the attention he needed. *If her parenting skills were better—if she was more organized— these outbursts wouldn't happen,*" she thought. Whenever she spent time one-on-one with Tucker, it brought out his sweet disposition. The idea that Tucker's behavior problem was a disorder rather than a parenting flaw was slowly taking root in her consciousness even though she always knew autism was associated with behavioral issues. She knew he functioned better when she functioned better and was more consistent and organized. But keeping that pace was exhausting. She didn't want his label be an excuse. Meredith had viewed his autism traits as his hand flipping, his excellent memory, and his desire for order only. Adding behavioral problems as a part of his autism made Meredith feel hopeless. She fought against that feeling. She couldn't stop him from using his memory or requiring order. Could she stop him from having meltdowns if this was just a part of autism? *How much can we change and how much do we accept?* she wondered.

Meredith, Dr. Fisher, and Tucker walked down the corridor to the self-contained special education classroom.

"Tucker, this is going to be your new school. We are going to see your new classroom, meet your teachers, and meet your classmates," Meredith stated matter-of-factly to prepare Tucker.

Dr. Fisher opened the classroom door.

The bright room and the sound of classical music brought a smile to Meredith's face. "I love the music. What a wonderful classroom," Meredith said.

"Yes, it is. The music is designed to not only keep the brain stimulated but also to create a calming effect," Dr. Fisher said with obvious knowledge and pride in the classroom applying the latest educational techniques.

"I know that song." Meredith brightened and turned to Tucker. "That is one of the songs that we listen to in the car."

Tucker tilted his head to the side and listened and smiled at no one in particular.

The brightly lit classroom had charts covering every wall.

Each desk had a schedule on the corner of it. All the students appeared to be engaged in learning either in small groups, with a teacher's aide, or with a therapist directing the activities. One group of three students was working on trying to guess the objects in a bag by using only their hands. There were some giggles emerging from this group. Two students were working with computers. Each student sat at the computer with a headset on and a teacher's aide sat between them occasionally pointing at the screen. Mrs. Canon, the special education teacher, was working with a group of four students around a semi-circle table when Meredith and Tucker arrived. When those students began working quietly in their workbooks, Mrs. Canon came over to meet Tucker.

She held out her hand to Tucker. "It's nice to meet you, Tucker."

No response from Tucker.

Meredith prompted, "Tucker, say hello to Mrs. Canon and shake her hand."

Tucker acknowledged Mrs. Canon with a hello and offered her a limp hand.

"She is going to be your new teacher, and this will be your new classroom."

Mrs. Canon put her hands on Tucker's shoulders and guided him over to a desk. His name was written on a lined card at the top of the desk. "We have been waiting for you," Mrs. Canon said and pointed to the card. "Tucker, this will be your desk in our classroom."

No response again, but Tucker did sit down at the desk. He rocked slowly. Meredith knew that rocking was a coping skill for Tucker. She felt her heart speed up a bit engaging her into a fight or flight mode. This could go either way.

As soon as they left the school, Tucker began, "I want to go to my class at Cornerstone. I want to sit between John and Sarah. I want my desk at Cornerstone. I want John and Sarah in my new class. I want Mrs. Garnett in my new class."

Tucker continued to say the same five sentences over and over and over again as he rocked in the backseat of the car. His voice took on a rhythm as he kept repeating the sentences. Meredith rubbed her forehead like she had a headache. She didn't respond to Tucker but just stared ahead. On the next block, they pulled into Tucker's favorite fast-food restaurant. She didn't ask him what he wanted because he always got the same thing. He sat down at a table while Meredith placed the order. When she brought the food to the table, he took his food and went to a separate table. Meredith watched a young couple order and sit across the restaurant —together — in one of the booths. There were no school-age children in the restaurant just couples or singles. She watched as a couple in their 50's came in and studied the menu as if they had never been in a fast-food restaurant.

Tucker came over, "I'm finished. Can we go to Cornerstone now?"

"Tucker, we are going to go to your new school this afternoon."

Tucker's voice was elevated. "I want to go to Cornerstone. I want to sit between John and Sarah. I want my desk at Cornerstone."

Meredith stated matter-of-factly, "We are going to Central. You will have new friends to sit between." She took Tucker's shoulders and turned him to face her. "Look at me," she said. "Your new class at Central is so much better than your classroom at Cornerstone. They have music and lots of helpers."

"I want to sit between John and Sarah."

"This afternoon you are just going to take a test. You can answer the teacher's questions, can't you?"

"Okay. And then can we go to Cornerstone and I can sit

between John and Sarah?" Tucker asked with force in his voice.

Meredith ignored his question, not wanting an outburst in the restaurant. "Let's go take the test at Central. I want you to show the teacher how smart you are."

"Okay, and then we can go to Cornerstone and I can sit between John and Sarah." Tucker's question was now a declaration.

◆ ◆

Meredith tried to change the subject. "I really like Central and Mrs. Canon. Maybe you could try out Central tomorrow."

"Okay, and then can we go to Cornerstone and I can sit between John and Sarah?"

When Meredith and Tucker arrived at Central after lunch, Tucker strolled into the testing room. She watched the testing behind a one-way mirror. If the question was hard, he didn't even try. He only said, "I don't know." Meredith's palms were sweaty as she watched.

Chapter 6

Jeff parked the car and waited for the pounding rain to ease up so he could make a run for it to the crisis center. Once inside there were two doors: one served men and one served women and children. Priority was given to women with children and to those who were in immediate danger from physical, mental, or emotional abuse. Jeff realized that even though Kate's issues seemed severe, she was way down on the list of people needing intervention.

Jeff watched as the counselor added Kate's name to the bottom of his list. The list itself looked in need with its curled and worn edges. Kate's name was two-thirds of the way down the list on the third page. Names on the top of the second page had been highlighted and crossed out.

Jeff inquired, "How long will it take for Kate to be admitted to a program for addiction?"

"It all depends. It might take six months or more. In the meantime, she needs to go to AA and stop her addiction."

"She's tried AA and she said it didn't work."

"She needs to try again. Recovery is a long process, and the main focus of our in-house program is getting people back to work and into decent housing. She'll receive support and one-on-one counseling here, but she needs to be and stay sober."

"She's in bad shape and six months is a long time to wait. She's so thin."

"Then get her to go to AA or get her in rehab or a hospital," the counselor said without looking up.

"What kind of rehab?" Jeff asked.

When Jeff spoke again, the counselor looked up surprised to see him still standing at the desk. Before the counselor spoke, he surveyed the man before him wearing a sports coat, button-downed shirt, and tie. "There are some private rehab programs near here. They are costly, but for some people they are the only way. The rehab is 24/7 for six weeks to three months and sometimes longer, and they get group and individual counseling to stop the addiction."

"Can I make her go?"

The counselor laughed slightly and shook his head. "No, not unless it's court ordered, and you can't make her stay either even if it is private pay. They are in the program at will." The counselor opened the side drawer of the desk and pulled out a single sheet of paper. "Here's a list of some private centers nearby. I have her name on our list, and I'll give you a call when we have an opening for her."

"I don't know what to do to help. She'll barely talk to me. I just found her and I don't want to lose her again."

The counselor's toned soften, "I know. Addiction is mean, and it doesn't spare people who love the addict either."

Jeff took the paper and went next door to "New Start," an organization helping people deal with homelessness by providing a safe place to sleep and a midday meal.

"I'm looking for Kate Harper. Do you know if she has been here?"

The lady, who looked like she might still be struggling with an addiction herself, eyed Jeff and then checked her records. "I'm really not supposed to tell you, but she was here overnight two days ago."

"I would like to get a message to her. Would she be able to phone me from here if I left my number?"

"Sure, you can leave a note for her on the bulletin board. I can't guarantee she will be back here or that she will call if she sees the message."

Jeff wrote for Kate Harper on the top of the card. The attendant handed him a push pin, and he positioned his card near the middle of the bulletin board.

Jeff started to leave but was blocked by a man walking back and forth in the lobby quietly flipping two fingers in front of his face. A sick feeling settled in Jeff's stomach. He thought that could be Tucker someday if he didn't have someone to look out for him. He watched the man for a few moments and then edged around him to leave.

The sad, worn area of town gave way to bright linear patterns as Jeff drove from downtown to his planned neighborhood. The image of the man rocking and flipping his hands at The New Start Center kept coming up into Jeff's mind. Most people could navigate the loss of a few paychecks or bad breaks. But for the disabled, any life event could leave them homeless with no understanding of how to even access the system of safety nets.

Jeff pulled into the pick-up lane at Cornerstone. "How about pizza?" he asked as the girls surged into the car through every door. When they arrived home, Tucker and Meredith weren't home yet so he placed the pizza on the counter. As soon as Meredith and Tucker walked in the door, Isabelle gave her report. "There is going to be a magician at school tomorrow."

Tucker was instantly hooked on Isabelle's enthusiasm.

"He's gonna make something disappear!" Isabelle related. When she noticed she had her audience's attention, she spread her arms out in full theatrical style and said, "Tomorrow will be so much fun."

"I can't wait to see the magician," Tucker said while slightly flipping his fingers.

"Tucker, we're going to Central tomorrow," Meredith said. "Remember, Mrs. Canon and your new classmates?"

"No!" Tucker demanded, "I'll be at Cornerstone tomorrow. I'll see the magician, and I'm going to sit between Sarah and John!"

"Mom, why can't Tucker go to Cornerstone tomorrow. Just for tomorrow. Let him go with me," Isabelle whined.

"No, he's going to Central," Meredith said then turned to Tucker, "Tucker, we're going to Central tomorrow. Remember your new class with music? It'll be fun."

Isabelle left her pizza on the counter and let Ashlyn, Clare's neighborhood friend, in the front door.

"Clare, Ashlyn is here," Isabelle yelled down the stairs. She went over to the computer that sat in the living room area of their open concept home, leaving Ashlyn waiting for Clare.

Tucker started staring at Isabelle, who had sat down at the computer to play a game. "I was going to play the computer," Tucker said.

Isabelle turned and shrugged her shoulders at Tucker. She had a slight grin on her face, and she took a full second to blink her eyes at him.

Tucker bounded over to the computer desk and grabbed the computer tower and threw it to the floor. Isabelle's mouth dropped open, and she put her hands on her hips and yelled, "Mom!" She stood there glaring at Tucker and waiting for justice to be served.

Instead, Jeff swooped in and grabbed Tucker and sat him on the couch and yelled, "Isabelle, go to your room!"

Isabelle's eyes widened at the injustice. When she recovered, Isabelle started, "What about Tucker? He's the one—"

"Go to your room, Isabelle. I'll deal with Tuck."

She stomped out with her arms folded across her chest. She darted her eyes toward Tucker.

"Tucker, go to your room!" Jeff demanded. Tucker just kept sitting on the couch. Jeff wanted to ask Tucker, Why? Why did you do this? But he knew there would be no real answer just an I

35

don't know. Instead, Jeff sat down and unhooked the cables from the back of the computer to survey the damage. He unraveled the tangled equipment. Meredith came in and started picking up papers that had scattered on the floor. Neither one acknowledged Tucker, who stayed on the couch.

They heard a door slam. Meredith looked out the door and saw Ashlyn running out of the yard heading home. "Oh no, Ashlyn. I forgot she was here," Meredith groaned. Ashlyn was an only child so sibling fights were not part of her daily existence. Meredith dialed Ashlyn's mother and spoke in a lukewarm tone, "I just wanted to let you know Ashlyn is on her way home."

Mrs. Eckerd said, "I see her coming into the yard now. Thanks."

She said good-bye offering no explanation to Mrs. Eckerd.

Meredith dusted under the computer while Jeff reassembled all the wires. With the computer system back up and running, they sat down at the dining room table. Meredith picked at her pizza. Tucker got up from the couch and went downstairs, and Isabelle peeked into the kitchen and then headed downstairs too.

"We really should punish Tucker or Isabelle or both. At least he should go to his room like I told him," Jeff said.

"You do it. I've already been the heavy once today," Meredith said, but Jeff didn't get up.

The voices of Isabelle and Tucker playing a video game together in the basement filtered up to where Jeff and Meredith were sitting. The kids were obviously over whatever started the conflict. "Well, at least no one is heading to the emergency room." He took a bite of pizza and then changed the subject. "Did you see the news the other day about a boy with autism who wandered away from his home?"

"No, what happened?"

"Well, they searched for him for two days and then found him in a pond near their house. Unimaginable. The sad part was

36

the parents said they'd only left him for maybe a couple of minutes. He was nonverbal so he couldn't even respond to their calls. And who knows, he might've been afraid of the search team and hid from them. It was astonishing to me that none of the searchers found him before he drowned in the pond. Anyways, it kinda reminded me of our last canoe trip when we lost Tuck in the woods. It was scary, but at least Tuck answered our calls."

"But remember, we yelled, *Tucker, say what.*"

"And he did." Jeff grinned. "I remember hearing his little voice saying, *what*. It was one of the best sounds I have ever heard. But that just about did me in. After we found him I remember we tagged team who was going to watch him. We were like guards changing duty."

"I remember being exhausted after that trip too. I guess that is why we stopped camping," Meredith said. "Camping used to be fun but—"

"We need to go again," Jeff interrupted. "Tuck is older. I think it would do him good to run around with no fences or sidewalks. He needs it. Plus, I've done some research and there is this new device that looks like a wristwatch, but it actually contains a GPS that can be tracked with a cell phone. Ever since I saw it advertised, I have been thinking about camping. I know Tuck would wear it since he loves watches. It's even waterproof. As long as we go somewhere we can get a cell signal, if he had the GPS watch on and he wandered away, we could track him and find him."

"It sounds kinda like 'Big Brother' watching, but I do like it."

"Remember, technology is our friend. I think it would do us all good to get away for the weekend. Clare was just a *baby* the last time we went. She doesn't remember camping. I saw her little *inside fire pit* she made in her room, and it made me want to take her camping. We NEED to take her camping."

"I guess so. Our canoes are still good," Meredith said.

I think together Myla and Isabelle could probably handle a canoe on their own now. . . with a little work. Plus Myla and Isabelle can help keep an eye on Tuck. It's a win-win. We need to do it."

Meredith looked at Jeff while shaking her head, no, but smiling at the same time. "Okay, let's do it."

"This weekend then . . . you and me and four kids." Jeff smiled. He opened the bookmarked page on his phone and ordered the GPS watch. "I did 2-day shipping. We should have it by this weekend. We need to air out those sleeping bags. We are going to the woods."

Jeff was right. Tucker loved the GPS wristwatch and took great pleasure in announcing the time in both the 12-hour and 24-hour format. Switching between the two was easy for Tucker, and he was oblivious to his sisters rolling their eyes when he routinely announced it was 2100 hours and time for bed. During her planning period, Meredith continued to walk to Mrs. Garnett's class at Cornerstone. She would peek in the door and look at Tucker's empty chair and desk pushed up against the wall. John and Sarah now sat next to each other. There was no place for Tucker anymore. When she returned to her room, Meredith would log-in on her phone and see the little green dot that represented Tucker's location. Tucker and his watch were at Central. Meredith would smile at her phone. She could still check on Tucker.

Meredith heard her phone indicating a text as she and Tucker were on their way home from Central. She handed the phone to Tucker. "What does it say?"

Tucker read, "You are near the Conoco on the corner of

Broadway and 2nd Street. Bring me a bag of ice for the cooler and a candy bar."

"Text back, funny," Meredith told Tucker.

Meredith went into the convenience store near their house and got the ice and the candy bar. She got Tucker an Icee, his favorite treat, and headed home to start packing.

Chapter 7

"I want to get on the road by 9 AM," Jeff said as he was loading the car.

Tucker came up and handed Jeff two pieces of paper. "Here, Dad."

"Did you print these out yourself?" Jeff said looking at the printed maps routing the location to the camping area. "Thank you, Tucker," Jeff said admiring the map and noticing that one route was the exact route that Jeff himself had printed out. Tucker smiled at Jeff. Clare walked by wearing her new bright pink life jacket. Jeff playfully picked her up by the shoulders of the life jacket. Clare squealed with delight. But Jeff was making sure the jacket was a perfect fit and would protect Clare if she needed it.

Clare ran into the garage when Meredith called her name. "Clare, I have something for you." Clare looked silently up as her mom solemnly presented her with own paddle complete with a pink ribbon tied around the handle. "Keep this with you. This is yours—only yours."

When the other girls and Tucker saw Clare with her new paddle, they silently went into the garage and took their paddles down and carried them to the car.

They rode in silence for the first 20 miles as they left the city. When nothing but forest lined the state highway, Meredith rolled down her window. "I love the smell of the forest." She took in several deep breaths. Jeff deeply breathed in the earthy air too and let his mind—for the moment—release the images of Meredith with her black eye, the man at the homeless shelter flipping his hands, and Kate's gaunt appearance.

"How about one of the snacks you packed?" Jeff asked.

Isabelle had her arm out the window feeling the power of the wind as they drove. She started singing a song that they had learned at church. Myla joined her. Tucker didn't play his DS but listened to sounds of his sisters' voices.

The weather forecast was 55° for the night and 70° for the daytime. By late afternoon, the tent was up and the fire blazed. Jeff and Meredith propped up in the lawn chairs watching as the fire settled down to glowing embers. "I feel like a genius every time I log-in and see Tucker's location. I can actually sit in this lawn chair," Jeff said as he leaned back and closed his eyes.

Meredith said, "You definitely are a genius." She looked at the girls walking and talking at the waterline of the lake. Clare was still wearing her new pink life jacket. They were picking up mussel shells. Isabelle was using her paddle as a hiking stick. Myla was showing Clare the shells. Tucker followed along behind the girls. Something caught Tucker's attention and he darted into the trees.

Meredith instinctively started to get up. "I'll check."

"Wait. Stay right there," Jeff picked up his phone and saw the green dot representing Tucker. He had stopped just out of their view but not out of the GPS range. Jeff turned the phone for Meredith to see. "He's fine. We have great cell reception here."

In a moment Tucker reappeared. Meredith looked at Jeff, leaned back in her lawn chair, closed her eyes, and smiled letting the last rays of sun warm her face.

The kids were in view but not within earshot—a rare opportunity for adult conversation. Meredith began, "I've tried to call my sister a couple of times. I thought she might be able to give me some insight about navigating the school system. I haven't been able to get in touch with her yet. Her phone goes right to voice mail. I knew she was upset with me, but it's hard to believe she continues to not take my calls."

"You're right. She is probably mad. I think you were a bit rough with her about her new guy. But let's not talk about it. Let's not talk about the school, or work, or your sister. Not here. Not now. Let's just enjoy this evening." He paused and pressed himself back into the lawn chair.

The kids started running back toward Jeff and Meredith. It

was a foot race and Isabelle and Myla were the only contenders with Myla gradually leaving Isabelle behind. Clare and Tucker ran, but Tucker's goal was to keep pace with Clare, which was effortless for him. He wasn't competitive; he was a follower. At the end of the race, Tucker flipped his hands and walked on his toes in what they all called the *dance of joy*. Tucker did this when he was happy. Jeff got up and danced with Tucker. The girls joined in too and they all danced and laughed in the middle of the forest with no one watching—no meltdowns, no evaluations, and no tears just dancing in the cool night air.

The kids with bellies stuffed full of Graham crackers and marshmallows crawled into the tent. There was a faint scent of bug spray, but the cool evening air dominated their senses. Four paddles leaned against the tent. Jeff crawled around and zipped each kids' sleeping bag up and kissed them on the forehead. He began telling Kipling's The Elephant Child from memory to the four exhausted kids. He had only made it through the first part when the sound of steady breathing told him that each child was asleep. Jeff could hear Meredith rummaging around in the car, and as the flashlight beam came closer to the tent, he quietly untangled himself from the sleeping kids and went up behind her and wrapped his arms around her waist. "Did we forget anything?"

"I was checking to make sure I had our paddles. I know the kids have theirs. Tomorrow when we launch these canoes out onto that peaceful lake, I don't want any tears or screaming over paddles from you to disturb the peace." She winked at him and handed him his own paddle. He inspected it by rubbing his hand along the rough edge. She put her and Jeff's paddles inside the canoes. Everyone would have their own paddle, but teamwork would be required for forward motion.

Chapter 8

"Mom, Clare is roasting a hot dog for breakfast," Isabelle reported.

"That's okay," Meredith said as she was cleaning up the plates from the breakfast of western omelets that turned into scrambled eggs.

Indigent that she hadn't thought to eat a hot dog instead, Isabelle went to the cooler and started her own alternate hot dog breakfast. Tucker watched but ate his usual breakfast of bananas and yogurt.

"You and Myla should be able to manage with Clare. I'll have Tuck and Isabelle," Jeff said as hoisted the canoe up onto his shoulder. "And I have the paddles," he yelled back over his shoulder. Tucker followed as Jeff carried the canoe to the water's edge to wait for Meredith.

Meredith smiled. "Myla, you and I are going to carry our canoe over our heads. Clare, get the paddles."

Jeff started giving out instructions. "Isabelle, you get up-front and steady the canoe while Tucker gets in." Isabelle climbed in, but worry lines etched her forehead. "I'm going to hold the canoe from here. You won't get away from me." Everyone seemed to hold their breath as Tucker stepped into the canoe as if he was stepping onto a concrete floor. The canoe rocked. Isabelle grabbed the sides trying to steady it. Jeff just smiled. "Whoa there, partner."

"Sit down, Tucker," Isabelle yelled as she gripped the sides of the canoe.

Jeff pushed off and jumped in. As they watched the swaying canoe leave the bank, both Meredith and Myla tried to steady an imaginary canoe with their hands. Jeff laughed. As the rocking subsided in Jeff's canoe and they began some forward motion, Jeff shouted, "Come on girls!" His shout startled some ducks on the lake causing them to take flight. They landed a short distance away. Tucker flipped his hands and squealed in delight causing the ducks to take another short flight and the canoe to bob back and forth in the water with Isabelle still gripping the sides.

Meredith's launch went smoothly. Clare settled in the center of the canoe with Myla up front and Meredith pushed off within minutes of Jeff.

Meredith started teaching Myla the finer points of paddling a canoe and how to imagine the paddler's box. "Pull the boat toward the paddle. Pull the boat toward the paddle," Meredith repeated.

Tucker started rocking and flipping his hands in the canoe sending ripples across the turquoise lake which rocked Myla's canoe.

"Tell Tucker to stop making waves," Myla yelled.

"We're fine," Meredith said as she steadied the canoe with her own paddle.

Chapter 9

Jeff turned the car into the driveway around 3 o'clock on Sunday afternoon. The kids were piled in the back asleep with slight sunburns across their noses. Canoes rested on top of the car and the back was loaded with dirty clothes.

"Looks like we have a visitor," Jeff said when he saw Brenda — their neighbor and the mother of Clare's friend, Ashlyn — standing on the porch when they arrived. Brenda had her hand on Ashlyn's shoulder.

Clare's eyes popped open when she heard Jeff speak. When she saw Ashlyn, she started scrambling to collect the shells she had found on the camping trip. "That's my friend, Daddy."

Jeff winked at Meredith and said, "And so it is."

"Hey, Brenda," Meredith said as Jeff nudged the other kids awake.

"Meredith, we came over to see if Clare could come over and play. It looks like you have been out of town. Sorry, we didn't know."

Clare ran up to Ashlyn. "I have my own paddle. I went on a canoe ride on the lake. We saw a snake and I found a turtle. Dad wouldn't let me keep the turtle because the turtle needed to find its mom. But I did keep some mussel shells." Clare opened a grimy hand and showed the mussel shells to Ashlyn.

Ashlyn looked into Clare's hand and then looked up at her mom with wide-eyes seeking approval. Then she looked at Clare and asked her well-rehearsed question, "Do you want to come to my house to play Barbie?"

"Let's play here," Clare said.

"I can't," Ashlyn said with downcast eyes.

Brenda bent down to get on Clare's and Ashlyn's level.

"Clare, Ashlyn wanted you to come down and play at her

45

house," Brenda sang.

"It's fine if they play here," Meredith offered.

"I was hoping Clare could come to our house." Brenda now turned serious and stood to face Meredith. "Ashlyn was here when Tucker and Isabelle had a fight over the computer, and it just makes me too uneasy about Ashlyn coming to Clare's. I'll be honest. Tucker's behavior traumatized Ashlyn. She was in tears when she got home. I know it must be difficult with Tucker's problems." She paused measuring each word. "We adore Clare. She is always welcome at our house, and she and Ashlyn get along so well. I hope you understand."

Meredith felt like she had been slapped as reality came rushing back. Tension returned to her shoulders. Her joy evaporated. She bit her bottom lip to keep from saying, *If you can't accept all my kids then you can't have Clare at your house.* But she knew that would punish Clare. So instead, Meredith said, "I'm sorry Ashlyn was upset by Tucker. He was having a bad day. He had just changed schools," Meredith stopped. *Why did she always feel the need to explain herself? She didn't need to explain herself or her kids to anyone including Brenda,* she thought. Then she said, "Let's get them together another day. I think Clare is tired from the trip." Under her breath Meredith said, *That was just a brother-sister fight. You should be here for one of his meltdowns. Then you would really be traumatized.*

Meredith looked at Clare who was holding her Barbie doll tucked under one arm and her paddle under the other. When Ashlyn and her mother left, Clare began to whine. "I just wanted to play Barbie and show her the mussel shells from the lake." She threw her paddle down on the driveway.

"I'm sorry, Clare" She rubbed Clare's back. "But really I need you to be my helper because we have a lot to carry in." Meredith turned Clare around and guided her towards the car. "You and Isabelle can play dolls after we unload."

Meredith picked up Clare's paddle and held it up to show

46

Jeff. "Her first ding in her new paddle."

He smiled a sad smile.

Chapter 10

"Work is done, next dinner, then homework, then bed," Meredith said as she and the girls were driving home after picking up Tucker from Central on Friday.

"Mom," Myla said drawing out the word, "I wish you would quit saying that. You have said it over and over all week. It's getting a little annoying and, besides, it's embarrassing. It makes you seem crazy."

Tucker started flipping his hand and grinning. "Dinner, homework, then bed. First school, next dinner, then homework, then bed.

"First school, next dinner, then homework, then bed," Isabelle joined in the chant.

"Mom," Myla said enunciating each sound. "Make them stop."

"Sorry, Myla, I'm just trying to survive the week."

"I hope you don't have a chant for Saturday," Myla huffed, crossed her arms, and took a deep breath. She then reached into the backseat to try and hit Isabelle who was safe out of Myla's reach.

"I guess Saturday could be a no chanting day," Meredith said smiling.

"Yes, let's definitely make it a no chanting day," Myla said with crossed arms while emphasizing the word definitely.

"It has been a good week though."

"Well, you wouldn't let Gloria come over. So it hasn't been a good week for me."

"But you did ace your science test? I'm hoping all that studying each night paid off."

"I think I did really well on it today." Myla's tone soften. "There was only one answer that I wasn't sure of."

"See, focusing and hard work pays off," Meredith said and then turned her attention to the younger kids. "Okay, guys, hold it down. Saturday is officially a no chant day. But for Sunday start thinking about pancakes, church, and naps," she said emphasizing naps.

Chapter 11

"How was Sunday School?" Meredith asked at the door of Isabelle's and Tucker's class. Tucker headed right past Meredith. She reached down and grabbed his hand, and he jerked it away and looked up at her and announced, "I want to go to Cornerstone."

Jeff and Meredith stopped in their tracks and looked at each other. Their smiles vanished as they exchanged an uneasy glance. Meredith did her best to remain calm on the outside.

Isabelle, always the reporter, pointed to a boy about Tucker's age standing with his father and said, "Dillon is in Tucker's class at Central."

"Really?" Meredith asked with interest. She looked at Dillon and saw no indication he was a special education student—much less in a self-contained classroom. About that time Dillon's mother appeared with a two-year-old on her hip. When Dillon skipped over to his mom, Meredith spoke to Dillon's mother. "Hi, I'm Meredith. I just found out your son and my son, Tucker, are in the same class at school. Tucker started last week."

"I'm Sarah," she said and then turned to Dillon. "Wow, Dillon, do you know Tucker from school?"

Dillon's bright eyes and curly hair matched his little sister's except in color. Dillon's curls were tamed down and blonde. "Hi, Tucker."

Tucker didn't respond.

"Tucker say *Hi* to Dillon," Meredith prompted.

"Hi, Dillon."

Dillon's mom exclaimed, "You are going to love Mrs. Canon. She is so creative."

Jeff and Meredith locked eyes for a moment. Jeff took Tucker's hand leading him out of the situation and giving Meredith some time to talk. "Come on, Isabelle," he said, "let's go get Clare."

Dillon's mom, Sarah, continued, "Mrs. Burke and Mrs. Crawford are so organized. Dillon has learned so much in their class."

"So far I have been impressed," Meredith said.

"We should get the boys together sometime." Dillon handed his mother a drawing that showed primitive stick figures—very juvenile for Dillon's age. Sarah led Dillon off praising his artwork created in the Sunday School classroom. Meredith followed Sarah down the hall.

"What about next Saturday?" Meredith asked trying not to sound desperate.

Sarah looked at Meredith and briefly held her breath. "Sure, that should work," she said breathing out.

Meredith found Jeff and the kids in the sanctuary. "I asked Dillon to come over next Saturday," Meredith whispered to Jeff as they sat waiting for the service to begin. "Maybe it would help Tucker at Central if he had a buddy."

Jeff and Meredith picked up their conversation after church while clearing the plates from the table. "What's Dillon's disability? He seemed fine to me."

"I know," she shrugged. "But maybe he'll be a friend to Tucker."

"Maybe—" Clare and Isabelle ran into the kitchen interrupting Jeff.

"Quiet time," Meredith said as she grabbed Clare, picked her up, and gave her a playful kiss. The girls began to move in slow motion towards their rooms without complaint.

"I am extremely powerful," Meredith said as she lie down next to Jeff on Sunday afternoon. "They may not be sleeping, but they are all quiet in their rooms."

"Truly amazing," Jeff said. He was quiet for only a minute and then began to quiz Meredith. "What do you know about Dillon? That seemed a little quick to jump out there and invite him over. We don't even know why he's in the self-contained classroom."

"Does it matter? Are you going to be like Brenda?"

"Of course not. Good point, it doesn't matter."

"Well, he seemed fine to me. But I can tell he doesn't have autism—maybe dyslexic or something like that but definitely not a social disability like autism. Kids with autism always stick out socially, but kids with academic disabilities mostly fit in socially. There is only one other kid in the class that I think might have autism. The rest must have an academic disability."

"It's strange. Tuck can read like nobody's business, but he can't play a board game without someone coaching him. He's smart enough. He ought to be able to memorize social rules. I'm gonna work with him some more this week on taking turns playing the video game. He and Dillon will probably play video games?"

"That's a great idea. I'll work with him on offering Dillon a snack. The girls, especially Isabelle, are such sweet caregivers and they just cater to him. I guess it's easier or it's just what they are used to doing."

"It would be nice if Tuck could just have a friend over rather than us planning an autism intervention."

"I know, but I can't help it. I'm going to get some books for the intervention fun though. There are some books in our school library about making friends. Tucker and I have read them before, but I'm going to check them out and read them again to refresh his memory before Dillon's visit — I mean the autism intervention."

Chapter 12

Meredith and the girls walked in the kitchen lugging bags of groceries.

"Wow, you'd think the Queen of England was coming over," Jeff said as he started looking through the groceries in the homemade cloth bags that Meredith and Myla had made.

"Mom bought ice cream," Isabelle declared solemnly. "Real ice-cream."

"What else did you get?" Jeff asked as he started rummaging through another bag.

"Cookies," Isabelle announced and rolled her eyes towards Meredith as if her mother had lost her mind. Then she looked at her dad and wordlessly placed the oatmeal raisin cookie on the counter for Jeff to see she was telling the truth. She placed a pineapple next to the cookies. "This has to wait until Dillon arrives. But we are going to cut it before he gets here."

"I wish Dillon would come over every day," Jeff said opening the package of cookies.

"You are supposed to have your fruit first," Isabelle instructed Jeff.

Jeff picked up a handful of cookies and motioned for Isabelle to follow him. Isabelle, Tucker, and Clare all followed Jeff out the kitchen door. As Meredith was finishing coring the pineapple, the doorbell rang. Isabelle came running—with Tucker behind her—when she heard the doorbell.

"Welcome, Dillon," Meredith said as Sarah and Dillon entered the front door. "Tucker, take Dillon in the living room and you guys can play some video games."

Tucker said nothing but walked into the living room and powered on the game system. He did look back to see if Dillon was following him. *That's positive,* Meredith thought. Tucker quickly flipped his hands but then stopped himself and handed the control to Dillon. Isabelle joined the boys as they played video games. Meredith started cleaning the kitchen counters to be nearby if needed, but she didn't want to hover. She hoped having Dillon over would give Tucker an ally at Central and then he wouldn't continue to talk about sitting between John and Sarah. Maybe he could sit by Dillon. Dillon and Isabelle came into the kitchen and sat at two of the barstools.

"Let's get a snack," Isabelle said to Dillon as she greedily popped some pineapple chunks into her mouth. "Do you like pineapple? We also have ice cream."

"What kind of ice cream?" Dillon asked.

"Vanilla and we have strawberries or pineapple for a topping."

"Tucker, do you want some ice cream?" Meredith asked him from the kitchen hoping to lure him into the conversation.

No response from Tucker.

"Mom, can we go outside?" Isabelle asked.

"Sure," Meredith said. She walked over to Tucker and said, "Dillon went outside with Isabelle." Tucker just continued to play. "Tucker, don't you want to play with Dillon and Isabelle?" she asked as he tapped Tucker on the shoulder. Tucker looked at her, paused the game, and then looked around. He went outside with Isabelle and Dillon who were both swinging and talking. Tucker took long strides as he walked several times around the wooden swing and fort set. Meredith watched from the window. Tucker eventually climbed the ladder of the fort and sat on the platform and rocked and flipped his hands. He was nearby but not engaged.

The threesome had come back inside for another snack when the doorbell rang. It was already time for Dillon to go home.

"Do you have to go?" Isabelle pleaded.

Tucker's eyes darted from Dillon to Isabelle to Meredith as he searched for the clues to know what to do. Meredith rescued

54

him by saying, "Tucker, tell Dillon good-bye and thank him for coming over.

"Good-bye, Dillon. Thank you for coming over." Then he went back and sat down and restarted the video game.

"Maybe Tucker can come over to our house sometime," Sarah suggested.

Meredith thought, *I wish he could but…*

"Can Isabelle come too?" Dillon asked.

"That would be fun to have Tucker and Isabelle come over? We will do that soon."

"Good-bye, Dillon," Isabelle said. As the door closed, Isabelle ran over to Tucker and tapped him on the shoulder and said, "Let's go swing, Tucker."

Tucker jumped up and followed Isabelle. The video game music still played.

Meredith again watched from the window. They were both swinging this time and Isabelle was telling Tucker something. Tucker only smiled at Isabelle, but he never responded even though Isabelle kept talking. Isabelle and Tucker did have a relationship. It wasn't typical, but it was something. They had an understanding.

As she watched them, she noticed that as Isabelle was happily talking away, Tucker would occasionally glance at Isabelle with a smile. It was enough. For today . . . in the backyard . . . it was enough.

Chapter 13

Meredith opened the door to start loading the car with backpacks and lesson plans. The chilled air instantly raised goose bumps on her skin. She called back into the house, "Be sure and get a jacket." The ride to school was unusually quiet. The cool temperature had calmed down the sentiments of settling into the school year.

The light sweater Meredith had chosen didn't keep her from feeling chilled in her classroom. She decided to button it up to try and get warm as she graded papers while eating her lunch at her desk. Mrs. Riley peeked her head in the door. "Mrs. Howard, you have a phone call in the office."

Meredith hurried to the office. It had to be Jeff or Tucker since the girls were with her at school.

"Mrs. Howard, we need you to pick up Tucker from school. There has been an incident with another student, and we have Tucker in the office."

"Is he hurt?" Meredith asked.

"No, he's fine, but you need to pick him up. Tucker attacked another student so effective immediately he will be suspended for three days. We have a no tolerance policy for aggressive behavior."

Aggressive behavior— not again, Meredith said aloud to herself as a wave of nausea hit her. She took several deep breaths to steady herself. *Not again,* she thought. Well, he is impulsive but aggressive implies the desire to hurt someone else. Tucker didn't have the desire to hurt anyone but . . . sometimes people got hurt anyway. She thought of her black eye and felt a wave of nausea hit again. Meredith knew the world would classify Tucker as aggressive or violent. Her emergency room record would even validate that classification, but she knew there was no malice. Aggression implies intent. But for Tucker, damage to things and people were simply collateral damage to meltdowns, frustrations, and sensory overload.

Dr. Fisher was standing by the serenity fountain waiting for her. He ushered her into his office. Meredith blurted out her greatest fear, "Did Tucker hurt another student?" Fear for other students was one of the main reasons she hadn't protested at Cornerstone when Mrs. Riley expelled him. Deep down she knew the potential was there for another student to get hurt and she couldn't bear the thought. And in her mind, Meredith rationalized that Central was better equipped for Tucker. But now that didn't seem to be the case. Suddenly she was frantic over the safety of the other students and felt she hadn't been straightforward enough about Tucker's behaviors.

"No one got hurt this time. But it was luck!" Dr. Fisher began.

Meredith thought to herself, *There is that word again.*

"Tucker threw his lunch box towards a group of students. This wasn't shoving books to the floor. This was an overhand throw towards another student."

"Did the kids say something to Tucker? What had the kid done?"

Dr. Fisher looked surprised at the question. "As far as I know, the student did not do anything to provoke Tucker." His forehead was wrinkled, and then he leaned back in his chair to study Meredith.

"Tucker always has had a trigger for his meltdowns. Sometimes it's hard to figure out, but he has never started a fight. There has to be a reason," Meredith insisted. "Was there a teacher present?"

"There was a teacher nearby and she did not see any provocation. Mrs. Howard, Tucker wanted to hit the other student. He wanted to hurt him. It was lucky it was just a lunch box. We have a no tolerance policy for acts of aggression. I know Tucker has only been here a short time, but he needs to learn that aggression is not tolerated."

Meredith knew Dr. Fisher had to be wrong. Something must have provoked Tucker. Meredith also knew the pain of being in the way when Tucker was provoked.

They drove home in silence. All she knew was that he threw his lunch box at another student. No one was hurt . . . this time. Meredith didn't even know her son anymore. He used to be a compliant little guy and now he's just added *aggressive* to his list of labels.

At the house, she sent Tucker to his room for his bad behavior at school. He didn't feel punished. He simply complied. When Meredith went into his room, she noticed how sparse the room had become. No pictures were on the wall. Those had long ago been jerked down. His empty bookcase stood collecting dust in the corner. All of his favorite toys had been torn up or thrown. The thrown toys had a new home— sitting on top of the kitchen refrigerator. The drywall had several holes in it where Tucker had used his elbow against the wall. One hole stood like a scar on the wall, repaired but never painted. The others were just open wounds in need of repair. A book lay on the floor where it had been tossed.

Meredith picked up the book and climbed on the bed pulling Tucker close to her. With Tucker tucked in the crook of her arm, she read the book out loud to him. The book had icons in the story which corresponded to the buttons that made a sound. She read to the icons and then Tucker would chime in with the word and push the button just like he did a few years ago when this book had been his favorite.

"Let's read it again," Tucker said.

After the fourth time, Meredith looked around the room. This desolate scarred room would make anyone feel bad about themselves.

"Tucker, you want to fix up your room this week?"

"Okay."

Jeff came into the house and called Meredith's name with obvious anxiety in his voice. Tucker threw the book at the wall.

She sighed as sadness washed over her at Tucker's response to hearing Jeff's voice. She picked up the book and placed it on top of the bookshelf and went into the living room.

"I got your message. What did they say at Central?" Jeff began.

"Tucker got suspended for three days for throwing his lunch box at a kid in the lunchroom."

"I told you not to get him that old-fashioned metal lunch box. You should have gotten him one of those soft lunch boxes."

"That is not the point," Meredith said looking shocked at Jeff's reaction.

"How could they suspend him? He barely has started! I can't believe this is happening again!" Jeff ranted, pacing back and forth.

"He just got suspended, not expelled this time."

"And that makes it better?"

There was a sound from Tucker's room as he threw something against the wall . . . again.

"Keep your voice down," Meredith chastised Jeff and then changed the subject. "Even though he has been suspended, Tucker's appointment with the behavior specialist is still scheduled for tomorrow. And then Friday we have the educational planning meeting regarding the test results from the academic testing and the behavior test. Other than that, Tucker and I will be home at least until Friday unless you can stay with him?" Meredith asked.

"I can't . . . not this time," Jeff said.

Chapter 14

Jeff drove downtown for a lunch date with Kate. He had been so surprised when she called. He practiced several different conversation scenarios out loud in the car on the way to meet Kate. He found her sitting on the bench in front of the huge window that said, "The Right Step Day Program." She looked as good as expected for someone living on the streets. Her clothes were clean. She seemed nervous as she got in the car. They drove to The Blue Plate Special, a nearby restaurant with well-known plate lunches. Kate looked out of place in the restaurant filled with business men and women on lunch.

Jeff jumped right in, "Kate, I'm glad you called. I want to get you some help."

"Tell me what you really want," Kate said and chuckled. She looked up and saw Jeff staring at her as if he just tasted spoiled milk. She turned serious and said, "I'm beyond help at this point. Don't bother." She looked down, and her eyes lost their sparkle with the last sentence.

"Kate, I'm sorry. I'm not very good at this. I want to listen. Tell me why you called? What can I do?"

"I was hoping you could let me borrow some money. I could get a hotel and get cleaned up so I can see Meredith."

"Okay, I can do that. But I still want to get you some help—some real help. I talked to a counselor and there is help available."

" I know. I know. One day at a time. Right now, the days are long. I fight, but I don't think I'm gonna win. I'm just so tired." Kate took both hands and covered her face. She ran her fingertips under her eyes. Jeff thought she was about to lay her head down on the table. He looked around to see if anyone noticed. "Just forget about me. I'm lost." She paused and some resolve returned to her face. "It was nice of you to buy me lunch and all but . . . really I just wanted to talk to you about seeing Meredith. I miss her."

Jeff looked at her and he knew he couldn't walk away. It

would be like leaving the scene of an accident when people are crying in pain. "Kate, I want to help you out of this. We all have bad luck. Anyone of these people here could end up in your situation. They think they wouldn't, but it could happen to anyone. Most people are just one paycheck away from the streets. If people think they are in control, they are just kidding themselves."

The waitress picked up the salad bowls and then sat a plate of chicken fried steak smothered in mashed potatoes and gravy in front of each of them. Jeff winked and said, "Don't tell Meredith as he sliced into his steak." Kate smiled at Jeff. Even though both Kate and Meredith were thin, Kate ate more like one of the guys while Meredith measured the environmental impact of each food choice.

"Your situation is a lot like Tucker and his autism. People want to believe it can't happen to them. They want to find a reason— something to avoid or some special thing to do. I have had people ask me if Meredith took a certain drug or if we let him watch too much TV. It's all so absurd sometimes. If someone does the right therapy or buys the right products or eats the right food, they think they can insulate themselves from *catching* autism. That just doesn't happen. And I guess what annoys me the most is the implication that Meredith or I did something wrong or made some kind of mistake. Don't get me wrong, we have made mistakes— no doubt about that. But Tuck being punished for my mistakes is a stretch for my mind."

Jeff saw a shift in Kate's attitude as she assumed a more professional tone. "Tucker is such an interesting and unique kid. The girls are precious too. I don't understand some people's attitudes. When I worked as a child advocate—in my other life— so many of the kids were treated like throw-away kids because of a problem in their family." She paused and the weariness returned to her face and then to her tone of voice as she continued, "The last family I worked with had a precious four-year-old. I was working to get him out of the home. This system gives the parents too many chances. He disappeared. I looked and looked for him. I can't find him. I'm still looking everywhere I go. I wonder if he is on the street with his mother. I guess the system started to get to me. I hate it—I gave up or gave in. I don't know which. I just don't have the strength anymore to try. I want to find him. It's exhausting." She placed her elbows on the table and propped up her head.

"Kate, I'm not giving up on you. So don't give up on yourself. I'm not giving up on Tucker either." Jeff took a breath and looked off into the distance, and a weariness came across his face. "I'm exhausted too but from dealing with Tucker. I guess we are just two tired people."

"You are one strange guy," she said and looked around the room at the people in the restaurant. "I use to be one of these purposeful people in this restaurant, but something happened. I'm not sure what started it or what it was. But I definitely didn't win the breakup."

"You will yet," Jeff said. "Will you go with me to talk to a counselor?"

Kate's face clouded. "I've been to AA. I do great at the meetings but can't seem to stay on track. I always fall off. I don't have the resilience for another fall. I think I'll just stay down. I'm not like Meredith. She keeps going no matter what. And if I could just get cleaned up and see Meredith, she could help me put some perspective on my situation. She's my touchstone, but I don't want her to see me like this."

"Okay, I'll give you the money and let's get you some help. Kate, please. . . you can do this. There are other options— private programs."

"Please," she said stringing out the words. "I don't have that kind of money laying around. Besides, it's not gonna work."

"Kate, you want to see Meredith, right. Well, she wants to see you too. She thinks you're avoiding her because you're mad at her over what's his name. I bet she's called you 20 times in the last month."

"Really?" She smiled a sad smile then she sighed. "Give me a few days to think about it. What do you want me to do?"

"Get help. Go to a program. I've been researching options. There are some decent choices nearby. Meredith needs you, and I want you to be a part of our lives again. And that little boy you were talking about— you may be the only hope for kids like him."

Her elbows were on the table and her hands were covering her face again. She placed her folded hands in her lap and looked at Jeff. She mouthed, okay. Her eyes didn't match her words.

"Okay," Jeff said then smiled, "Okay, Let's go."

"Not right now. How about in a couple of days after I clean up a bit?"

"Okay, I'll make the arrangements and I'll pick you up in two days—same place—same time."

"It just seems like too much—"

Jeff interrupted, "Kate, you're our only family. You know my sister checked out. I don't want you checking out too." Jeff gave her the money for a hotel hoping that was what she was really using it for. He was surprised at his own thoughts. He left her back at the bench and held up two fingers.

She waved and smiled back.

Chapter 15

On Friday, Jeff showed up for their first Individual Educational Planning meeting with Meredith to get the results of the testing and recommendations of the school. Even though Tucker was suspended, he was allowed to go to the self-contained classroom and play on the computer. The diagnoses were read out loud as if Dr. Fisher was calling numbers for a bingo game. Mild autism, mild intellectual deficit, social delay, oppositional disorder, and obsessive-compulsive behavior—the words hung in the air of the room. Meredith put her hands together almost like she was praying and tapped her lips lightly with her index fingers as she waited for the team of professionals who had summed up Tucker in a ten page report to begin their dissertations.

Dr. Brick, the psychologist, began with his justification for the label of oppositional disorder. His attire of a loose-fitting button-down collared shirt with a loose tie gave him an appearance of being relaxed. But his words were stiff. He slid the incident report across the table. Jeff and Meredith read the incident report from when Tucker threw the lunch box. This incident had happened in the lunchroom and the child involved was not a special education student as Meredith and Jeff had assumed. *The lunchroom is not a good place for Tucker*, Meredith thought. The noises and smells always sent Tucker into sensory overload. First the chair incident at Cornerstone . . . in the lunchroom and now the lunch box incident . . . again in the lunchroom. The other child was a sixth grader in a regular classroom.

"Did the other student in this incident report get suspended also?" Jeff unclenched his teeth and asked hoping there had been a balanced discipline approach.

Dr. Brick motioned for Dr. Fisher to have the floor. He replied, "From all appearances, Tucker attacked the boy without provocation. So the other student did not receive any consequences."

"That is not like Tucker at all. His meltdowns usually have a reason. Did you ask Tucker's classmates about what happened?"

"No, but we did ask some students that witnessed the assault. As far as the onlookers could tell, Tucker assaulted the student for no reason. I'm not saying that something did not set Tucker off. I'm just saying that whatever caused Tucker to react the way he did was not apparent to the other students."

"How come you didn't ask any students from Tucker's class?" Meredith asked.

Dr. Fisher looked at her as if the answer was obvious, but he did not respond.

"Where were the teachers when all this was happening?" Jeff demanded.

"There was lunch staff and a teacher's aide nearby. But again, no one saw Tucker being provoked."

"The staff needs to be more alert," Jeff fumed. "I think this is a failure of the staff to monitor the lunchroom environment, and our son is being punished because the staff was not paying attention."

Dr. Fisher looked at Jeff to acknowledge that he had spoken, but Dr. Fisher neither agreed nor disagreed. "The cause of the assault does not matter. That the assault occurred is a serious issue and demands a strict behavior plan. This is important for Tucker so he knows limits and for the safety of the other students." He then simply began to present the behavior management plan that Tucker would now have in place along with his label of aggressive.

The behavior management plan was laid out and it mostly focused on positive reinforcement. The staff in the self-contained classroom where Tucker would be educated had training in physically restraining students, and the plan included the use of restraints if necessary. Tucker would eat lunch in the classroom and would get to join the other students as a reward for good lunchtime behavior. If the aggressive behavior continued, Tucker would be placed at Hillside Behavioral Health, an alternative school for students who are mentally disturbed. "A placement at Hillside is not appropriate. That place is like a prison environment. I toured that facility, and Tucker does not belong there. Most of the students there have been involved with the legal system," Jeff stated.

"I realize that it's a placement of last resort, but here at Central, we are not equipped to handle a student with aggression. But for now, we will implement behavior management in the classroom. If things deteriorate, we may need to consider other options."

Jeff and Meredith looked at each other. Neither one smiled.

"First, we will remove him from the lunchroom, and he will have to earn back the privilege of eating with the other students."

Jeff and Meredith both knew the reward for Tucker would be not eating in the lunchroom. He would not be trying to go back to the lunchroom with all its noises and smell that overwhelm his sensory system. Sensory overload usually began with rocking or humming. An unexpected loud noise could be enough to send Tucker into a "fight or flight" mode. These reactions were often interpreted as aggression. But in reality, Tucker was simply trying to escape to stop the noise, the smell, or whatever the uncomfortable or fearful sensation might be.

"I think Tucker will enjoy eating in the classroom. It's much quieter, and noises can be upsetting to him," Meredith offered.

"So do you think the noise of the lunchroom caused Tucker's aggressive behavior?" one of the people across the table from the Howards asked.

"No, he doesn't act aggressively when he has sensory overload. I can tell when he is in overload because he rocks slightly and sometimes hums. It doesn't happen very often. We lead a rather quiet life."

Meredith and Jeff bantered back and forth with the professionals whether Tucker was exhibiting aggressive behaviors or experiencing meltdowns due to sensory overload. The more Jeff and Meredith tried to explain Tucker's behavior, the more it seemed like they were trying to defend or justify his behavior. Without thinking, Meredith used her black eye as an example of Tucker's lack of understanding of social situations. The discussion went downhill from there, and Meredith decided she was doing more harm than good for Tucker and decided to shut up.

Jeff rescued her by saying, "We need a couple of days to consider this IEP for Tucker. There are a couple of items I would like to think about and talk about with Meredith."

"That is fine. Just sign that you attended the meeting. But be aware, the plan can go into effect without your consent. The rest of the members of the team have agreed on the behavior plan. Feel free to contact us if you would like to amend the plan in any way before the one-year review. Mrs. Canon will be sending home weekly reports to keep you updated on Tucker's progress. I'm confident that once he gets acclimated to his new school and classmates, he will do fine."

I wonder what makes him so confident, Jeff thought as he clenched his teeth and looked at the members of the team who had decided what was best for Tucker after spending collectively 6 hours with him. He gritted his teeth knowing that speaking his mind would get him on the bad side of the professionals sitting across the table from him, and he knew that Tucker might need their help. Meredith had already done enough damage and she looked wounded. She knew her insight didn't matter to the team unless it was on a behavioral scale of 1 to 5.

For a moment, no one said anything. The air grew stale in the room as the professionals looked at the Howards and Jeff stared back. Meredith was looking down at her hands clinched neatly together on the table. Her knuckles were white. She decided to excuse herself to pick Tucker up from the self-contained classroom and lied about starting his new routine on Monday. She just needed to breathe in some fresh air. She did feel bad for abandoning Jeff and not including him in her excuse. But Jeff could handle himself. She just wanted to have Tucker with her away from the "professionals." Jeff glanced at the door willing Meredith to appear. His elbows rested on the table with his hands clasp. No one had spoken since Meredith left. When Meredith appeared at the conference room door holding Tucker's hand, Jeff jumped up and headed for the door not acknowledging the professionals who stood up for parting niceties. Jeff grabbed Tucker by his other hand and both were unaware of the social faux pas.

Once outside, Jeff and Meredith smiled at each other. Jeff took a deep breath and let it out slow. "Well, that was pleasant," he said sarcastically.

"Absolutely lovely," Meredith replied playing along.

"Sir Tuck, will you and the lady accompany me to the kingdom of Chuck E. Cheese?" Jeff asked as he bowed at the waist.

Meredith curtsied, smiled at Jeff, and said, "They probably think we are nuts too."

"I'm beginning to feel crazy."

Chuck E Cheese was sparsely populated since it was a school day. Twenty dollars of tokens would keep Tucker blissfully occupied. Tucker enjoyed the noises he made playing the machines. He could control these noises; they were predictable. Tucker went off to play while Meredith and Jeff had some time to discuss the meeting. They automatically positioned themselves where they could see the exit and the play area.

Jeff began, "How can that group of people think Tuck would ever belong in a place like Hillside Behavioral Health? That place is for emotionally disturbed individuals. I'm not sure why Tuck *assaulted* the other student, but I don't think we have the whole story. I feel like we have been robbed — in open daylight — and there is no one to take the crime report. They just start the plan no matter what we think. I'm not sure why they even wanted us at the meeting. I think what annoys me the most is that they said we were part of the team, but we aren't going to get to play. I'm still thinking Tuck needs his own aide who can be with him to help with the social matrix he can't seem to navigate. Then he could settle in and be at peace. But I guess you noticed the reaction I got when I suggested that."

"They looked at you like you had lost your *ever-loving mind*," Meredith said in her best southern accent as she shook her head in disbelief at the professionals' understanding of Tucker. "I know he can do the work; he just needs social support in the regular classroom."

"The plan isn't bad except the part about Hillside Behavior Health. They would eat him alive at that place. It just bothers me because it seems like it's a threat. They seem to have all the right papers and all the right professionals and all the right equipment, but it just seems heartless—no compassion, no soul."

"It'll probably be fine. We are overreacting. It's hard to have your child *clinicalized*—I'm not sure if that is even a word." Meredith began flipping through the handbook she received at the meeting. She opened to the section on what to do if you disagree with a committee decision. She quickly read the information and then summarized it for Jeff, "The handbook says we are entitled to a second opinion. We could get a second opinion from someone who sees Tucker as a capable young boy with sensory issues, not just a defiant aggressor who needs placement in a facility for violent students. His social skills and sensory issues are the problems not so much his academics. If we could get the label oppositional disorder removed, then Hillside wouldn't be a valid alternative.

Meredith dog-eared the pages about the process for disagreement, and she made notes about her thoughts in the

69

margin. She told Jeff, "There is a list of parent advocacy groups here. We need to call an advocate."

Jeff nodded in agreement as he finished his pizza.

"I'm going to call Kate and see if she had any recommendations," Meredith said and pulled out her phone. Kate was an advocate for children in the foster care system. "Kate must have had experience with something like this before," Meredith said.

Jeff set his pizza down and watched Meredith and wondered if Kate might answer. He hadn't thought about her cell phone.

Meredith held the phone up for Jeff to hear the recorded message—*I'm sorry the number you have dialed has been disconnected.*

"Well, Kate must have changed her number," Meredith mused, "That is just like Kate. She is probably still mad."

"At least she's not aggressive," Jeff said and rested his elbow on the table with his chin in his hand and smiled at Meredith. Meredith smiled back and rolled her eyes.

He thought momentarily about telling Meredith about Kate coming over on Saturday, but he decided against it. *What if Kate just used the money for alcohol?* he thought and was surprised at himself that he didn't trust Kate. He knew if Kate were a *no show,* Meredith would insist on finding her, but Jackie—the counselor Jeff spoke with—had said that Kate needed to make this decision on her own. Meredith would push her.

"Regardless of Kate," Jeff said, "we need to do what we think is best as his parents. Professionals see things differently. He is our son, and we love him and we need to make the decisions that are best for him. Kate would probably just look at this through professional eyes. We are in this for the long-term outcome of a well-adjusted, productive, happy adult. We want what's best for him for his life, not just one school year," Jeff said trying to put perspective on the situation.

"You're right. We can let him go back to Central under the new behavior management plan and see what happens," Meredith said and then continued, "It's not a bad plan. It just seems like they look at the effect and not the cause. The cause is a sensory issue. But I do think his teachers are excellent. If it gets to the point where they place him at Hillside, I'll pull him out, but I think it's just a threat."

Jeff started, "I agree. At this point, he just needs understanding of his disability and his sensory issues. If they force him and restrain him, it will break his spirit. He is just socially immature for age. He coexists with the other students, but he doesn't connect. We just need some time. We don't have to agree and if anything we don't like happens, we will pull him out

Meredith said, "Absolutely."

Jeff looked at his watch. "I'll take Tucker home and you pick up the girls."

Meredith called the advocacy number as she waited in the car for the dismissal bell.

When Meredith and the girls lumbered into the house under the weight of heavy backpacks and lunch boxes, they all stopped in the doorway. Tucker was sitting in a chair facing the wall, and Jeff was sweeping up glass from the kitchen floor. Jeff relayed the events to Meredith ejecting each word. His fists were clenched. "Tucker knocked the dishes off the table . . . the breakfast dishes. . . to the floor when he asked me where you were, and I said that you were at" —Jeff spread his arms out and held them out like a magician revealing his surprise— "at Cornerstone."

From his chair facing the wall, Tucker muttered an automatic, "I'm sorry."

"He's . . ." Jeff started to yell at Meredith but then turned to Tucker. "You're not sorry." Jeff then turned back to face Meredith,

71

"This is too much for me today!" Jeff waved his hands around to include the girls, Tucker, the mess, the meeting. "I need to focus on work right now. I can't be helpful here tonight. I'm going to the office. Missing work today for the meeting has already put me behind. I have a million things still to accomplish today, and I was hoping to work at home tonight, but I can't . . . I can't . . . I can't work here. I need a place free of distraction. Call me if you need me. I can't stay here. It's no good . . . no good. I need to focus!" Jeff dumped the glass into the trash, picked up his briefcase, and left with an "I'm sorry" just like Tuckers.

Meredith, the girls, and Tucker watched as Jeff stormed out of the house. The girls stood with their backpacks still on their backs and their lunch boxes still in their hands. Meredith still held a stack of books mingled with papers to grade that she had picked up from her substitute. They all silently watched as Jeff left the house. Tucker looked at them and dropped his head and said, "I'm sorry, Mom."

Meredith went over to Tucker and put her arm around his shoulder pulling him close to her and said, "It's okay, Tucker. Daddy is having himself a meltdown. She sat the books on the table and looked at the back door that Jeff had just walked out. She kept thinking Jeff would come back in and say he was sorry and hug Tucker too, but then she heard the car backing out of the driveway. She looked at the girls and could tell they were waiting for something also. "Just leave your backpacks in the kitchen for homework time later," Meredith said so the girls would quit staring at the door and then her. She looked at Tucker. She knew the difference between bad behavior, impulsive behavior, and sensory overload. And so did Tucker. This was just bad behavior and both Tucker and Meredith knew it. Apparently, so did Isabelle because she hung back a bit waiting to see what Tucker's punishment might be.

Meredith looked at Tucker and gave out the punishment, "No DS for you tonight. Go get it and bring it to me."

Tucker left and returned shortly with his DS. He handed it up to Meredith.

"Tucker, you know what you did was wrong?" Meredith asked.

"I shouldn't have gotten angry and knocked the dishes off the table but I . . ."

Meredith interrupted Tucker, "There is no *but.*" There is no reason to break the dishes."

Tucker didn't argue he only said, "I know."

Isabelle had heard the punishment and was secretly pleased. She pressed her lips together to suppress her smile. She always delighted in justice. The punishment phase was over so Isabelle called out, "Tucker, let's go swing."

Tucker looked at Meredith. There was a pause as Meredith looked at Tucker. He was looking up at her in her eyes. Those blue eyes looking at her made her feel happy. She smiled at him and said, "Okay, put your jacket on and you can go."

Tucker put on his jacket and ran off with Isabelle to the backyard.

Meredith sat down at the table and ran both hands through her hair. Her day wasn't finished either. She had more work to do too. There was dinner, dishes, homework, papers to grade, and bedtime, but she just sat there trying to figure out if Tucker's issue were simple or complex. It was hard to decide.

Chapter 16

Jeff drove downtown at lunchtime on Saturday to pick up Kate and take her to the rehab center. He pulled up to the bench where he had found Kate two days before and where he had left her, but this time she wasn't sitting there. He pulled over and waited. After 30 minutes past, he went into the Right Step Day Program and asked if anyone had seen Kate Harper or had heard from her. No one had any information so he left his number again. He drove around the downtown area hoping to catch a glimpse of her — but no luck.

Kate was expected to check-in to rehab this afternoon so he drove out to tell Jackie, the counselor at The 4:12 Center, that Kate wouldn't be arriving. The 4:12 Center was the rehab Jeff had chosen for Kate after careful research. The center's name was a reference to the verse from Ecclesiastic 4:12—A cord of three strands is not quickly broken. The center's rehabilitation focused on the individual, God or the higher power, and establishing community. These three things working together are what bring real change to people and their lives.

"These things never seem to be straightforward and easy. It has to be her decision to change. You can't force her. She will just start blaming you if things don't work out," Jackie said.

"She seemed so sincere. She said she wanted to see her sister — my wife— and I gave her some money for a hotel to get cleaned up. I probably shouldn't have done that?"

"You don't know what she did with the money, and you need to be supportive but don't let her start depending on you or using you. You can't co-sign her lies."

"I just want her to be okay. I want to have her back in our lives. My family is going through some challenging times right now. I haven't shared much about it with Kate, but I know she would be there for Meredith if she only knew."

"I hear what you are saying, but what YOU want won't help

Kate. Kate has to want recovery herself. It's up to her how she's going to live her life. You'll be wasting your money if you talk her into starting rehab when she's not ready. But when she is ready — and hopefully that will be soon — the potential for real change is there. I have seen people start rehab and make remarkable progress because they want it. She has to want it. People only change when the pain of staying the same is too great. We also call that *rock bottom*. She hasn't hit rock bottom yet."

"She can't be too far from it. She is thin and sickly looking. I barely recognized her when I happened upon her weeks ago."

"Everyone's rock bottom is different. Some people hit it quickly and early before their lives are too outwardly affected, and some people lose everything including their health before they are ready to make a change. Rock bottom is the lowest point someone can go and it's also the turning point where people start making changes to improve their situation."

"What should I do if she calls again?"

"Take her to lunch like you did before. If you're worried about her health, you might bring her some portable food. If she asks you to pay for a hotel, then you can pay for the hotel, but don't give her the cash. Be honest and don't buy into her lies. If she thinks you believe the lies, she may start believing them too. I'll give you some resources for people who love an addict. There are family meetings that will help you understand Kate better."

"Thank you." Jeff took the materials. "I'll try and make it. But it's *iffy*. I have a son with autism that needs a lot of attention right now. He's been expelled from one school and suspended from another. My wife has been missing a lot of work so I'm working hard to stay ahead. It's a day-by-day thing."

"That must be hard."

"It is, but we are working a plan to get him the help he needs and fortunately business has been good so I'm staying ahead."

Chapter 17

"Mom, you know we need to go by and pick up the driver's ed book so I can study for my permit," Myla announced with authority as they walked to the car after school. She shot a smile at Isabelle. "I want to take the test the day after my birthday so I need some time to study."

Meredith raised her eyebrows and looked over at Myla. "I guess we can do that," Meredith responded.

"I will be the first one in my grade to get my driver's permit. The day after I pass the test, I want to drive to school. I told Desiree I would be driving to school soon."

Meredith didn't make any commitments but only said, "We'll see." Myla dug through her backpack to retrieve some gum and handed a piece to Isabelle in the backseat. Meredith noticed that Myla was indeed changing.

October 28 was Myla's birthday, making her one of the oldest students in 8th grade. She liked this and it seemed to bring some authority to her status because she was older than everyone else in her class.

"Can we do the braids with ribbons and feathers again this year at your birthday sleepover?" Isabelle asked with expected eyes. "I want to look exotic," Isabelle said emphasizing the word 'exotic' while flipping her hair up with both hands. "Everyone at school has told me how exotic I look." Isabelle tilted her chin up and closed her eyes obviously enjoying using the word, 'exotic'.

Each year on Myla's birthday, she and her mother planned a sleepover for her friends. It always involved a late night movie with popcorn in the living room. This year her October 28 birthday would fall on a Friday night making this an extra special birthday.

A cloudy look crossed Myla's face and she looked down at the floorboard of the car and put one hand up by her mouth and rested her chin on her palm. "I'm too old for a sleepover. That seems sort of childish. I'm going to be fourteen and driving. A sleepover is way too juvenile."

"Juvenile?" Meredith repeated. "That's nonsense, Myla. Fourteen is a great age to have a sleepover," Meredith spoke and then waited for Myla to argue, but there was nothing, so Meredith continued. "I was thinking pizza and pedicures for the theme for the evening. I talked to Eva— she teaches 4th grade at Cornerstone and has a daughter who is studying to be a cosmetologist— and she said her daughter could come over and do everyone's nails. I don't think that is too juvenile. Do you?"

"Mom, well . . . it's. . . I'm just not in the mood for a party."

"What do you mean not in the mood?"

"Well . . . Dad seems to be stressed out and I don't want him to yell. What if Tucker has one of his moods and throws something? I would be horrified. It has gotten around school how Tucker threw the chair and got kicked out of school. Isabelle told everyone that Tucker gave you the black eye. Desiree's mom already told her that she can't come. She didn't say, but I know it's because of Tucker. Gloria said she might not be able to come either."

Meredith felt her heart sink and she said, "I see." Meredith wasn't sure if she felt anger or embarrassment at Myla's report. On the one side Meredith was embarrassed because she had confirmation that other families—typical families—considered her family strange. But she also felt anger at being judged. Meredith fluctuated between the two emotions and then was overcome with sadness when she looked at Myla. They rode in silence for a while. Meredith didn't trust her own emotions.

Myla had already realized the "no-win" situation of her life, but she never complained about Tucker. She was just making another adjustment for Tucker in her life of many adjustments. She did not choose this and it could make her either better or worse.

"I wonder if we had the party at the Civic Center Hotel if Desiree and Gloria could come. There is an indoor swimming pool.

We could do our pedicures after a swim, have our pizza, get our nails done, and watch our movie," Meredith suggested.

Myla's face brightened at the prospect. "A pool party in October? Now that would be cool. Do you think they could come?"

The tension left Meredith's shoulders as she took a deep gathered breath and smiled at Myla's sudden enthusiasm for a sleepover. "Let me make sure I can get a reservation and then I'll call and ask their parents."

As they were walking into the house, Myla hugged her mom, "You're the best."

It did so happen that Desiree and Gloria were both suddenly free for the birthday swimming party at the Civic Center. Eva's daughter gave Myla a sample of 10 nail designs to choose from for the party. Nail designs dominated lunch conversations. The group determined that each girl would get a balloon on the index fingernail because the nails were done at the party. Of course, Isabelle and Clare joined the fun at the pool, pizza, and pedicure party. Jeff stayed home with Tucker missing his daughter's 14th birthday party.

Meredith called Kate again, hoping to invite her to Myla's party. This time she got an answer, but the person hadn't heard of Kate. The number had been reassigned. Where was Kate? Her anxiety was growing, but she tried to talk herself out it.

Chapter 18

Meredith had been five years old when Kate was born, and Kate had been a long awaited *gift* for Meredith. She even took baby Kate for her show-and-tell in kindergarten. Meredith took great pride in all of Kate's achievements. The day that Meredith walked Kate into school to start kindergarten, she was as proud as any parent would be watching a child meet a milestone. And then Meredith thought about the day she left for college and left Kate alone with their mom and dad who were struggling to get along. Kate had said, *Please, don't leave me here with those two.* But she had. She left Kate to manage in the increasing hostile home environment when Kate was only Myla's age. Meredith remembered saying, *Oh, it's not that bad*, but Meredith was glad to leave and leave the conflict behind. Soon she was busy with studying and friends, and the hostility was out of sight and out of mind.

At Christmas break from college when Meredith visited home, she was alarmed at Kate's withdrawal and how disengaged she had become. Meredith talked to her parents almost as if they were quarreling children about their anger and how it was affecting Kate. Her parents took Meredith's insight to heart and decided on counseling and came through the midlife crisis, and they were better friends on the other side. However, the counseling didn't take with Kate, but she did seem to rebound and bloom in the new found freedom and refuge that college provided. And Kate wanted to help others in crisis and majored in social services and landed a job as a child advocate for children in the foster system. Meredith knew Kate could give her some insight into Tucker's situation, but it looked like Kate had disengaged once again. Meredith still had to help Tucker even if she couldn't find Kate.

Chapter 19

Meredith called Mrs. Wilson, a special education advocate listed on a website, who had worked with many families and schools helping design programs and service plans to benefit both the school and the family. The schools and families both had a very fine line where they would compromise, and Mrs. Wilson had successfully brought both parties to that line in more than one situation.

As soon as Meredith began talking to Mrs. Wilson, she could tell that Mrs. Wilson enjoyed a challenge and confrontation was something she enjoyed. She was glad to have Mrs. Wilson on her side. From their conversation, Meredith learned there were two alternate schools in their area for students with behavior issues. One school, Hillside Behavioral Health, which they had learned, was geared to meet the needs of students with severe behavior issues related to truancy, drug use, violent offenses, etc. The other alternative school was a private school for students with special needs and behavioral issues. Only Hillside Behavioral Health, which was part of the local school system, was brought up in the meeting, and the mention of it seemed like a threat. Central would have to pay the tuition to the private school that was independent of the public school. The private, alternative school for students with special needs was called Amicus, Latin for friends, and it had a well-trained and educated staff. A therapist was assigned to each student's family. Amicus considered special needs a family affair not just a label for educational services. Of course, Jeff and Meredith could pay the tuition themselves, but at $35,000 a year this was out of the question financially for them. Even the scholarships did not get the tuition down to a doable level. One of the main reasons Meredith worked at Cornerstone was the half-price tuition. Cornerstone wouldn't even be possible for the girls without a tuition discount for teachers and a discount for multi-students.

"From what you have told me so far, Amicus might be the

best placement for Tucker, but he will not get a personal aide there," Mrs. Wilson stated over the phone. "The trick in these situations is the definitions of *most appropriate* and *least restrictive* environment. These are vague terms and can be interpreted a variety of ways. The public school will argue that the public setting gives Tucker the opportunity to be with non-disabled students and, therefore, is the least restrictive."

"That's true, and I want him to be able to engage with all people, not just disabled people. We want to give Tucker the best possible outcome so he will be happy and productive throughout his life."

"I understand. That is exactly what all parents want. However, many times, the school districts simply match the *most appropriate* to the programs that they have and are already in place. This is a battle for you and your family. You are battling for Tucker's future," Mrs. Wilson said with all the determination of a coach giving a sideline talk to the players.

"Central seems well staffed, and I do like Mrs. Canon and wouldn't want to jeopardize Tucker's place in her class. He has done well with her," Meredith said. "We just don't want the label of oppositional disorder and the threat of Tucker being sent to Hillside Behavioral Health. I feel like I need to educate the staff at Central about sensory disorders and impulsiveness. I think Mrs. Canon gets it. She was in the meeting but said nothing. I guess if she wants to keep her job, she won't go against the administration."

"This situation is so much more than the classroom teacher. Don't get me wrong. The teachers are very important and can make or break a kid. But it's the attitude of the administration. At Central, the administration is older, and rather than work with families, they consider forcing a hearing a cheaper option. Few families proceed as far as a hearing. It's a difficult journey. Many times the school district will make some concessions during the progress. Even at that, it sometimes seems the administration at

Central considers the few that push the issue cheaper than reorganizing and accommodating every child whose parents insist their child's behavior necessitated an independent learning environment. In all fairness to the school, it's probably hard to determine who actually needs help and who is making excuses for their child's failure. The ones who really need it push for change."

"Just talking about this makes me anxious. It seems so overwhelming," Meredith said and took a slow breath to slow down her breathing and frustration.

"Change is slow, but it's coming. There will be new administrators as the current ones retire. And some families in your district have already won. Most families can't endure the long battle to a hearing," Mrs. Wilson said.

Determined, Meredith said, "Well, I can make it— for Tucker and for the families behind me."

"Then visit Amicus," Mrs. Wilson said and then continued, "so you can see for yourself if you want to ask for this option. I think the school is great, but you need to see if Tucker likes it. Then you will know whether Amicus or an aide at Central is your preferred choice. If you choose an aide at Central, you can ask that the staff get training in sensory issues. Of course, that doesn't help Tucker right now. The staff at Amicus already has had the training. Just don't expect the administration at Central to say, *okay* on either one. They think Tucker is a behavioral problem. Remember, they didn't even mention Amicus existed. So get ready for the fight ahead."

Chapter 20

Meredith pulled up in front of Amicus. It had a semi-circle of brick steps that led up to a landing and then more steps to the door. Large paned windows lined up on both sides of the door. She knew it was a school and there was a small marquee by the front door, but it could have also been another type of business or even a small church. It was well-maintained but not award winning in appearances like Central.

Meredith had prepared Tucker for the visit by telling him about Amicus. "Tucker, remember that we are going to see a different school today. You know what Cornerstone school is like and you have been to Central. And this is another school. Do you remember the name of it?"

"Amicus"

"And remember you are not going to stay today. We are just going to look around and see if we like the classrooms and meet the teachers."

Tucker nodded and said, "Okay."

They arrived early and sat in the car. Meredith didn't want to rush Tucker and create any anxiety for him. She talked about the outside of the school while they sat in the car. "The building is brick and it has lots of big windows. I see a playground on the side with a nice fence. The students don't have to worry about the ball rolling too far away. There are four brick steps going up to the building and then three more steps. How about let's go inside and see what it's like inside?"

"Okay."

The entrance walls were pale blue and the office clearly marked. They entered and asked for Mrs. Staten stating they had an appointment. Mrs. Staten emerged from her office. She clapped her hands together and then held out her hand to Meredith. "Hi, Mrs. Howard, I'm Mrs. Staten. I'm so glad you came here for a visit."

Meredith wanted to back up immediately. Mrs. Staten was about 5'11" and in her late 50's. She had a warm smile and dark hair. She bent her knees slightly, placed her hands on her knees, and looked directly at Tucker. She waited for him to look at her and then started, "This must be Tucker."

"Yes, Tucker say, *Hi!*" Meredith prompted but got no response from Tucker. He was looking up at Mrs. Staten as if she was acting strangely. Tucker then made eye-contact with Meredith with a questioning look about Mrs. Staten. The eye contact and nonverbal communication that took place between Meredith and Tucker had already made Meredith's day regardless of Mrs. Staten and her bold behavior. Tucker did not say anything. He just looked down at his hand and silently placed his thumb against the index and ring finger and started flipping his hand.

"Tucker, I want to show you my school. Will you come with me to see the classes?"

Tucker said, "Okay." Then he put his hand down.

The first class they observed had six students working with two adults. The elementary age students were sitting in the front of the classroom in a semi-circle with both teachers present. Mrs. Staten explained that this group was involved in an activity called *social studies* time. Each student participating had a social goal based on a developmental model of relationship building. Relationship building and social interaction was a big part of the student's day. She explained further that students with autism become more socially delayed as they age because they tend to enjoy solitary activities like video games and computers. At Amicus computers are only used as a social opportunity. Two students can play a game together. The students must interact even with free time at the computer. Social communication is built into every part of the students' day and is one of the highest priorities at Amicus. Meredith was struck at how the students seemed to be enjoying their social games.

They didn't enter any of the classrooms but looked in each

room through tinted windows. The second classroom had bubble columns against one wall. The lighting was indirect lamps with no overhead fluorescent lighting. Just looking into the room made Meredith feel relaxed. One student sat on a therapy ball at his desk. Others were in comfortable chairs. Tucker was mesmerized by the bubble columns. Everything seemed purposely placed.

"Parents are encouraged to come and observe as much as they want," Mrs. Staten said after she greeted a parent in the hall. "Observations and weekly meetings, along with counseling for parents, are the two factors I attribute to the high rate of generalization of social skill, behavior skills, and adaptive functioning that the students achieve."

Meredith was impressed by Mrs. Staten's statement—the students achieve. Meredith already liked Mrs. Staten's attitude.

"Behavioral skills are written for each student and evaluated weekly. The school uses a variety of approaches for achieving behavioral success, and the goals are written to address anything that might interfere with the learning process. A behavior might be as simple as not making eye contact. If a student is not watching, they cannot learn. Some students' behavior goals start with learning to watch. Other students' behavior keeps them from participating in family outings due to the student acting inappropriately or disrupting. So the student is systematically taught the appropriate behavior. Kids without natural social compasses need to be given direction to navigate society. This is possible with the right education. As these skills are learned and become automatic, families and students function better."

"I can see that," Meredith said.

She knew it was Tucker's inappropriate behavioral response that had caused problems at Cornerstone and Central. Tucker had to learn how to respond in each environment. He generalized little from situation to situation. The only thing that crossed over many situations was Tucker's sensory overload responses and his impulsiveness.

Meredith confided in Mrs. Staten. "Tucker shoved a chair at Cornerstone, which caused him to be expelled. At Central he threw his lunch box. The staff said he was aggressive. They even used the word assault. I tried to explain that he wasn't aggressive—impulsive maybe, but not aggressive. Central didn't seem to understand and just cited their no tolerance policy for aggression."

"We hear those kinds of stories from a lot of new families. Behavioral issues are one of the top reasons parents choose Amicus for their child. We recognize the difference between inappropriate behavior caused by external factors and aggression, which is caused by internal factors. Learning behavioral strategies for stressful situations would be a goal for Tucker. That goal would be broken down into manageable and observable steps for Tucker to learn. He would learn and practice those steps here. You would know the steps because you would be attending therapy sessions and parent-staff meetings. You would be a key player in helping him generalize those skills to home."

For the first time in a while Meredith felt like there were answers and real direction for Tucker. She knew she didn't have the answers. She felt like she had been treading water for so long and was getting so tired, and she was starting to sink. Mrs. Staten had thrown her a life preserver. Tucker wouldn't just be managed. He would achieve. He wouldn't spend his life being kicked out and ostracized because he didn't understand social rules. He would learn to be a part of the group.

"In addition to the behavior plans and social plans, each student also has an individualized education plan. I understand that Tucker is working on grade level. Is that correct?"

"Yes, and I have seen him make great strides. His reading comprehension is his lowest area and this includes word problems in math. It's not the actual math computations but the understanding of the word problems."

"What program is he in now?"

"He's at Central Elementary right now."

"We do receive tuition funding from some public schools for many of the students here. Mostly the schools agree to pay half the tuition. This is the about the amount per student they would spend if the student were being educated in their own school district. So it ends up being a wash for the school. When we go back to the office, I'll have you fill out forms for a scholarship. We do extensive fundraising for scholarships and many of the students receive a partial scholarship in addition to funding from the public school."

"That would be great," Meredith said and then continued with a lower tone, "I just don't know how to nor do I have the time to help with his behavioral needs. I feel like his behavior problems are ruining his school life and our home life."

"Our goal is to give you back your life and enjoy your child, not manage him. You know Tucker isn't happy when he is frustrated and doesn't know what to do. I'm the parent of a son with autism. He is an adult now. He was the reason Amicus was started. There were no schools available. The public schools were not an option for us. The programming was too narrow to benefit my son, and most of the staff had never had training for autism, and some had never even heard the word. So I started teaching my son at home. After we had started home educating, I wanted a peer group for him and met a few other mothers with similar goals for their children and Amicus began. I have my degree in special education. One of the other mothers was an occupational therapist. My husband is a physician specializing in neurodevelopmental disorders. So we began. I'm telling you this because I want you to know I understand where you are coming from. I was like you and wanted something better for my son. It was worth it and now I see other students and families living up to their potential and living lives of hope."

"How old is your son?" Meredith inquired.

"He's 25 now. And he is still autistic, but that is part of who he is, and I have discovered that for me, autism is not something to cure. It's simply a character trait — like shyness. My son works at a job he enjoys. He has a group of friends he sees socially. And lately he even has a girlfriend." Mrs. Staten smiled as she related all this to Meredith. "I can say he is happy and enjoys his life. He lives in his own apartment. He uses public transportation and knows the bus system backward and forward. I don't think he is finished learning just because he is out of school. He is happy, but I'm not sure by societal standards if he would be considered happy or even successful. But I've learned that society's standards don't apply to happiness. Happiness is an individual standard. We each have to find our own peace. We all have to work the steps to bring back joy and control in our lives. The hard part is the steps are different for everyone. Each person has to find their own way. One of the biggest challenges I see with our students and parents is for them to learn to love and accept themselves."

Meredith followed Mrs. Staten back to the office and collected application forms, scholarship forms, and questionnaires. They passed a line of 5 students walking down the hall. One of the kids waved and said *Hi* to Tucker. Tucker didn't wave back but rolled his eyes and grinned slightly. Meredith already knew a behavior goal for Tucker—wave back at people who wave to you. They would practice that goal while they waited to start at Amicus.

Meredith had found where she wanted Tucker, but the path there would be rocky.

Before lights out, Meredith made the rounds, talking and praying with each child a few minutes. Tucker was lying quietly in bed looking at a book. His DS was plugged in for recharging. He was a study in contrast— so typical and quiet one moment and the next destructive and loud. His surrounding might seem chaotic, but he would follow the same bedtime routine among a chaotic mess including plugging in the DS right before bed. He seemed calm in clutter, but then he would get mad about some random something. The randomness put an edge on Meredith's demeanor as she always watched for signs from Tucker that he was about to get out of control. Her new strategy was to let the nearest item be a casualty. She did not want to be a casualty again or have the girls in the way. From now on she would keep important things like herself out of the way. The ER visits cost more than a vase. She sat down on the edge of his bed.

"Tucker, tell me about what happened in the lunchroom the other day with the boy when you threw your lunch box."

"The boy used a mean voice. He said, *Idiot.*"

Meredith gasped slightly. She hadn't expected such a clear and direct answer. "What? What exactly did the boy say?" Meredith asked Tucker knowing he had perfect recall of conversations.

"Oh look, there is a new idiot in the class of idiots." Tucker even did the inflection as Meredith imagined the boy would have said the remark, making it cruel.

"And then you threw your lunch box at the boy?" Meredith asked.

"No, then Dillon said that it's not nice to call someone names."

"And?"

Tucker said, "Then the boy said, *Oh look, the other idiot doesn't want to be called an idiot either.* Then Dillon said, *Stop it.* That boy with the mean voice made an angry face at Dillon and me. Then I knocked over the trays and threw my lunch box at him."

"You knocked over trays too?" Meredith asked and then shook her head. "Okay, thanks for telling me," she said, matter-of-factly, even though she was getting mad.

"I'm sorry," Tucker said with downcast eyes.

"It's okay, Tucker. You were right about the boy being mean." She kissed his forehead and said, "I love you."

As Meredith was turning out the light and started to close the door behind her, Tucker asked, "Mom, what's an idiot?"

"It's a bad name to call someone. It means someone who's not smart."

"He was using a mean voice and Dillon was mad."

"Did you tell this story to the teacher?"

"No, she said, *We can't throw our lunch boxes.*"

Meredith took a deep breath and blew it out slowly in an attempt to control her emotions. "Tucker, thank you for telling me what happened."

"Can I go back to Cornerstone?"

"No, but I'm going to make sure that boy isn't mean to you again."

Meredith put a sticky note on her computer screen that read, *Call Dr. Fisher.* She knew she wouldn't forget, but she had to get it off of her mind.

Meredith called Mrs. Riley, "I need a sub for Monday. I have another meeting at Central about Tucker."

"What time is your meeting?"

"I don't have one yet, but I will be meeting with Dr. Fisher."

Meredith was mad, and she wanted to talk to Dr. Fisher immediately — lucky for him it was the weekend. Bullying was unacceptable. Tucker was the target and he knew it was wrong. He wasn't assaulting the boy; Tucker was standing up for himself. Now that is *normal behavior.* Meredith planned to be prepared for her meeting with Dr. Fisher. She sat down at the computer and typed in, *Bullying Policy.* She found students with special needs are at a higher risk for being the target for bullies, and that bullying can be in many forms. There are federal civil rights laws to protect special populations from bullying. The school would need to respond appropriately or be in violation of the law. She read the school's no tolerance policy about bullying. Dr. Fisher will be hearing about this and she wanted the bully expelled.

Next she typed, "Obsessive Compulsive Disorder," Tucker's new label thanks to the behavior specialist at Central who had diagnosed Tucker with Obsessive Compulsive Disorder (OCD). She found OCD frequently occurs with autism, the symptoms often begin in preteens, and the preteen can get upset with changes or unexpected events. The behavioral specialist was right on this one. His recent destructive outburst, intentional or unintentional, must be related to OCD. She thought about the night recently as they were reading together. And when Tucker heard Jeff's voice calling out, he threw the book. Jeff was unexpected. We can't use the unexpected to justify bad or destructive behavior. Isn't most of life unexpected? It would be impossible to keep everything in the same routine—same time, same place, and same people. Tucker needed a strategy to deal with inevitable change. Is it possible to help someone expect change? Can the rule—everything changes—be the rule that doesn't change. She thought about the serenity prayer she had seen. It had something about change and about wisdom.

Meredith knew that something for Tucker would be new and different tomorrow and every day after that. Maybe she could make a game out of the change. Let's find the change? It could work. We can't change that change happens. Meredith loved circular reasoning. She smiled at that thought. But hatefulness and bullying would be something that changed for Tucker starting tomorrow. She would not allow her child to be labeled aggressive because of someone else's hateful remark. She thought about the misguided and hateful remarks she had heard over the years—institutionalize him, he's just lazy, a good spanking will fix him.

Chapter 21

Jeff's small accounting company had steadily grown over the years. He kept the books for several small businesses and one medium size business. The end of the year always had Jeff working long hours. The end of the Medicaid fiscal year and the beginning of tax season kept Jeff busy back to back. He was glad for the work and hoped that sometime soon Meredith could be a full-time mom. Her teaching job had been their base salary for the years that Jeff was growing his business. Now his job almost covered their living expenses while Meredith's job was for tuition and the extras. Soon he thought he would probably even be able to swing the private school tuition for the girls if Meredith didn't return to work. Things were moving along as planned. And the timing was right because Tuck seemed to need lots of attention right now. Jeff was busier at work now and he couldn't give Tuck that attention. But one thing troubled him. He felt like he was the trigger for Tuck and he didn't know how to fix this. He always seemed to say the wrong thing at the wrong time. But with Meredith freer, she could be the keel to their lives.

The best thing Jeff felt he could do right now was work. By working he was providing a way for Meredith to eventually be at home full-time which would help Tuck. With Tuck better, the girls' lives would also improve. It had become hard to live with the tension of a possible outburst, meltdown, aggression, or whatever it's called always looming over every interaction. The house looked more and more sparse as decorations and furniture became casualties of the frequent outbursts or were removed to safer locations. The girls smiled less and less. There was always a clouded look on Myla's face as she tried to de-escalate Tucker by getting the younger girls out of the way. Meredith relied more and more on Myla. Jeff knew that wasn't fair to Myla. She was becoming older before her time. Myla deserved a childhood, too.

But for now Jeff had to concentrate on work. The fiscal year had just passed and now it was nearing the end of the calendar year, and the companies he kept the books for were making end-of-the-year decisions based on his projections. Plus his biggest client, Parker Dental, had asked for a detailed analysis of all assets and liabilities. Truthfully, Jeff was happy to have work as a distraction and a way to not be at home. He loved his job, his own business, and he loved numbers and the order they created. The office felt peaceful. He was secretly glad he had a pull-out sofa for long nights at the office. He told himself again, *The best thing I can do for Tuck, Meredith, Myla, Isabelle, and Clare is work.* Tucker desperately needed Meredith's time and needed her to be at home. *If Tuck can be okay, the girls will be okay, and the worried looks can be removed from their faces. If the girls and Tuck are okay, then Meredith will be okay and then I'll be okay, too.* He opened Excel on his computer to make his family whole again by making a weekend of numbers.

Chapter 22

Sunday morning Jeff pulled up in the driveway from his Friday and Saturday nights at the office. He was ready for church and he actually looked refreshed. Meredith had Isabelle and Clare lined up for hair details of ponytail and pigtails. Clare wanted the hair ties with butterflies on them because she loved butterflies. Tucker was playing his Nintendo DS on the steps when Jeff pulled up.

"Tucker, you were the man of the house this weekend while Daddy was at work."

"Yeah."

"Did you take care of Mommy and the girls?"

"Yeah."

"Since you were so good, how about a milkshake after church?"

"Yeah."

At the door of the Sunday School class, Tucker abruptly stopped. A couple of the kids said   to Tucker and Isabelle.

"Tucker, what's wrong?" Meredith asked.

No response.

"Tucker, go with Isabelle to your Sunday School class."

No response.

Isabelle took Tucker's hand and he hit her hand away. Isabelle looked at Meredith.

"Go on to class, Isabelle. I'll take Tucker with me today."

Jeff and Meredith sat with Tucker in a cafe area used for the youth. They bought Tucker a bottled water from one of the machine and sat and waited for the girls to finish Sunday School. "Do we dare stay?" Jeff asked.

"Clare's class is singing in worship today. I don't want to

miss it. Let's try to stay," Meredith quietly told Jeff.

Tucker lightly hit the table with the side of his fist.

Meredith shrugged her shoulders not daring to speak out loud again. "What happened?" Meredith mouthed to Jeff.

"No idea," he mouthed back.

Neither one smiled. Neither one spoke for fear of saying a word that would begin a downhill spiral of Tucker's nearly out of control behavior. He was keeping it together, but barely. They waited, surveying the area like secret service officers trying to detect an intruder.

Tucker hit himself with his palm to his forehead. Jeff looked at Meredith. "Let's walk," Meredith mouthed and took Tucker by the hand as they walked the church corridor waiting for Sunday School to end and the worship service to begin. "We can leave after Clare sings," Meredith quietly told Jeff.

The organ music whirled around the sanctuary as early service attendees were leaving and late service attendees were arriving and swapping their seats. Clare was with her group getting ready to perform. The Howards took their usual seat about 1/4 back from the front.

Helen and Sam Sawyer, a 50-something couple, always sat behind Jeff and Meredith and the kids. Each week Helen spoke to each of the kids giving them positive words about their appearances or behavior. Tucker even acknowledged Helen's comments.

Isabelle turned around and reported to Mrs. Sawyer, "Tucker started going to Central."

"How do you like Central, Tucker?" Mrs. Sawyer asked.

"A mean boy called me an idiot," Tucker stated matter-of-factly without looking up at Mrs. Sawyer.

Helen's eyes widened and she told him that she was sorry and then the service began. Sam and Helen looked at each other shocked at the report and Tucker's uneasiness spread to them. Tucker's behavior had been off this morning and the worship service ended up being no different. Tucker squirmed and loudly bumped his elbows against the back of the pews. The October cold and flu season had just begun, and Meredith noticed that anytime a parishioner coughed or cleared their throat, Tucker was bumping his elbow against the back of the pew. Meredith moved Isabelle in between her and Jeff to get up close to Tucker. She put her arm around him hoping to muffle the sounds of the coughs. To Meredith it began to seem that everyone in the church must be sick. With each cough, Tucker jumped, and his elbow blows to the pew became louder and louder. Jeff cleared his throat and looked at Meredith with wide, questioning eyes.

Meredith mouthed, "I'm going to take him out." She whispered to Tucker to leave. Going towards the back someone coughed and Tucker hit the wall with his elbow. Meredith struggled to get him to the back. Eyes from the congregation darted between Tucker and the minister.

Finally out, she walked Tucker to the fellowship hall and waited for the end of the service. Frustrated and nearly in tears, she knew going to church shouldn't be this hard. Jeff and the girls found them after the service sitting in the car. Meredith had been crying. She told Jeff, "I can't do this anymore. Cornerstone, Central, name-calling, behavior plans—everything is starting to get to me. It's just getting too hard for me."

Jeff nodded and the other kids silently climbed into their seats.

The family drove away from the church.

Chapter 23

At 9:00 a.m., Tuesday morning, while her class was in art, Meredith called Mrs. Wilson again, and her thoughts rushed out without any order. "The evaluation included the labels of autism, mental retardation, OCD, and ODD. I've been doing a little research, and I don't agree with any of the disorders except autism and possibly OCD. The worst part is that Tucker was called an idiot, and then he was suspended for assaulting the student when he was just standing up for himself. The other student didn't get disciplined. I went up to the school on Monday, and Dr. Fisher said they would check into the name-calling. I was glad he at least took it seriously. But, I want to get that second opinion we talked about. An aide for Tucker would allow him to participate in school without being a target. He needs an adult present. I don't want him to have bad social experiences like the name-calling. Social experiences are challenging at best and negative experiences such as the name-calling create further difficulties for Tucker. And the Amicus school is no doubt the best setting for Tucker.

"Meredith, slow down. You are all over the place with your information. You are talking about an aide at Central, bullying, attending Amicus, and you're not even happy with the labels that are being used for the programming decisions. You need to pick a focus and go with it," Mrs. Wilson said.

"I just don't know what to do. I'm wanting some— something. I know don't what it is," she stammered trying to collect her thoughts. "I need help NOW! Amicus seems way out there in the future and like something I'll never be able to have for Tucker. The aide at Central might be a possibility? I really like Mrs. Canon . . . I don't know. I just don't know what to do. That's why I called you. I need some help . . . some direction . . . somebody not so close to the situation."

"Well, we need to get a good idea of Tucker's skill set so the first step should be to request a second evaluation, an Independent Educational Evaluation (IEE). The school must consider the findings and the recommendations from the second evaluation. The law states that the school pays for the IEE and does so with reasonable promptness. With a recommendation for Amicus or an aide, then it might be easier for Tucker to transfer to Amicus or have a personal aide. But you need to decide what you want to fight for. Do you want Amicus or do you want an aide?"

"I think I want Amicus, but I think getting an aide is more likely."

"Decide what you want not what you think is more likely. Getting payment for Amicus or getting an aide are both expenses for the school district. At Amicus, Tucker won't have an individual aide and if you think an aide is best, let's go with that. But you must decide what you want to fight for."

"I'm fighting for Tucker."

"Yes, and you're his mother and in your gut what do you think would help Tucker achieve his best outcome?"

"I don't know."

"Well, I know it's hard. That is why we need another opinion and recommendations from an Independent Evaluator. That process will hopefully bring some clarity. Tucker will have to stay put and be labeled as the school deems for now. Give the school a 10-day deadline to schedule the IEE. Tucker can stay in his current setting while the request is in process."

Meredith composed herself as her students started filing back in her class. "Okay, thanks," she said as she clicked off the phone and brought herself back to a competent teacher rather than a disheartened and uncertain mother. The anxious feeling did not subside the rest of the school day until she was at Central picking up Tucker. He smiled at her when he saw her and her anxiety rushed away.

She saw Sarah as she was picking up Tucker. Dillon was gathering up his things. He stuffed his papers into the backpack creasing them and tearing them as he forced everything in his

98

partially unzipped backpack. Tucker unzipped his backpack and folded the flap back neatly as he placed his books inside. Then he carefully put each paper into his pocket folder and then methodically put the pocket folder in his backpack. Tucker put on his backpack and adjusted his shoulder straps so the weight was evenly distributed and walked over to Meredith.

Meredith spoke to Sarah as Dillon continued to crumple papers down into his backpack, "Tucker enjoyed having Dillon come over the other day."

"Dillon enjoyed it too. He kept talking about Isabelle and how much fun he had."

"We will have to do that again soon."

Tucker stood by Meredith patiently waiting. Dillon was still forcing his supplies down into his backpack.

At bedtime, Meredith came into Tucker's room after reading Clare to sleep. She could hear Myla and Isabelle talking in their room. Meredith noticed several small bruises on Tucker's arms. "What happened?"

"That boy with the bad voice pinched me."

"What?" Meredith asked holding her breath waiting for a response.

"That boy with the bad voice pinched me."

"What? When?" Meredith asked.

"He said invisible words—words without his voice. Like this." Tucker mouthed the words, "Idiot, idiot, idiot."

"Then what? Did anyone tell the teacher?"

"No, but Abby wanted to go home."

Meredith pictured Abby, an adorable little girl that used a walker, understanding the hurtful words and the intent behind them. Tucker was lucky— in a way —that he didn't comprehend the social atrocity occurring. He knew what was happening was not right, but he could not fully understand the meanness and prejudice behind the words.

Meredith was restless. Dr. Fisher had said he would take care of the verbal abuse, but now the bullying has escalated to physical contact. She knew she was clenching her teeth together but couldn't seem to stop. She paced the floor and looked at the clock that stated 2 am. She unsealed the letter to the school district requesting the IEE, read it again, and sealed the envelope again. The school was required to "decide promptly" following the request but what does decide promptly mean? Promptly probably gets decided by the school just like least restrictive environment.

She thought about curly haired Dillon with the bright eyes. He didn't deserve to be called names either. Tomorrow was Wednesday—actually today was Wednesday since it was the early hours of morning— and Tucker had three more days this week. Her eyes felt hazing from lack of sleep and worrying over Tucker's bruises and the wait for the IEE. The wheels of change move slowly at the administration office at school. She thought about waiting in the Central school office for a prompt reply to the IEE request. More importantly she needed prompt action to stop the bullying. Tucker needed guidance to take a confusing, noisy, and unpredictable world and make sense of it by applying some rules and organization to the chaos. He also needed protection from pinches and hateful words. The hate filled words that made Dillon angry and made Tucker throw the lunchbox were bad, but this physical abuse was too much. Dr. Fisher would also be informed about the physical abuse when she handed him her letter. Suddenly a dispute over a label seemed insignificant to her son being physically abused. The boy who pinched Tucker and said hateful things was truly the disabled one.

Meredith went into the girls' room to visit with them before bedtime. Isabelle was already in her bed. Meredith sat down on the edge of Isabelle's bed and brushed her hair back out of her eyes.

"I miss Tucker being at Cornerstone. It's just not the same without him."

"Tucker misses it too. If I could go back and fix everything, I would, but I can't."

Isabelle was a natural beauty with skin that tanned evenly. Her brown hair hung slightly off her shoulders. Mostly she kept her hair tucked behind her ears but sported a ponytail whenever the occasion demanded a "dressed-up" look. She walked with the gait of a natural born athlete, but other than playground fun, she had not participated in organized sports. This spring was to be her sport's debut on the soccer field. She had the competitive drive to be successful at sports, but she also loved books and was able to use her imagination to create drama through her observations all around her. She could easily grow up to be a television reporter because of her ability to make the most boring day into an interesting story interwoven with details. The attention she got from her imaginative tales and fact reporting neither embarrassed her nor made her feel superior. As a performer, she was able to command attention from her audience whenever she desired. It was just who she was and she did not regard her abilities as a special gift.

She was a gift to Tucker and she and Tucker were exactly 14 months apart with her birthday in January and his in March. Tucker had been her first audience. As she learned to walk, he would lie on the floor and watch her move about the room. She didn't remember a time when Tucker wasn't her audience. He made the perfect audience because he adored Isabelle and enjoyed everything she did. Isabelle in turn had been Tucker's best teacher. By following and mimicking Isabelle, Tucker had enjoyed the world as only children can. They were a perfect pair—the performer and the audience.

At the playground, if Tucker ever got distracted, Isabelle would bring him back to the game by calling to her audience. "Tucker, watch me or Tucker, kick the ball." Tucker's eyes would smile even if his face did not, and he would fix his gaze on Isabelle. Isabelle's playmates had all accepted Tucker's presence just outside of their circle of play as he watched Isabelle. With Tucker at Central Elementary, Isabelle at times felt his absence at her school. She would look off to where she knew he should be watching her and she would feel lonely. A performer without her audience is a lonely thing. At home, Isabelle enjoyed her lead role as Tucker's guide and interpreter.

Tucker was lost without Isabelle to interpret the world for him at Central. When he didn't know what to do at Cornerstone, he could always watch what Isabelle did and then follow her lead. If he didn't get the sequence just right, Isabelle would swoop in and have Tucker watch her. But at Central Elementary he wasn't sure who to watch and follow. The world of sounds and instructions were confusing to him. He was never sure if a voice was talking to him. If Isabelle were with him, she would have been able to say, "Tucker, Dillon is talking to you." Then Tucker could listen. But now with all the voices around him from all the people, the computers, and the intercom, Tucker had no idea what to listen to. He decided to rock with his eyes closed to help quiet the constant noises around him.

Chapter 24

On Friday, Tucker threw a tantrum when Meredith pulled up in front of Central Elementary. Meredith tried to get Tucker out of the car, but each time she pried his hand off of the door handle, he grabbed another part of the car. He repeatedly banged his head against the back of the seat. Isabelle began crying and pleading on Tucker's behalf.

Meredith near tears herself spoke to Myla, "Call your Dad and tell him I need him to meet me at Cornerstone."

Myla complied without question. "Dad is on his way."

Jeff knew not to question Meredith about why because why took too much time and energy. He knew action was needed from the sounds he heard in the background. Analysis would wait until later.

Meredith turned to Isabelle and Tucker, "Okay, you guys win. We are leaving. Tucker, you do not have to go to Central today."

Tucker immediately stopped and relaxed unapologetically. Isabelle wiped her tears with the back of her hands, but her face was still clouded. She tucked her brown sun-streaked hair behind her ear and sniffed trying to resolve the crying. Isabelle knew she had won this battle, but she also knew the war was still going on.

At Cornerstone, Myla took Clare and they both made it to class just as the tardy bell rang. Meredith moved quickly through the sea of students and asked Mrs. Earnest to watch her students for a few minutes. Mrs. Earnest nodded. Meredith mouthed, "Thank you!" and headed back to the car. Isabelle was unable to compose herself enough to go to class just yet. Jeff stayed in the car with Isabelle and Tucker.

"What happened today, Tuck?" Jeff quizzed.

"I don't want to go to Central. I want to go to Cornerstone and sit between John and Sarah." His sentences came out between

103

sharp breaths. "I want my desk back. I want to see Isabelle," Tucker cried which was uncharacteristic of him.

"Well, you have to go to school. Mommy's got to work and I've got to work. Clare and Myla went to their classes. Isabelle's getting ready to go and you need to go to your new class at Central."

Tucker began to rock as he held onto Isabelle's hand. He hit the back of the seat with his elbow. Jeff wearily rubbed his forehead with his right hand and thought. *When am I going to learn that 'tough love' doesn't work with Tucker?*

Isabelle became Tucker's voice, "A boy at Central is mean to Tucker. He called him names in a bad voice. Look what he did to him." Isabelle held up Tucker's arm and pulled up his sleeve.

Jeff looked at the tiny bruises from the pinches Tucker had been receiving. There were a couple of larger bruises on his upper arm. He had a falling feeling in his stomach but braced against it. "Isabelle, you don't know that someone did that to Tucker. He could have gotten those marks a million different ways."

"But he told me . . ." Isabelle began as Meredith emerged from the doors of the school.

Meredith looked at Isabelle's red eyes and tear-stained face and knew Isabelle was in no condition to go to class. When she saw tears on Tucker's face, her eyes filled with tears. She looked at Jeff and asked, "Can you take Tucker and Isabelle to the office with you?"

"There is no way I can take Tucker and Isabelle to the office today. I'm meeting with Parker today. We are going over his end-of-the-year projections. This is going to be a long meeting. We are going over a complete summary. I expect it to take most of the morning and possibly part of the afternoon. I cannot reschedule with him. He is my biggest client. Several department heads are attending this meeting and it starts in 30 minutes!" Jeff said while drumming on the roof of the car.

"Fine, Mrs. Riley is not going to like this. Give me a few minutes to tell her that I'm not going to make it to class today."

"Hurry!" was Jeff's only reply.

◆ ◆

When Meredith, Tucker, and Isabelle arrived home, both Isabelle and Tucker bounded down the basement steps as if nothing stressful had transpired that morning. Meredith called the school, "Tucker Howard won't be at school today."

"Be sure and bring the doctor's note when he returns," the receptionist said stating the school policy.

"He's not sick. I'm keeping him home because he is. . . upset," Meredith said trying to come up with words to reasonably explain his absence. I couldn't get him out of the car didn't sound right.

"Well, then he will have an unexcused absence. I'll make a note of that."

"I need to speak with Dr. Fisher."

"I can ask him to call you."

"Okay. Do you happen to know if the school has made a decision about the Independent Educational Evaluation?"

"There had been no decision made about the IEE."

Her next call was to Mrs. Wilson. "I couldn't get Tucker into school today," she began and then told her the story about the pinches and the bruises. "I'm guessing he got the large bruises yesterday."

When Mrs. Wilson finally spoke after a long pause, her voice was firm. "First, I want you to take pictures of the bruises. You need to document what is happening. Make notes of Tucker's emotional decline since the bullying started. Keep everything factual and list dates and times. This obviously is beyond educational programming. We are now into a safety issue."

"Okay, I can do that," Meredith said. Having something to do kept her from wilting on the floor in utter despair. She wiped the silent tear from her face.

"Make a copy of the first letter and write another letter. In this second letter request the Independent Education Evaluation again and end with a statement saying Tucker would not be able to attend school and request homebound instruction. List your reason for nonattendance as a concern for his safety. He is supposed to stay put in his placement during the IEE request, but in this situation, that is not a good idea. So this letter will let them know why you are keeping him out. This will put pressure on the school district to comply since you are worried about his safety. Give them ten days to reply."

"Okay," Meredith said but her words betrayed her. Her faith was wavering because all the steps took so long. "What should I do with Tucker since I have to work?"

Again, Mrs. Wilson was quiet on the other end of the phone for several moments. Finally she said, "I know it will be a sacrifice to keep Tucker home. Do you have anyone who can watch him?"

"No, no one. There is no one that can handle Tucker," Meredith said. She and Jeff were on their own, and Jeff brought in most of the income so that left her to take care of Tucker.

"If you don't pressure the school, the abuse and bullying will continue."

"I know. It's a *no brainer*. This has got to stop. I just don't know how to tell my principal," and she added quieter, "or Jeff."

"There is the family medical leave act."

Meredith was trying to hold on to improve Tucker's situation. The idea that the family situation would deteriorate for Tucker's to improve hadn't crossed her mind. This realization had her sitting down to finish the conversation with Mrs. Wilson. "It's not going to be win-win, is it?" she asked.

Mrs. Wilson voice was now soft. "No, these situations can

106

take a terrible toll on families. The divorce rate is high." She paused. "You don't have to move forward if you don't want to or can't afford to. Think about it—really think about it. This is not an easy road and that is why many families don't go against the school."

Meredith was silent as she stared into the empty living room. She thought about her students who were counting on her and her own girls and the things they would give up.

Mrs. Wilson's voice brought her back. "Meredith, are you still with me?"

"Yeah, I just don't know what I'm going to tell Jeff. He is just so busy right now. We haven't talked lately."

"You have another thing you need to do and that is report the bullying. The other students in Tucker's class probably know who this student is and he needs to be stopped. This may have been going on even before Tucker started Central. But it's your responsibility to report it. The school is required to respond to bullying of a disabled child. And be sure the other moms know what is going on."

Meredith told her that she had already talked to Dr. Fisher twice, but now Tucker was suffering emotionally so she would call him again. She hung up the phone and sat it on the coffee table and continued to stare. She felt heavy and wasn't sure if she could stand.

Isabelle shook her arm. "Mom, we're hungry."

"Eat your lunches out of your lunch boxes." When she looked at the clock, she realized that she had been in the same spot for several hours. She only had an hour before it was time to pick up Clare and Myla, so she sat down at the computer and typed the heading of the letter: Independent Evaluation - Second Request.

Her intuition told her Tucker would not easily recover from the trauma at Central. It frightened her how his world was getting smaller and smaller. Central was a difficult place and Tucker would not be changing his opinion. A thought established became an unbreakable rule.

She couldn't pinpoint when it started, but Tucker had been closing down for some time. Like the aperture of a camera closing to block out glaring light, Tucker was closing down to block out challenging situations. His focus was becoming intense and the surroundings blurry.

Over the summer, there had been gradual changes that were almost unnoticed—a small adjustment here and a small adjustment there—but looking back, the sum of transformations was significant. Meredith hoped getting back into the school routine would help Tucker's behavior settle back down, but school seemed to bring a new set of rules that Tucker did not or could not change. When Tucker shoved the chair, that act had launched the family onto a merry-go-round of changes that Meredith wasn't sure when or if they would stop. She suddenly wasn't sure if she could handle the change either. Her hands froze over the keyboard. She stared at the screen. She had to summon the courage to move forward and to continue to type the letter. When she sent this letter, there would be no turning back. She wouldn't be able to teach at Cornerstone any longer.

After a long meeting with Parker, Jeff made it to the Friday afternoon family meeting hosted by The 4:12 Center for current and prospective families. Jackie had encouraged him to attend. He was early and paced back and forth at the back of the room. There were muffins, bottled waters, and some coffee on the table. Jeff downed two bottles of water while he waited, crushed the empty containers with his hand, and tossed them into the trash. As each person came in the room, they nodded at Jeff and took a seat. Jeff finally took a seat on the back row when Jackie arrived and motioned for him to sit.

He listened to the stories and discovered that there wasn't a checklist to follow for how to get an addict in rehab. He had come to learn everything he could about addiction so he could put those things into practice and save Kate. But what he discovered was that it wasn't that simple. Each person's addiction and recovery were different. He was disappointed. How could something be accomplished without a plan? He liked black and white. Gray zones made him uncomfortable. He waited around after the meeting to talk to Jackie. They sat in two chairs at the front of the room.

Jeff leaned over and put his elbows on his knees as be began, "A couple of the people lost contact with the addict they loved and I don't know how they made it. It's not in my nature to walk away. This is driving me crazy." Jeff got up and started pacing. "I need to know what to do to make this happen."

"The only thing you can do is let go. If you get too involved in the addict's life it will drive you crazy. That is why you need to turn your life over to the care of God. These steps help restore sanity to the people who love an addict."

"But, Jackie, I can't let go of something I don't even have. I haven't been able to find Kate. I've driven downtown at least three times a week for the past couple of weeks, and I haven't seen nor has anyone I asked seen her. I want to put some of these principles into practice, but I can't even find her."

"Then you are at the beginning where you admit that you are powerless. This program is about keeping your sanity even though Kate is deep into her addiction."

"Sanity right now is difficult. Besides looking for Kate and worrying that she is dead somewhere, my son — Tuck who has autism — won't go to school. He's the type that makes rules and once a rule is established, it's almost impossible to change. This morning he wouldn't even get out of the car, so I had to go to the school to help my wife. She wanted me to take Tuck. Meredith thinks I can stay home at the drop of a hat because I have my own business, and I have been able to be flexible and let the kids hang out with me at the office. But today I couldn't. I had a meeting and I need to go back to the office when I leave here." He started walking toward the door.

Jackie got up and followed him. "I'm glad you came to the meeting. And when you find Kate and if she agrees to treatment, we will be here. Jeff—" Jackie paused and waited until Jeff made eye contact with her. "— keep coming to the meetings."

Jeff stopped by the gym on the way to the office. He had to run.

Meredith was pacing the floor rehearsing her speech to Jeff. She had to tell him that Tucker would not be going to school and that she was going to stay home with him until the school did the right thing. Then the phone rang.

"Hey, I'm not going to make it home. I'm still covered up with work. I'll probably be here all weekend."

"That's okay." Meredith hoped he didn't hear the relief in her voice. He didn't even ask about Tucker and Isabelle. He didn't ask. She didn't tell. She wouldn't have to face him today and say she wasn't going back to work for a while. She was mentally exhausted, and Jeff was one fewer person to worry about. She felt lighter. She went in to check on Tucker and Isabelle; they stopped their video game and looked at Meredith with no smiles on their faces— just frightened heavy looks.

Clare came in and started whining, "I want Ashlyn to come down and play."

"That is not going to happen."

"Why not?" Clare asked jumping up and down in place. Her whining grew louder.

"It's just not."

Myla was just sitting on the couch listening to music and

110

holding a pillow. Isabelle came in and leaned on Meredith. She put her arms around her mom's waist and asked, "Are you going to make Tucker go back to Central?"

Crying with no tears, Clare had collapsed to the floor still whining and demanding an answer to *why not.*

Meredith didn't have an answer for either child. She couldn't even decide what she wanted other than she wanted everyone to be okay and to stop worrying and whining. The balance was broken—the delicate balance between work, husband, and kids. And now she separated the kids into two groups—Tucker and the girls. She didn't want to think about the girls and then Jeff and then Mrs. Riley. "Let's not worry about anything. How about we go camping tonight?" Meredith asked the girls surprising even herself. Isabelle looked shocked and then a smile spread across her face delighted. Clare stopped whining and looked up at her mom with tears now streaking her cheeks. There were no arguments or bargaining. There was entire agreement.

Myla helped load two canoes on top of the car. Meredith threw in the tent, sleeping bags, a few supplies, and an empty cooler. She double-checked and made sure she had the paddles. She left Jeff's rough-edged paddle hanging in the garage. Not one whimper was heard from the kids as they pulled out of the driveway with maybe a couple of hours of daylight left and headed to the grocery store to fill up the cooler. Myla and Isabelle made eye contact with each other when they saw their mom put cokes in the cooler. They knew she must have lost her mind. The camping area was a 45 minutes drive. The cool air made breathing deeply possible. At the campsite, Tucker danced and flipped his hands in the air as Myla and Isabelle worked to light the campfire. Delighted with their fire, the girls joined Tucker in his dancing around the fire. Meredith assembled the tent. With the last stake in place, she stood and stretched her back and felt the tension of home leave as she watched her kids—all of them—enjoying the campfire. The insect noises had gone with the summer. An owl hooted in the distance causing the kids to stop and listen. Another owl answered. Clare silently distributed hot dogs as each child listened for another owl call. With bellies full of hotdogs and s'mores, the group settled down in the tent. Meredith reached out and held Tucker's and Clare's hands. Isabelle looked at her mother and instinctively reached out and took Tucker's other hand. Myla took Clare's other hand. They lay listening for the owls. The cool night made sleeping easy.

Chapter 25

No whining, no tears, no heavy faces as the breakfast of apple slices and almond milk over granola was devoured. It was wonderful how easily the kids got along on a camping trip. No more worried looks from Isabelle and Tucker. There were no whines from Clare. Monday morning seemed like a world away. There were no distractions and even Tucker joined in the activities. Taking the kids around the lake in a canoe without Jeff presented some challenges, but after the last canoe outing, Meredith knew Myla had reached the point where she could effectively steer the canoe. Isabelle could guide Myla as needed. So with Myla at the stern, Isabelle at the bow, and Clare balanced in the middle, Meredith launched the girls amid squeals and splashes. Clare once again proudly wore her bright pink life vest. Then Meredith took her position in the stern and had Tucker climb in while she steadied the canoe. Only his tennis shoes got wet as he quickly climbed in and knelt in the bow. Tucker and Meredith joined the girls on the calm lake just seconds later. The lake had a slight chill, but the calming effect that Meredith always felt on the water was there, and apparently the kids felt it too. The paddles efficiently cut through the smooth water giving forward momentum. Even though Meredith knew they were all at the mercy of the water, the tranquility was worth the risk. They navigated the canoe while the sun danced on the surface of the quiet waters.

Saturday passed peacefully with a break on the same sand bar island for peanut butter sandwiches and cokes — a rarity that the kids seemed to think made them more mature. The island had a sandy beach that provided the entertainment for an afternoon of sand castles. Shortly before dusk geese landed in the water and fed in the shallows. Leaving their sandcastles behind as monuments to their presence, the kids quietly loaded into the canoes and solemnly took a wide berth around the geese as their oars notched the water steering them back to the campsite. The stillness of the lake captured and quieted their souls. Each with quiet longings to return, they all packed up the camping supplies. Peace had been restored to the group. They drove home as the sun left the sky on the cool Saturday night. Only one night gone but everything seemed different. Jeff had not yet arrived home.

Chapter 26

Tucker was rocking and humming. His stress was palpable.

"We are not going to church, Tucker," Meredith said hoping to remove some stress; she was biting her nails, a nervous habit that she did when she was anxious. "We are going to do Sunday School together at the kitchen table, okay."

Tucker came to the table with the girls but continued his rocking and humming.

"Tucker doesn't want to go back to Central tomorrow. He's afraid someone will hurt him." Isabelle reported as if she was receiving a mental message from Tucker.

"No one is going to hurt Tucker. I already told Mrs. Canon and Dr. Fisher about the boy who hurt Tucker," Meredith told Isabelle.

Tucker looked at her out of the corner of his eye but continued to rock.

"I'm not going to school if Tucker has to go to Central," Isabelle said. "I'm going to stay with Tucker."

Meredith suppressed a smile at Isabelle's loyalty to Tucker. "Isabelle, you are an amazing big sister to Tucker." She turned to Tucker, "Tucker, you don't want Isabelle to miss school, do you?" She didn't wait for an answer but just continued. "You know, Mrs. Canon won't let anything happen since she knows about the mean boy.

Tucker stopped rocking. "I'm going to stay with Isabelle," he said without looking up.

Meredith sighed. *I guess we could all go live in the woods*, she thought. *None of this would matter then.* She was speechless, even worse she had no thoughts about how to solve the problems before her and no ideas of the future. Making Central do the right thing and quickly was her hope. If only Central keeps the bully away. If only Central would assign one of the aides to Tucker exclusively. *If only . . . If only . . .*, Meredith said to herself more than once. There were so many *if onlys*. It seems out of her control. She couldn't make Central do anything. They were at the mercy of the school district, and she had no assurances for her own children.

But Monday loomed and she had to face it. She felt like curling up on her bed and rocking herself to sleep. But she knew she would give it one more try. *If only* everything goes okay on Monday it would mean last week's blow up was a fluke. She still had the unmailed letter to Central on her desk. She had to try one more time — try to be "normal" one more time. All she had to do was drop Tucker off and go to work. *I'll hang onto this letter because Tucker just might go to school*, she thought. Denial was her best friend.

Chapter 27

But denial left and reality rushed in to take its place on Monday when Tucker refused to even get in the car. Not only did Isabelle cry again but Meredith was in tears as well. Tucker grabbed a chair in the kitchen. Meredith kept trying to pull him towards the door. The chair fell to the floor as Tucker held on tightly to anchor himself to the house. Meredith sat down on the kitchen floor and leaned against the wall looking at Tucker. Without being asked, Myla called Jeff to come home so she could go to school. Jeff arrived and Myla and Clare ran out to get in the car. Meredith stayed sitting on the floor.

Isabelle just stared at her. Tucker was sitting on the floor near the overturned chair rocking and flipping two fingers in front of his eyes. Meredith finally got up and went to the kitchen sink to wash her face with cool water. When the panic had passed, Meredith got up and soaked a dishcloth with cool water and washed Isabelle's face. "Go play," she said. The kids lingered moving only into the living room. Meredith took several deep breaths and then called Mrs. Riley hoping to sound like this was a short-term glitch in the routine, but in the back of her mind, she knew this was going to be a long road. As she talked to Mrs. Riley, Tucker—eavesdropping— paced in the living room. Meredith watched him as she talked on the phone distracted by Tucker hitting himself on the forehead alternating with the palms of both hands. She said, "Mrs. Riley, I'm going to be out this week. I need to stay home with Tucker today and possibly the rest of this week."

"What is going on?"

"It's hard to explain. Things are not going well. There may be bullying going on. I'm trying to get Tucker settled at Central, but it's so . . . so hard." She couldn't concentrate on the conversation as she watched Tucker strike himself again and again. Meredith tried to hide her concern about his behavior. Her "friend," denial, kept her going. "I spoke with a special education advocate named Mrs. Wilson and she suggested I keep Tucker out

117

of school a few days to put pressure on the school district. I'm asking for a second opinion. I hope to have some answers from the school this week." She knew it was a lie when she said it. The school wouldn't give her an answer this week. And at this point, she knew deep down, the school didn't have an answer neither did another's professional opinion. But she was searching and hoping because she had no answers either. She put the letter requesting homebound instruction, while the IEE was being completed, in the mail.

"I'll make arrangements this week for a substitute for your class. Keep me posted and let me know when you hear from the school district. I know Tucker has some special needs and the right situation can make all the difference. I wish we had more services available at Cornerstone."

"Me too," Meredith replied softly.

"If possible, could you give me a little more advanced notice if you're going to be out? Stay in touch."

I wish I could know in advance too, Meredith thought as she hung up the phone. And with that the conversation ended. "Tucker," she yelled, "quit hitting yourself. You are not going to class at Central today." She called Central and asked to pick up his books so she could work with him at home. Then she called Jeff. "Will you go to Central and get Tucker's books since he wasn't able to go to school again today."

"Can't you do it? I have a lot of work here."

"I couldn't even get Tucker to get in the car—much less into the school to pick up books."

"Alright, but you have got to stop babying him."

Meredith hung up the phone. She thought, *Well, he is clueless.* Tucker had quit hitting himself and was staring at Meredith. "You can go play." This time he and Isabelle went to the basement.

Jeff came home at lunch with the books. Tucker was outside swinging and singing at the top of his lungs. "Well, he seems happy today," Jeff said. Meredith nodded and smiled. Jeff changed the subject. "I haven't seen Desiree and Gloria around here lately."

"They don't want to come over here. You don't even want to come here," Meredith said

"Ouch," Jeff said

Meredith shook her head. "I'm sorry. I don't know what's wrong with me." She started over in a more civilized tone. "I guess I didn't realize how strange our home life had become until Myla's birthday party. It seems most of her friends don't accept invitations to our house. But they are still going to the mall and hanging out, just not here — which is in a way a relief. Same with Clare's little friend, Ashlyn. Clare plays at Ashlyn's now that Ashlyn can't come over here."

"It does make me sad that the girls have to adjust so much for Tucker," Jeff said softly looking away from Meredith. "You have got to get him under control."

Before dinner Clare marched in the house. She had a headband holding back her bangs and it matched her glasses perfectly. Her arms were full of Barbies and Barbie's clothes. "Does Tucker always have to be at home? I wish he would go away so that Ashlyn could come down and play. I'm tired of carrying all my stuff to Ashlyn's house. It's not fair." She stomped her foot.

So Isabelle's fiercely protective and Clare is ready to throw him to the wolves, Meredith thought. She did feel bad for Clare, but there was nothing that could be done. Tucker was always home, and the girls never got a break from his "rules" except when they were at school which had its own set of rules. "I'm sorry, honey," Meredith said. There wasn't anything else to say. Nothing could be changed.

"Tucker should just hit those boys back. It isn't fair. Ashlyn can't come over. Those mean boys should stay home from school, not Tucker. They are the mean ones. It's just not fair," Clare repeated and stomped her foot again.

"I agree. The mean boys should be the ones to stay home. Clare, you know Tucker needs us to be understanding right now."

"You don't let me stay home and I don't like to go to school."

"Yes, but that is a little different. Someone is hurting Tucker at his school."

"He should hit them back. I don't like that boy."

"Me, neither."

Clare collected her armload of toys that she had carried back from Ashlyn's house and went downstairs. Within a few minutes, Meredith saw Clare outside swinging on her belly. She would run fast and the swing would lift her up. Her unbuttoned jacket allowed the cool evening air to embrace her, but she didn't seem cold at all. She just dangled her arms. Her hair nearly touched the ground as she swung back and forth. When the swing slowed down, she did it again. Clare had three band-aids on her leg over what she called 'tiny ant bites' that no one else could see. The band-aids were in the shape of a "C" on her calf. Meredith could tell that Clare was talking to herself but couldn't hear the words she was saying, but Meredith could tell Clare was content and that made Meredith smile.

Clare ran into the house to report that she had seen a lightning bug, and it wasn't even summer anymore. This sighting was a marvel to Clare and made her feel enchanted the rest of the evening. Meredith heard a bang from Tucker's room and headed to see what was broken now.

Chapter 28

Kate called Jeff from the New Start Day program. He immediately left work and drove to meet her and found her sitting on the same bench. She looked like she had aged a year since he saw her last. Kate smiled a weary smile at Jeff, but he could tell she was glad to see him. "Hey, Jeff," she said when she got in the car, but she didn't make eye contact. Instead, she leaned her seat back and closed her eyes. Jeff drove to a fast-food chain planning to get the food and eat in the car so he could talk privately to Kate. He ordered the food and drove to the park and pulled in one of the spots.

"Kate, here is your food," Jeff said gently nudging Kate awake.

Kate sat the car seat upright and rubbed her hands over her face and then took the food. Her dull brown hair hung over her face as she unwrapped the burger. "Thanks."

Jeff waited. *Should I mention her not showing up,* he thought. *What would Jackie say?*

"Kate, have you thought any more about entering rehab?" Jeff asked and immediately regretted his choice of openers.

"Jeff, I appreciate your concern. I don't need rehab. I can stop anytime I want. It was a hard break-up and I'm going to take some time off. I plan to get myself together and back on track soon," she said between bites of her hamburger.

"Yeah, you said that last time — it was a hard break up. But that break-up is over. It's time to move on." Jeff shook his head in disbelief of what he had heard. "Are you telling me you are choosing to live this way to get over your break-up?" He paused and shook his head. "Kate, listen to yourself."

Kate looked down again at her food and didn't answer. She set the burger down and started to wrap it back up. Her hands had a slight tremor.

Jeff's voice softened, "Kate, we care about you. Your mother has been calling Meredith wanting to know what happened to you. Meredith thinks you're not answering her calls because you're mad at her. Your mother's getting ready to file a *Missing Persons* report on you. I told them I saw you downtown at a diner and that you were fine. I only lied to spare their feelings. But I'm not going to do it again. If you don't take me up on the offer of rehab, I'm going to tell them where you are and how you have been living."

"No . . . Jeff. Please don't," Kate pleaded, the strain obvious on her face. "I don't want them to see me this way. I don't . . . I don't . . . I wish you would have never found me." Kate was silent for several seconds. "Good old mom, ready to file a missing person. She was always tracking me down," she snorted. Then she turned sideways in the seat to face Jeff. "You don't get it. I've been to the 12 steps meetings. It doesn't work for me. That *one day at a time* crap doesn't work for me. I can't face having to live my life 'one day at a time' for the rest of my life," Kate said mockingly.

"How do you think I live? Try living with an autistic child with OCD. I can't even make it to *one day at a time*. It's *one moment at a time*. I live in crisis management on overdrive. Meredith could call me at any moment. Tucker could have hurt her or one of the girls. He could have run away, been suspended, or torn up the house. When I'm at home, I'm on patrol. I don't know how Meredith spends so much time with Tucker without going insane. So don't give me I can't take the *one day a time*. You're lucky; you can take it day by day. No one else is depending on you." Jeff's voice was elevated. Kate's pitiful attitude only annoyed him.

Kate was still looking at her food and then quietly said, "You're right. I get it. My problems are of my own making. Your's —not so much." Kate stared ahead unwilling to make eye contact with Jeff. "I know I messed up. Was mom really going to file a missing person report?" she asked and looked at Jeff. Her eyes were rimmed with tears.

"Yeah, she was." He chuckled slightly. "I don't know how you have made it this long without her finding you. You're just lucky right now that she is preoccupied with your dad. She still might have filed the report. I'm not sure, but I did try to act like everything was okay with you." His voice grew firm. "But no more. You need to call your mom even if you don't take me up on the rehab. She's worried and Meredith's sad. Meredith thinks you pushed her out of your life, and she is blaming herself and she doesn't need any more stress right now."

"Okay, I'll go," Kate said abruptly.

Jeff asked, "What?" He had mentally prepared a speech to convince her and he was only getting started.

Kate spoke softly, "I'll go." And then she said louder, "I'll go."

"Good." He smiled unsure of whether to continue his speech. *Less is more,* he thought to himself and said, "Okay, let's do this." He started the car.

Kate rubbed the palm of both hands down the legs of her jeans. She wasn't sure she made the right decision. "You have got to promise me not to tell Meredith or Mom, not yet. I don't want them to see me like this."

"Okay, if you go, I promise."

"Thanks." She took another bite of her burger.

Jeff handed her a sack with some granola bars and dried fruit in it that he had brought with him as Jackie suggested. "These are for later."

Kate and Jeff didn't speak. Jeff hit the automatic door lock and pulled the car out of the parking space. He kept glancing at her as they drove. He felt like Kate might jump out of the car. Kate picked at the sandwich still on her lap as they drove. Thirty minutes later, they pulled past some stone gates with a small sign that read, The 4:12 Center. Jeff parked and ran around the car and opened the door for Kate. She got out but still didn't speak. He opened the door and they entered into a large atrium with stained concrete floors and several small seating areas tucked around in corners. The round check-in desk had a clinical look and feel to it, but the clusters of seating areas looked homey. Jackie, the counselor Jeff has met with about Kate, came around the counter and greeted Kate. Kate's eyes were wide and she did not smile but extended her hand.

Jeff mouthed to Jackie, "I hope you have a place for her?"

Jackie nodded at Jeff and then spoke to Kate, "Let's get you settled and then we can do the intake." Jackie took Kate's arm and led her up the staircase. Kate looked back down at Jeff as she ascended the stairs. Jeff was staring up at her. The receptionist gave Jeff some forms to complete. He got to the question about court ordered placement or voluntary placement. He wished the rehab had been court ordered, but he checked voluntary knowing Kate could walk out anytime she wanted and he couldn't stop her and might not be able to find her again if she left.

Jackie returned. She smiled at Jeff. "Good job. You got her here."

Jeff sighed and smiled back. "I was so surprised when she agreed. I actually couldn't believe it because it was easier than I thought." He was talking fast. "What's her first step? What's next?"

"We're going to let her rest for the night. She is showering. We'll give her some scrubs to wear, but I suggest you pick her up some outfits—something comfortable."

"Can you let me know if she leaves? I know she is here voluntarily, but I want to know if she leaves," Jeff said.

"I'm not supposed to. I'll check with Kate about giving you access to her records. That's part of the forms she'll be signing."

Jeff completed the paperwork and wrote a check for $5,000 for the first week of rehab. Jeff's excitement turned to panic at losing track of Kate. "Can I see her before I leave?"

"Sure. As she gets started in the program, she will be earning her right to have visitors, so I'll keep you up to date on when you can visit her again." They went up to Kate's room. Jackie knocked. There was no answer. She slowly pushed open the door. Kate had on the scrubs and she was asleep on the bed with a towel wrapped around her wet hair.

"Don't wake her," Jeff said relieved that he knew she was safe for the moment. "I'm not sure I said the right thing, but she is here."

Jackie eased the door shut. "What matters is that you got her to come here voluntarily. You need to continue coming to the meetings for families, and if you can come a little early, I can update you on her progress."

Chapter 29

By the second week of being home with Tucker, Meredith had not heard from the school. She called the office on Wednesday and spoke to Dr. Fisher.

"The school will consider the results of an Independent Educational Evaluation. You are welcome to schedule it, but right now I don't have any funds allotted for an outside evaluation," he said emphasizing now, and then he continued slowly. "Right now, the school will not be able to pay for the evaluation. If you wait, I should be able to get some funding. If you want to pay for it and get it done, as soon as you have the results, we can have a meeting to discuss the evaluation."

"Okay, thank you. I'll get that taken care of immediately."

Meredith hung up from talking to Dr. Fisher and called Mrs. Wilson who gave her several evaluators' names to call. The bad news was the waiting list could be quite long for an evaluation and the school said they would not pay. Mrs. Wilson listed the names of evaluators that had worked with families that had students at Amicus, the independent alternate school. She suggested Meredith call one of those evaluators because they would know the services available at both Amicus and Central and would be able to make the best recommendations.

"You need to press the school on paying for the evaluation. They are trying to negotiate," Mrs. Wilson said.

"Maybe so, but it will delay the whole process, and I need something to change for the positive for Tucker right now."

"Yes, it will take longer, but it's the right thing to do."

"I just can't wait."

Meredith hung up and called the first name on the list. There was an opening in March, four months away! The second name had a canceled appointment open up on November 28, the Thursday after the Thanksgiving week and only about three weeks away. Meredith took the appointment.

Next was a call to Mrs. Riley. "I'm going to need to be off at least until the end of November. The earliest I could get an appointment for an evaluation was November 28."

"Since the appointment is November 28, and you've already used up your time off with pay, I'll ask the board to grant you a leave of absence using the Family Medical Leave Act until after Christmas. This will give you a couple of weeks to meet with the school and get Tucker going in a positive direction."

"That could work. And thank you so much," Meredith replied hopefully. "You have been more than understanding."

"You're welcome. I'll prorate the girl's tuition discount for the days you were here. We can get back on track with payroll deductions when you return. And I really hope all works out well for Tucker and your family."

"Thanks." Meredith hung up the phone and puffed her cheeks out with a quick exhale. The thought of the tuition cost gave her a panicky feeling. The girls had already made so many concessions she couldn't take them out of Cornerstone. If she had to use their savings, the girls were going to stay at Cornerstone. *Calm down, this is only a couple of months. You can handle this,* she told herself, but it felt like she was asking herself a question and was uncertain of the answer.

The next call was to Jeff. She was biting her nails while she waited for him to answer. Thankfully he was busy. "What's up?" he asked in his *talk quickly and give me just the highlights* voice.

"I scheduled Tucker an evaluation for November 28. Central agreed to use the findings from the independent evaluator for his diagnosis and placement considerations."

"How much?

"$2500."

"Is it covered?"

"No, they don't have the funds allotted right now," she said imitating Dr. Fisher's voice. "But they did agree to use the information in the report for placement and services."

"What about insurance?

"None — I already checked."

"What kind of evaluation is this?"

"It's a behavioral and academic evaluation."

"What's involved?"

"It's a couple of hours with Tucker and then a couple of hours with us. Tucker will take some test and we will fill out some more questionnaires about how we see Tucker. His teachers will fill out questionnaires and then the evaluator will take the test results, the questionnaires, and our interview and determine the diagnosis and make recommendations for the school."

"Why are we doing this again?" Jeff asked and then paused.

"Why?" Meredith repeated, shocked by his question. "You tell me? Do you have a better idea?" Meredith confronted him and then was silent. She had no words. She couldn't believe he didn't know *why*.

Jeff broke the silence. He had focused only on the dollars so he asked again in a softer voice. "When do we go for the evaluation?"

"November 28th."

"The appointment is almost three weeks away. Then by the time we get the results and meet with Central, several months will have passed. What do we do in the meantime?" Jeff asked skeptically.

"I keep Tucker home. I already called Cornerstone and asked for a leave of absence. Mrs. Riley is speaking with the board about me being off until Christmas. That will give me time to get Tucker settled and off to a good start and I'll be back in my class when school starts back up in January."

Jeff spoke breaking the silence. "So you won't have a paycheck for the next couple of months?" Jeff's voice shook with disbelief and then he was silent again.

"No, I won't," Meredith said timidly. "And. . . it gets worse." She didn't even want to continue, but she did, "We will have to pay full price for the girls' tuition for those months. Mrs. Riley said they could start the payroll deductions back up when I return to work."

"Let me get this straight," Jeff said with disbelief. "The evaluation is $2500. You won't have a paycheck for the next two months which is a loss of $8000, so we are down $10,500 so far for the next two months. Then add the girls' tuition of $1650 a month for two months. So now we are down about $12,000 for the next two months." Jeff groaned. Silence invaded again. He bit his bottom lip as he considered the numbers and thought about the $5000 check he just wrote.

"I'm sorry. I don't know what else to do."

"Well, the girls could go to Central," Jeff interjected knowing Meredith would never agree to that arrangement.

"This should only be for a couple of months. They need to stay at Cornerstone. It has been a hard year so far. We can't ask them to give up their school. We have our emergency savings and I think this is an emergency," Meredith pleaded.

"Give me some time to go over the numbers. We will probably have to use part of our emergency savings, but I might be able to swing some of it or most of it short term. Is there anything we can do without for the next couple of months?" Jeff asked and then thought about Kate. *I can't put her back out on the street.*

Meredith suggested, "Well . . . I could try to cut back on the groceries. Since I'll be home more I can cut coupons and I'll be cooking at home. No eating out."

"That's not going to make up $12,000. Let me work on it. Okay? I gotta go. I gotta get back to work."

Jeff hung up.

Meredith called her sister again. No answer. Meredith wasn't sure whether to be annoyed or concerned.

Chapter 30

The day before Thanksgiving, there was a knock on the door. Meredith opened the door to see Helen and Sam Sawyer, the elderly couple that sat near them when they used to attend church. Helen was holding out a pumpkin pie.

"Happy Thanksgiving," Helen sang with a smile

"Happy Thanksgiving to you, too," Meredith replied searching her mind for a possible reason for the visit. She looked at Helen and then Sam and then the pie.

"We just wanted to drop this pie off to go with your Thanksgiving dinner," Helen said breaking Meredith's long stare.

"Oh . . . come in." Meredith stumbled on her words. "I'm sorry the house is a mess. The kids are out of school and—

Helen interrupted. "No worries here. I was hoping we could visit for a moment. I noticed you and your family hadn't been to church in about a month. Are you attending somewhere else?"

"No, we haven't been." Meredith searched her mind for a logical and acceptable explanation but was coming up blank.

"I'm glad your family is well," Helen said. Meredith continued to stare at her so Helen asked, "They are well, aren't they?"

"Yes, everyone is fine," Meredith said leaning forward still waiting for what Helen and Sam wanted from her.

"I hope you don't mind, but I noticed your son at church. He has some type of disability?"

"Yes, he does," Meredith said bluntly as she felt anger flare up inside her, and her cheeks grew warm.

"I had a son with a disability, too," Helen started. "He had Down's syndrome and some other issues. This was many years ago. The doctors suggested I put Brian, our son, in an institution and basically forget about him." She paused and looked down.

"Well, I didn't do that. I kept him home with me." She looked up at Meredith. "I wasn't a working mom like you and I had time to devote to him. I couldn't bear the thought of leaving him in an institution. I'm glad I never had to make that choice."

Meredith nodded and the anger drained out of her. "That would've been hard," she said realizing the reason for the visit. "Please, have a seat."

"He passed away a few years ago. He had heart problems," Helen said and then looked down.

Meredith said in a barely audible voice said, "I'm sorry to hear that. I never knew him."

"It's okay. I was lucky. I had the joy of having him with me his whole life. He never had to be without me. He had a good life. We did everything we could for him. Oh . . . but it was hard at times. Most people's attitudes at the time were the disabled needed to be separated from society. I think that was to protect society so others would not have to think about those less fortunate. There were no special schools or services available to help families so we just managed the best we could."

Meredith shifted from side to side and looked back for any of her kids. She wanted to change the subject. She didn't want to talk about the disabled or about Tucker being disabled. *Please stop talking,* she thought. She sighed because her guilt kicked in when she realized people like Helen just managed on their own. Meredith focused on what Helen was telling her.

Helen continued, "I did have someone who helped me, though. I had a dear friend who stayed with Brian so Sam and I could go out once a week. She probably never realized how important that was to us even though I told her each week. She would just say it was her privilege and that she had fun. Brian loved her too. She and I are still good friends; she is my best friend. I think besides Sam here, she was the only one who truly mourned when Brian passed on. She loved Brian despite his disabilities. I tell you this because I want to help you. I want to do for you what my friend did for me. I bet you two don't get to go out as a couple, and I know you're not coming to church anymore. I know you don't know us very well. But I can take the girls to church. I would love for them to go to church with me. They can sit with me in the service after Sunday School, or I can come and watch all the kids so you and your husband can go out."

Meredith was shaking her head 'No' but didn't say anything.

Helen continued, "Think about it. I've been where you are—in a way. Every family is different because every disabled child is different, but every family needs support." Helen got up and patted Meredith on the hand. "I'll call you in a few days."

Meredith mumbled, "Yes, and thank you . . . for the pie . . . and for the offer."

Helen hugged Meredith, and she and Sam said good-bye. After Helen and Sam had left, Meredith stood staring at the pie for a couple of minutes as she considered the offer they had made and wondered why they would care. It was amazing that someone noticed and cared, yet she was sad that they couldn't go to church together as a family. They always seemed to have to *divide and conquer.*

Chapter 31

Jeff felt the pressure. Numbers were important to him. He made his living with numbers, and the number that was important to him right now was $12,150, the number he was down in his budget. Not to even mention Christmas occurred in one of those months, and he had a commitment to Kate! Meredith and Jeff had agreed not to get each other a gift, but that didn't make up for $12,150. Some of the deficit would come out of the budget, which would be maxed out, and the rest from the emergency savings account. This was an unexpected event and it justified dipping into the emergency account. He had planned well and had a fully funded emergency fund. He was busy at work which meant he would be replacing the money as soon as possible. Jeff had been hoping that Meredith could be a full-time mom soon. This would give him an opportunity to see how the budget handled it. End-of-the-year accounting and getting ready for taxes made for long hours. His clients paid a monthly fee for his services, so he didn't realize extra income during these long hours, but he was thankful his accounting business had taken off just as Meredith had to take a leave of absence. He had actually thought this year would be the year they would get ahead and get some real money put back for emergencies, retirement, and maybe a new car. But it was not to be . . . just yet. Maybe next year when Tucker was settled, Meredith back at work, and they were receiving the half-price tuition again, Jeff could replenish the emergency fund. Then they could make some headway. Everything would settle down. They could take a great vacation, stash some money into their 401K, upgrade the cars, and get Myla a used car in a couple of years when she turned 16. He had been working his financial plan and it was paying off. He knew it's not if there is going to be an emergency; it's when. And then he thought of Kate—lying asleep on the bed at rehab—looking as fragile as a fallen baby bird. He rolled his shoulders trying to sit up straighter.

All these thoughts made Jeff's work therapeutic for him. He took a deep breath and looked at the numbers on his spreadsheet.

Work made sense. He could control the numbers. They added up. There was a loss or a profit. Home made no sense. Tucker was definitely calmer when Meredith was in charge. Jeff felt like he overwhelmed Tuck. Maybe he was too aggressive in dealing with Tuck. He certainly didn't have the knack that Meredith had, but he could tell dealing with Tuck was wearing on her. She seemed tired all the time—more tired than she had been while teaching full time. Now she seemed not only tired but just weary. They discussed how everything would work out after the evaluation, but that was still a few days away. Still they had no way of telling how long it would take the evaluator to write the report, for the school to meet on the report, and then for the school to implement the recommendations. *It will work. I'll make it work,* Jeff told himself. It was well thought out, and well thought out and well orchestrated plans work.

Jeff stayed at the office more than he stayed at home now. Being busy was a good excuse. After working 14 hours, he liked to watch some television and get some sleep. Home was too emotionally draining. The mental drain of work was easier.

Jeff arrived at The 4:12 Center, paid the next installment, and had 30 minutes before the family meeting so he could talk to Jackie. "How is she?"

"It's only been a couple of days, so she is still dealing with the physical withdrawals, but she is trying to work through it. You have heard of the term *rock bottom*? That is where Kate is right now. She's having to accept her own lies and dysfunction."

"She kept telling me that she was trying to get over her break-up."

"Exactly, she has been lying to herself and to you. And I think the fact that you told her that you would *out her* to your wife and her mother helped her to have a reason to change. What she was doing wasn't going to work much longer. You didn't co-sign her lies," Jackie said and smiled at Jeff. "It's hard to be so honest, but you did. And I think the break-up made her start questioning everything she believed in, and she couldn't handle it. There was also a child — a boy — who she was working with to remove from the home and that situation didn't end as she hoped. In that situation, she was doing the right things, but she didn't get the right outcome. She quit believing that she could make a difference. Everything a person believes in comes into question at rock bottom. It's from rock bottom that she will build her life again. She will have to let go of all that she has known to set herself free to live a new and different life."

Another counselor came into the office where Jeff and Jackie were sitting. "Jackie, do you want me to lead the meeting. We have a big group today."

"Go ahead and start. We'll be there in a few minutes," Jackie said to the other counselor and then turned back to Jeff. "Everything okay with you? Do you have any questions for me?"

Jeff looked away from Jackie and stared at the floor for several seconds before he spoke. "Same stuff with me. Meredith is still staying at home with our son while we pressure the school district into paying tuition for Tuck to attend a school for kids with autism and related disorders. We finally have an evaluation date and with the new evaluation, we should get some results and someone on our side. And we are paying the lady so she won't be trying to please the school district so she can get repeat referrals." Jeff shook his head. "I'm becoming cynical about the whole process." Jeff stood up. "Can I see Kate today?"

"Not today. She is still dealing with the physical withdrawals. She is angry and, now, she is blaming you. But that is no surprise at this point. I try to get clients moving forward in their recovery before they see family. She is wallowing around on rock bottom right now— so to speak. And the only reason I'm able to share so much with you is because she did sign a waiver for you to have access to her medical records. I encouraged her to do that because I think the more you understand, the better off she will be in the long term. And that is why it's so important for you to attend the family meetings. It will not only help you, but it'll help you understand her."

Chapter 32

Tucker demanded, "I'm not going to eat that chicken!"

"Okay," Meredith said as she quickly removed the plate from the table. She didn't ask for an explanation. She simply didn't want the food and the plate to end up on the floor.

"I'm hungry," Tucker stated.

"Then eat your chicken."

"I want Heinz ketchup with my chicken," Tucker informed Meredith.

Meredith had purchased the store brand ketchup because it was on sale and without thinking she concluded ketchup is ketchup. Silly Mom. But that is not the case with Tucker. Little things matter. The girls ate their chicken quietly and looked intensely at their plates. All three knew to not speak or make sudden changes when Tucker was on the verge of a meltdown. The escalation was hanging in the air.

"I want Heinz ketchup!" Tucker said pounding the table not with his fist — even though it was balled up — but with his wrist.

Clare slid her plate quietly from the table and went to sit on the sofa. Meredith didn't say anything as Clare and she made eye contact. Isabelle and Myla looked at their mom and then slid from their chairs and headed down to the basement with their dinner plates in hand. Tucker had begun to pound the table using his wrist and to kick the chair with both feet.

Meredith sat calmly at the table. She said, "If you want Heinz ketchup, you will have to go to the store with me so we can get some Heinz ketchup."

"You go to the store."

"I can't go to the store while you're upset. Let's go to the store together and get the Heinz ketchup," Meredith said in a monotone voice.

Tucker went and got his DS and got in the backseat of the car. He always sat behind the driver. Meredith quickly followed after she ran down the steps and alerted Myla to the fact that she and Tucker were leaving. Myla knew what to do—lock the door, check on Clare, don't answer the phone unless it was Meredith or Jeff. They drove away with Tucker in the backseat playing his Nintendo DS.

The girls switched on the television. They could watch whatever they wanted now that Tucker was gone, so they flopped down in front of the television with some more chicken on their plates. Clare sat by Isabelle, and they laughed at a cartoon as she pulled the meat from the chicken leg and dipped it in the store brand ketchup. Myla collected her's and Isabelle's plates and stuffed them in empty crevices in the dishwasher, turned the dishwasher on, and joined her sisters in front of the television.

Meredith drove to the smaller grocery store, even though it was farther away than the super center grocery store, to get the ketchup because there would be fewer people—which meant fewer opportunities for Tucker to get upset in the store.

"We are going to go in and get the ketchup and come right back out," Meredith instructed Tucker as if they were getting ready to undertake a covert mission. If Tucker knew what to expect, there was less chance of an outburst. Everything had to go according to the plan or there would be *hell to pay*. Meredith hoped she wouldn't see anyone she knew in the store. In they went straight to the ketchup aisle, through the self check-out, and back to the car. The plan was executed flawlessly, and Tucker had the Heinz ketchup sitting beside him in the backseat. Meredith thought how she didn't save any money buying the store brand ketchup that was on sale because she went back and bought the other plus she used extra gas. Every penny was important right now. She knew she was over-thinking buying a bottle of ketchup, but she just couldn't help it.

The girls heard the car pull into the garage. They switched

off the television and headed to the basement. Tucker came in and sat down at the table and ate his chicken with his Heinz ketchup. Meredith sat down on the couch and stared at the blank television and couldn't believe it was only 6:30. If only she could keep everything on schedule, have nothing unexpected happen, and have the correct items in the house, then the days would go much smoother. Try as she might, she couldn't seem to accomplish one ordinary day.

Tucker's rules wore her down. However, the rules were simple. It was just there was never a break from the rules — no downtime. It was a 24-hour 7-day a week job to follow the rules. They might help Tucker keep order in a confusing world, but they wore her out. They kept the unexpected out and kept the sensory overload down. Meredith could vary the time slightly but not the order of events. After dinner it was homework time. Meredith cleaned the kitchen while homework was done at the kitchen table and she was available to help. There was no television during homework, and Clare had to come to the table too even if she just colored. Tucker would bring his work to the table and do homework also even though he and Meredith had worked on his assignments during the day. She always assigned him homework just to accommodate homework time and his rules, but Meredith actually liked this rule of Tucker's. She remembered when she had started the homework time, but it was less structured. Now Tucker provides the structure because no one wants to deal with his rage plus everyone knows they really need to study each night. It amazed her that the girls complied with Tucker's rule.

Tucker casually interacted with his sisters and his mother during homework time. He had questions he would ask them as if from some script in his head. The questions were looped through every few days. He remembered previous responses to the questions, and if they changed their answer, Tucker would tell them their previous answers. It was as if Tucker was trying to catch them in an inconsistency. He wanted daily life to follow some kind of predictable pattern—a pattern he could count on not to change. He wanted life to make sense and the answers to always be the same. When Meredith would tell Tucker that the only thing he could count on was that things were going to change, he just seemed confused.

If Meredith tried to relate one of Tucker's obsessions to Jeff or a colleague, it seemed so ridiculous. To tell someone about the hassle of buying a brand that was on sale—which ended up upsetting Tucker—the girls disappearing from the table one-by-one, driving to the store to run in and grab the ketchup while avoiding as many people as possible, and then Tucker sitting down so sweetly and eating his cold chicken with his favorite ketchup as if that were the most natural thing in the world seemed strangely idiotic. So he had a favorite ketchup. It was hard to explain to others, but the ketchup was a big deal. The only person who would truly enjoy this ridiculous story was Kate. *Kate, what is going on with you,* Meredith thought

Myla's phone rang during homework time. Everyone stopped what they were doing and looked at her. Meredith nodded okay and quietly said, "quickly and then back to work."

Myla's answered and then held the phone down on her shoulder while she talked to Meredith. "Can you take me over to Gloria's tonight? She has friends coming over to watch a movie."

"I guess so. I can drive you over there after homework."

Tucker hit the table with his wrist several times and then started hitting his forehead with the palm of his hand.

Myla said into the phone, "I'll have to call you back. I might need to stay home and help my mom with my brother." Myla sat back down at the table. "Tucker, I'm going to stay here. I need to study my Spanish anyway." She smiled at Tucker who looked at her and relaxed.

Meredith's shoulders slumped forward. She sighed and looked across the table at Myla. When Myla's eyes met her's, she mouthed, "Thank you." Myla smiled back and then turned her

141

attention to her book.

We are his prisoners, Meredith thought. *But they don't even know it.* Myla must remember a time when Tucker was younger and easy going and the house was filled with laughter rather than rules, but she obviously accepted the change without resistance. Isabelle continued to champion Tucker's causes seemingly totally and blissfully oblivious to the fact that Tucker was autistic. Maybe she didn't care, or maybe it was because she has looked out for Tucker her entire life. Clare has never had a time of normal. Obviously the girls loved Tucker too, but the irony was the abnormal seemed normal to them.

Chapter 33

"What does someone wear to hear results of an evaluation?" Meredith asked as she looked through the clothes hanging in the closet. There were several discarded outfits laying on the bed.

"Wear the yellow top. It brings out your green eyes," Jeff said.

Meredith watched Jeff as he tied his tie again. She straightened it for him when he was done.

"This is ridiculous. We are going to hear the results of an evaluation. We are not going to meet the president." Jeff stopped and sat down on the end of the bed. "Why does it feel like we have so much riding on this?"

"We do. Our future will be determined by this evaluation."

"What if the school throws it out and says we considered it, but now we are going to do it our way?"

"I don't want to think about that," Meredith said and stared at Jeff as if he had just declared he could fly.

"Quit looking at me. Are you ready? Let's go. I don't want to be late. Where's Tuck?" Jeff burst out each sentence in rapid succession without waiting for an answer and then he left the bedroom. He came right back in and asked, "You do know the way to Dr. Holmes' office?"

Meredith bit her nails while Jeff and she drove in silence other than the occasional direction from Meredith. Tucker sang in the backseat.

While Tucker stayed in a playroom with the receptionist, Jeff and Meredith went into Sally Holmes' office.

Jeff shook Dr. Holmes hand and asked, "What placement will you be recommending for Tuck?"

"Have a seat, Mr. Howard, and we will go over the results."

Meredith gave Jeff a wide-eyed looked that said, *Be nice*.

The educational evaluator gave both Jeff and Meredith a copy of the evaluation. Jeff started flipping through the report as he quickly scanned it.

Dr. Holmes began, "Tucker is an amazing child. He has some impressive skills and some obvious deficits. As you know, Mrs. Howard, when you brought him in, I went through a battery of tests with Tucker including an IQ test." Jeff continued to scan the report while Dr. Holmes continued speaking. "I also had both of you complete a Behavior Rating Scale, and I had his teachers at both Cornerstone and Central complete the same Behavior Rating Scales but from a teacher's perspective. I spoke to Tucker's teachers at both schools and to both principals. I used all of this information to determine recommendations and placement for Tucker so he can achieve his maximum academic, behavioral, and social potential."

Meredith started biting her nails. Jeff reached over and took Meredith's hand — partly for his own comfort and partly to stop her from biting her nails.

"The first test measured intelligence and achievement. The second test measures the skills of decoding and word-reading ability, math reasoning, spelling ability, the ability to recognize stated details and make inferences, writing dictation, and solving calculation problems and equations. I want to present an overview of the results, and then we can look at the details. Let's begin with his mental processing score which was 85 and is the low end of average. Tucker has strength in sequential processing such as number ordering and word recall showing he has a great memory. His lower scores occurred when he had to work problems that were spatial, analogical, or organizational. I saw the same pattern on both tests. In basic reading and numerical operations, Tucker excelled. He can follow the rules for reading and is actually reading above grade level, and he can easily do math computation. However, his reading comprehension and math reasoning scores were low. He is good at following the rules of phonics and math. Actually, he is excellent. But when he has to apply these rules for reasoning, he is significantly below grade level."

Meredith spoke up. "That is exactly what I see at home. When we do his schoolwork, I have to give him hints or clues so he can answer the reading comprehension questions. I have him reread the paragraph where the information is found, and then he can answer the question if they are about details in the story. Comprehension questions requiring an inference are much more difficult for him than questions asking a specific detail. With the inferences, I talk him through the reasoning process to come up with the answer, but it's difficult."

"The testing picked up on that. His reasoning is his main deficiency. And as you probably know as a teacher yourself, most of reading in the early elementary years is about learning the rules of phonics, and then in late elementary, comprehension rather than phonics becomes the focus. And it's the comprehension that creates difficulties for Tucker. He has been able to get along so well in early elementary because it's fact based. He can apply and remember rules. But inferences and comprehension are very difficult for him, and they are also what make up so much of social interaction. I suspect that he may be acting out behaviorally because he is frustrated or simply doesn't know what is going on. He doesn't understand the social rules which have gotten more complex for him. So he makes up his own routines and this is where his Obsessive Compulsive Disorder or OCD comes into play. These obsessive compulsive tendencies plus the frustrations at the increased demand for reasoning and comprehension are what I believe are at the root of his behavior problems this year at Cornerstone and Central. Remember that social situations require a great deal of inferences and reasoning. We have to read someone's behavior, facial expressions, mood, and intent, and these social rules change constantly based on the person and place. I reviewed the responses from both of you and his teachers and principals. Everyone consistently documented Tucker's outbursts or meltdowns when an event occurred that did not follow a predictable pattern and that upset Tucker's routine. Each of the meltdowns documented was easily related to overwhelming sensory input or to a break in Tucker's routine by something new or unexpected. Considering all the results, I would classify Tucker as autistic and as having Obsessive Compulsion Disorder— both of which are categorically mild, and I believe with the right intervention, Tucker will be able to function well in the school setting. The test results gave me a picture of his autism. The behavior ratings gave me a picture of a student with OCD. So I'm recommending individual counseling for Tucker and family counseling along with speech therapy for pragmatics and sensory integration therapy to calm down his escalated behavioral responses. Obsessive Compulsive Disorder and the associated behaviors can be devastating to a person and a family. Your family needs to work with professionals while Tucker works with a therapist to minimize the effects of the OCD. Amicus has an excellent approach to integrating family and student counseling. You could also work with a private therapist. Both Amicus and Central have the other therapy services available. I'm also going to recommend that you take Tucker to a psychiatrist because there are medications available that help reduce the OCD symptoms."

Jeff held Meredith's hand a little tighter.

Dr. Holmes watched them both. "I know it can be hard to hear that your child has a disability. Do you have any questions about my report?"

"No, not about the . . . the label. We just need to know how to survive. It just feels like we have been barely hanging on these last few weeks. I know I just function in basic survival mode — always. It's so hard to balance Tucker's need and the needs of girls." Meredith took a deep, quick breath. "Our whole lives have been revolving around Tucker's needs and if he could be okay — again — then we will all be okay. Tucker has been home with me full time because I can't get him to go to Central. And I'm relieved that your impressions about Tucker are the same as mine. So I'm not crazy. He's not aggressive."

"No, you're not crazy." Dr. Holmes nodded. "Now you need to take this evaluation to the school district and work with them to get some help for Tucker and" — she paused — "for you."

Meredith attempted a smile and nodded. Then she listened as Dr. Holmes went through each test result. The autism was not new. So he was autistic. They could deal with autism. It was a part of who he was — his quirky self. They loved him the way he was. But the OCD was hard to deal with. It had been devastating and difficult for Meredith and the girls. His OCD was his attempt to organize a confusing world, but it caused everyone else's world to be chaotic. His rules were hard. He was somewhat predictable about certain things such as ketchup brands, people coughing, intercoms in stores, eating with his favorite fork and plate. But the intensity of his responses was unpredictable.

Meredith was leaning forward and sitting on the edge of her seat. "Your evaluation confirmed what I see with Tucker. It's difficult to hear, but at the same time, I can only work with what I know. Knowledge is power."

Sally Holmes nodded and said, "I can send a copy of the report to the public school and to Amicus, and I expect the public school to meet with you sometime this week to start implementing the recommendation. I checked with Amicus and they do have space available."

Jeff stood up and shook Sally Holmes' hand, "Thank you so much. With your recommendations and with your help, I think we can get Tucker back on track."

Meredith said, "Thank you."

"Call me if you need further information from me."

Meredith turned to Jeff as they left the building with Tucker in tow. "I can't wait to talk to the school tomorrow."

Jeff smiled.

Chapter 34

Dr. Fisher, Mrs. Canon, and several professionals they had never seen before sat across the long conference table from Jeff and Meredith. They each had their hands clasped and placed on the table.

"The school's only obligation is to consider the recommendations in your independent evaluation report. I've read the report. In our records we will remove the label of oppositional defiant disorder, and we will concur with the evaluator's assessment that the outbursts are a result of OCD and sensory issues related to his disability rather than defiant acts. We plan to have Tucker meet weekly with the school counselor to address the recommendation of individual psychological therapy, and he will stay in the self-contained classroom."

Meredith spoke up, "The self-contained didn't work before because of the bullying that Tucker was experiencing. One of Sally Holmes — I mean Dr. Holmes' —recommendations was placement at Amicus alternate school so our family could also participate in counseling. The school also has a highly qualified staff to deal with Tucker's behavior and his reasoning deficit in both academic and social situations. But more importantly, Tucker wasn't bullied there so he'll be willing to give it a try. I'm not sure I can get him to come back to Central much less stay. So I'm asking for Tucker to be placed at Amicus. We need the family counseling help so we can be consistent and help Tucker."

"Amicus is a very specialized private school. But at this school, we CAN provide the least restrictive environment, and we have an appropriate placement that can meet Tucker's needs and all the therapies recommended by Sally Holmes—except the family counseling. Mrs. Canon is excellent at parent communication and she will keep you informed," stated Dr. Fisher. "I'll check into the family counseling and get back to you. But I feel like our services here at Central can meet all the recommendations of Dr. Holmes."

"You might have the services, but the emotional trauma is not going to be easy to undo. I can't feel good about Tucker's placement here at Central. His behavior deteriorated when the bullying—both verbal and physical—started. This setting is not safe for him. And being in an unsafe environment is not what is best or appropriate for him. He has been traumatized by the situation here."

"Mrs. Howard," Dr. Fisher began, "we have a no tolerant policy at this school for bullying. The student involved with the bullying incident with Tucker and some of his classmates has been handled, and the situation has stopped. The student has been reprimanded and dealt with."

"Tucker won't care. It won't matter to him at all. He has already decided. He needs to be placed at Amicus. This is not a reflection on Mrs. Canon or your services," Meredith said looking over at Tucker's previous teacher. "This is about Tucker's disability. I think going to Amicus is the only way I'm going to get him back in school. I can't get him to come back here. Can you provide someone to drag him to school?"

"The school district is obligated to provide the least restrictive environment based on all evaluations. We have considered both evaluations, the school districts and your independent evaluator, and I feel that here at Central we have an appropriate and least restrictive placement for Tucker. We will start counseling services for Tucker. And the speech therapist will address social and pragmatic issues. And we can send a bus to pick him up."

"Who gets to define what's appropriate for him?" Jeff asked.

"This committee," Dr. Fisher stated.

"What if we don't agree with what the committee thinks is appropriate?" Jeff asked.

"There is a process to follow. First we can try informally to

149

work out the disagreement, then mediation by a third party, and then a due process hearing.

Meredith stared straight at Dr. Fisher. Her eyes showed no surprise. "Unless you can agree right now on the school district paying for Amicus, we need to take the next step," Meredith said — even though her hands were shaking.

Jeff cut his eyes over at Meredith wondering what had gotten into her to make her so decisive.

"The next step is mediation or we can go straight to a due process hearing with an impartial hearing officer."

"The only way I can see this working is for Tucker to go to Amicus. He's not going to be able to come here. He will not be able to overcome the abuse at the hands of the bully. His disability won't allow it," Meredith stated. "I need Tucker to go to school so I can go to work and he won't come here, not for classes."

Jeff was surprised at Meredith's determination, but he knew that they needed real solutions. Jeff found himself standing next to Meredith as she told the assembled professionals, "Thank you for your time. I guess I have to write another letter?" Meredith retrieved Tucker from the secretary who was watching him.

Meredith banged the dashboard with both fists when they got in the car. Tucker played his Nintendo DS in the backseat seated behind the driver oblivious to his mother's distress. She put her hands over her face and sobbed, loud sobs as her shoulders shook. The sobs came from deep inside. Jeff looked and felt helpless. All he could do was lean Meredith over so her head lay on his chest and put his arm around her. He had no idea what to say. Her response only added to his guilt of staying away — at work — so much. If she lost it, all would be lost. He had to get her to keep it together somehow.

Meredith spoke through the tears, "I need the school to help me. I need him to go to school and be okay. Why are they making this so hard? You know, I'm going to lose my job over this?"

Jeff leaned up and sat up on the edge of the seat. Until this point he thought his role was to be supportive of Meredith, but he suddenly realized his whole world could come tumbling down too if Tucker didn't go to school.

"I shouldn't have to choose between my children. If I end up staying home with Tucker, the girls will have to leave Cornerstone. That's all they've known." Meredith sniffed and wiped her face with both hands.

"I don't think we're to that point yet. We'll just work to get Tucker going back to Central. He can do it," Jeff said giving Meredith a pep talk.

"I need some type of professional help," Meredith laughed on the outside but inside she was serious. "Tucker needs help. He isn't a bad kid. He just needs a better mother."

"You're a good mother," Jeff said.

"No, I'm not. You're not around to see what goes on. I felt like I was barely keeping my head above rough water. This meeting was going to save me, but now I'm going down and it may be for the last time. I don't know why I thought the school would agree with us. Nothing has changed for Tucker. Nothing," Meredith said.

"We'll get Tucker back at Central. Our plan is still that you will be going back to work after the Christmas break."

Meredith stopped crying and stared at him through her red eyes. "How can you say that? I don't think so. I guess the plans have changed. How could I go back?" she retorted almost gritting her teeth as her sadness turned into anger at Jeff. "My teaching career is gone—all because this stupid school district doesn't understand how impossible it is to get Tucker back here. I might've had a chance with Amicus. Dr. Fisher said it was last resort, but I'm already there. I'm so stupid. What was I thinking?

Did I really think they would say okay? I seriously doubt I can get Tucker to go back to Central. I just don't have the strength."

"Well then, I guess Elvis has left the building," Jeff said in his announcer's voice.

Tucker said from the backseat of the car, "I didn't see Elvis."

Meredith stopped, looked at Jeff, and smiled despite the tears she was wiping from her eyes. "Tucker, that's an expression that means the show is over."

"What show?" Tucker asked.

Meredith was thinking about how to explain *what show*. When Tucker checked his GPS watch and said, "It's 11:30, time for lunch."

Jeff complied by starting the car and asking Tucker, "Where to, Tuck?"

Chapter 35

Myla kept checking the window and when she saw a white suburban, she called out to her sisters. "Isabelle, Clare, Mrs. Sawyer is here." Clare emerged dressed for church, but Isabelle came out in her play clothes.

"What's wrong, Isabelle? Are you not feeling well?" Meredith asked.

"I'm not going to church if Tucker can't go," Isabelle declared.

Meredith knew which battles to fight so she simply put her arm around Isabelle. "Okay, you don't have to go."

She grabbed a quick kiss from Clare and Myla as they bolted from the house.

Mrs. Sawyer poked her head in the door and saw Isabelle in her jeans and sweatshirt and asked, "Are you not going with us today to church?"

Isabelle shook her head, and Meredith rubbed Isabelle's back and said, "Not today,"

"Well, okay." Helen continued, "How was your meeting at the school?"

Meredith sighed, "Not good. Nothing changed."

"You keep working for Tucker. You know him best and you know what is best for him. When he gets settled, it will help the girls, you, and Jeff."

"I know. It will all be worth it in the long run."

"The girls will be in the music program next Sunday. Why don't I stay with Tucker so you and Jeff can go see the girls sing? I have watched them practicing," she said and put her hand together as if she was praying. "They sing like angels."

"That would be great! I'll ask Jeff."

She turned before leaving and said, "If it's okay with you, we would still like to take all the kids out to eat after church. I think it's Isabelle's turn to choose, and she said that she wanted pizza." Mrs. Sawyer then turned to address Isabelle, "So . . . can I pick you up for pizza after church?"

"Is Tucker going too?"

"Sure, if he wants to."

Isabelle brightened and looked at her mom. "Okay." And then Isabelle looked down and said in a humbled voice, "Thank you."

Tucker came out of his room after Myla and Clare left. The house was quieter, and he had Meredith and Isabelle all to himself, so he began talking about his favorite subject— airplanes. He seemed to know every fact about any airplane manufactured. His favorites were the military planes. It amazed Meredith each year when they went to the air show. Tucker would wear his *headset*, otherwise known as noise dampening headphones. He would squeeze his eyes shut if someone with a striped shirt walked by him. He wanted to see the planes so badly he managed to put up with stripes and noises.

At the air show, Tucker would go from plane to plane, reciting facts about each plane. He knew the names of the Blue Angel pilots and their *stats* as if they were baseball players. His memory of complex information amazed both Jeff and Meredith. They no longer double-checked his facts because they had found he was always correct. Meredith knew he could comprehend information because he would devour the books and atlases they gave him and he could relate that information. But could he use that information to solve a problem in a new way? Probably not but it didn't matter to her. They were still astounded. He could tell where a specific plane took off from, who the pilot was, the mission, whether the mission was successful, where the plane landed, and even where it refueled. If that information was in a book that Tucker read, it was now in Tucker's memory. He would ask Meredith questions about planes to see if she remembered.

"When did the Blue Angels first fly?" Tucker asked his mom.

"June 15, 1946," Meredith recited from memory. She was amazed how much information on aviation that she now knew.

"How high can an MQ1B Predator fly?" Tucker quizzed.

"25,000 feet," Meredith responded.

Tucker loved to discuss planes, and the question and answer sessions were predictable and enjoyable for both Meredith and Tucker. Meredith sometimes would give the wrong answer just to hear Tucker laugh at her ridiculous answer.

Chapter 36

Meredith was at the table working on the menus and grocery list. She had to be organized because it was almost impossible to make a trip to the store for a forgotten ingredient especially with Jeff working such long hours. She looked out the window when she heard a car pull into the driveway. To her surprise it was Jeff; he came in and kissed her.

"I want to spend some time with Tuck this afternoon so you and the girls can go out and have some girl time. Tuck and I can do some guy stuff. We may drive over to Central and walk around—a little desensitization therapy. Maybe I can get him to watch a ball game with me or play some catch. If all else fails, I'll let him beat me at one of his video games. I've wrapped up most of the details of the end-of-year books, and I have a breather here before tax season starts. And I want to spend some time with my son this afternoon."

"Really?" Meredith's face brightened. "That would be great. The kids — all of them— went out to pizza with the Sawyers. When they get back, we'll go out." Meredith smiled.

"This is very rare," Jeff said. "We are home— alone. This hasn't happened in . . . I can't remember the last time."

"I know. I took a chance and let Tucker go with the Sawyers to eat pizza. He was excited and Isabelle wanted him to go. Myla told me not to worry and Mrs. Sawyer said that she would call if there were a problem. So far no calls."

"Relax, Myla can handle him."

"I know. That makes me proud and sad at the same time."

"You worry too much."

A car pulled in the driveway; slamming car doors announced the arrival of the kids. Myla carried in a pizza box with a medium vegetarian pizza in it and sat in on the table. "Mrs. Sawyer said this is for you and Dad."

Isabelle was right behind with a pizza box with leftover pizza. Mrs. Sawyer opened the door and in came Tucker and Clare. "They were good — all of them," she said smiling and then waved and left.

Jeff grabbed Tucker playfully around the waist and lifted him off the floor. "Tuck, how about you and I play your racing game?" Meredith followed the girls into their room. "We are going to the mall," she said as she drew a circle in the air indicating just the girls. Both Myla's and Isabelle's eyes widened. "Just to look around though," she added. The girls needed no more explanation; they were ready to go. Girl time— it meant so much more to Meredith. It meant downtime. She wasn't on guard or having her attention divided listening or worrying. She could focus on her three daughters.

At the mall after they cruised through several stores, Meredith suggested ice cream. As they were sitting at a table in the mall corridor eating ice-cream, one of Myla's friends walked up wearing a candy-striped Christmas shirt. Meredith felt her breathing quicken until she realized that Tucker wasn't with her to object to the stripes on the shirt. Meredith leaned back in the chair and told Myla's friend, "I love your shirt." Myla looked at her mom with smiling eyes both knowing the same secret.

Isabelle had an audience at the ice cream shop. Always the observant comedian, she began to imitate different teachers and how they walked and moved. She demonstrated how Mrs. Ellen patrolled the lunchroom with her hands behind her back taking measured steps. Meredith began laughing and immediately her hands went to cover her mouth to dampen the sound of the laugh. She took a moment to regroup and put her hands down and enjoyed laughing with her daughters. She had made so many little changes. But this moment — this wonderful moment — with her daughters was all the more special because she didn't take it for granted. And that was a change too. Tucker had taught her to soak in the moments when all is right because everything can change in the blink of an eye. As they shopped, Meredith was able to glean some ideas for Christmas presents for each girl that wouldn't dig them further into their financial hole.

Jeff met Meredith at the door. "Do you want to know what the *little crapper* did while you were gone?"

Not really, Meredith thought, but she said, "What?"

"He stuffed a shirt and a DS cartridge down the toilet and flushed them. This was in the basement bathroom, of course. He never said a thing." Jeff started waving his hands around. "I had no idea that he had done it. We were together the whole time except when he came in to go to the bathroom, and I — stupidly— thought he needed to go to the bathroom, but nooo, he flooded the basement. I realized what happened when I went downstairs to get a load of towels out of the dryer, and I stepped in water up to my ankles. The toilet had been running for hours. I turned the water main off and spent 30 minutes trying to fish out the clog in the toilet with a plunger and then a clothes hanger. You can bet I was surprised when I fished out a T-shirt and a game." He paused. His lips were pursed tight together and his arms crossed. Meredith didn't say anything. She just stood there looking at him. He threw his arms back up in the air and said, "The DS cartridge is drying out on the back patio, and I put the shirt in with a load of laundry."

Meredith gently ran her hand over her hair pulling the strands back and resting her hand on the back of neck waiting and hoping for something helpful to come to mind. "Thank you . . . for doing laundry," Meredith finally said.

Jeff looked at her with a stunned look on his face and then just shook his head. He put his hands on his hips and started pacing back and forth as he continued his story. "This was not in the plan. We were supposed to have some guy time — bonding time. Instead, I spent 30 minutes with the wet vac getting the water up. There is still more water to get up. I just had to take a break."

"Did he say why he stuffed the shirt down the toilet?"

"Why? Is there ever a good reason to stuff anything down the toilet?" Jeff was talking with his hands again. Then he leaned closer to Meredith and added, "He didn't want you and the girls to go out without him."

"Ahh . . . that's sweet."

"Sweet? He didn't want to go. He just wanted you to stay here!" Jeff nearly screamed. He tapped his fingers on his forehead realizing the ridiculousness of the situation. "So much for guy-time"— Jeff leaned back and held his arm fully extended with his palms up — "unless learning about plumbing counts."

Meredith smiled at Jeff as he shook his head no but smiled back. Clare appeared with a wet Barbie and an armload of wet Barbie clothes.

"Oh honey, it's okay. Barbie's clothes need to be washed anyway and she needs a good bath. Let's rinse them off and lay them out to dry," Meredith suggested.

Jeff looked at Meredith, "I don't know how you do it. Too much reality for me today. I've got to go for a run or something. I'll work on getting *the rest of the water up*," he said emphasizing the words the rest of water up, "when I get back." He kissed Clare on the forehead. "Bye, my sweet girl. Daddy's got to run."

Meredith went to the basement and looked around. She said to herself, *It's not that bad.* The water wasn't ankle high. He is so dramatic.

Chapter 37

"Tucker, get your books out and get started on the next math assignment," Meredith said as soon as the pair returned home from dropping the girls off at school. "I have a phone call to make and then I'll check your work."

"The meeting with the school went horrible," she blurted out as soon as Mrs. Wilson picked up. *What is wrong with me,* she thought to herself.

"Did you request a hearing like we discussed?"

"Yes, but I haven't written the letter. I'm starting to lose hope," she said talking extremely fast. "I feel like Tucker is learning how to be irrational from me. He is probably watching me for pointers. He's listening to me right now." She smirked. "Actually the crazy thing is the crazier I get, the better he gets. He is starting to seem like the sane one. He probably thinks it's my turn to obsess." She paused trying to regroup.

"He is probably better because he is at home where the sensory load is lower. And staying at home, for someone who is used to working—like you—can be maddening sometimes," Mrs. Wilson said and then waited quietly on the other end of the phone. She heard Meredith take a deep breath.

Meredith began speaking slower and calmer, "This is not who I am. All of this has made me into a different — a meaner and angrier— person. I want myself back."

"The school is counting on you to give up. Remember when I said that most families can't make it through the hearing process. It's stressful. It's a *legal* battle," she said emphasizing legal. "You don't have to continue. I think Tucker's situation has been improved by what you have done so far, by stopping the bullying, and by getting the behavioral school off of their radar since there is now a distinction between a meltdown and defiance. Plus he is going to get counseling, Occupational Therapy, and Speech."

"I can't give up. I'm frustrated, but I'm not done yet, and

Tucker is actually doing better. If I put him back at Central with the counseling and therapies he might do better but"— her voice started rising in intensity — "I can't even get him to go to the classroom to pick up work much less leave him there. He'll go to the office with Jeff or me, but he won't let us leave him there."

"You are going to have to make a decision. Take 24 hours and think about it. And if you do decide to move ahead with a hearing, you must write another letter. This time request the hearing. The letter should list the reasons the school's program is not meeting the needs of Tucker. List the facts and describe the problems as they relate to the school and to Tucker's disability. Additionally there is a *stay-put* provision in the hearing process. The child has to stay in his current educational placement while the hearing is moving forward. Since you have been keeping him at home, just continue to do that and explain in the letter that staying in the educational placement offered by the school would be detrimental to your son's well-being. Be factual and clear about Tucker's regressions and fears in the current setting."

"I have documented everything since we started this process. I even documented phone calls to the school."

"Good. Send the letter by certified mail to the school. The school has ten days to send a response to the letter and then 45 days to complete the hearing process. In the meantime, start looking for an attorney. Winning a due process hearing without an attorney is nearly impossible."

Meredith started calculating the time frame. If she could get the letter in the mail tomorrow, the school district would receive it right before the Christmas break began. She wondered if the school would count the days during the break as part of the 45 days. If not then the count would start on January 5. Then ten days for the response plus 45 days after the response gave her an end of early March meaning another two months of having Tucker at home, another two months of no income coming in on her part, and another two months of full-price private school tuition. She dreaded bringing this up to Jeff. She could hear him say, *This wasn't the plan,* but she started the letter requesting a hearing knowing she would move forward with it and take Jeff's wrath if necessary. She had to move forward. There was no going back for Tucker. Feeling like you're getting painted into a corner gives focus to the only way out. It was Amicus or nothing. She called and left messages with a couple of the attorneys Mrs. Wilson listed who might be willing to take the case. Mrs. Wilson had told her to ask for attorney fees to be paid for by the school. At least they wouldn't have to find the money to pay an attorney. The advocate felt like the facts were on Tucker's side. Hopefully, the attorney would also.

Meredith finished the letter that day. She had it all in there in one page—concise and factual. She and Tucker drove over to Jeff's office for him to read it and sign it.

When Jeff heard the timeline he yelled, "Are. You. Kidding. Me." He said each word as if it was an individual sentence. You expect me to come up with full tuition money for the next two months. Meredith, this was not in the plan."

"I thought you would say that," Meredith answered back. "Not everything goes according to some plan."

"You've got to be reasonable. We barely made it through these two months. What you are asking is impossible." He rubbed his forehead and was silent for a few moments. Jeff knew he was in way over his head in more ways than one. After collecting his thoughts and quieting the need to scream, he simply said, "Let me put some thought to it."

"We could cut some more expenses," Meredith offered.

"What expenses? The few optional expenses we have are not going to make up the money," Jeff retorted.

"Well, do you have any better ideas? Should we just say that we change our mind, and they can send a bus to drag him kicking and screaming to school? I can't get him to go. Besides, it's just

162

not in me to sacrifice Tucker to the system. There is a better way, but we are going to have to fight for it," Meredith said.

"I know, I know, I know," Jeff said repeatedly while holding up his hands indicating stop and hoping to defuse Meredith. "Me either," he said quieter. "But someday Tucker will just have to learn to manage—especially if we don't win!"

"Manage!" Meredith enunciated the word sound by sound. "Then *you* take him to school. I won't and can't," Meredith said, emphasizing the word you, and then she stomped out of the room.

Why, Jeff said to himself as he rolled his eyes. *Why didn't I stop while I was ahead?* "Wait!" Jeff yelled and followed her outside. He held up his hands in surrender. "What if you go back to work and we get the half-price tuition for the girls? Maybe we could afford Tucker's tuition. In the short term . . . at least until I figure something else out. How much is it?"

Jeff's eyes widened when Meredith said, "$35,000."

Jeff asked, "A year? I can't come up with that amount. Do we have to pay it all at once?" He was shaking his head, *No.* "Not right now, anyway."

When Meredith saw Jeff's reaction, she began ranting because she was already primed for a fight. "Are your children more important to you than your savings account? You can make this work if you want to. But you are probably more interested in your savings account than in your child's well-being."

"That's low, especially for you," Jeff shot back. "I'm saving for our future and for our kids."

"Fine, send him to Central if you want. I'll go back to work. But I'm not taking him to school and you need to give the office your phone number. I won't be available to pick him up either."

Jeff clasped his hands behind his head and sighed and then began pacing. He knew he was asking the impossible. He couldn't work and take care of Tucker any more than Meredith could. Maybe some families can have it all but not if there is a kid with special needs in the mix. *Having it all* was definitely defined differently for families with a child with special needs.

"Well?" Meredith asked with finality.

Jeff didn't answer her. He had no answer. There was no good answer.

"You're cruel," Meredith blurted out taking Jeff's silence as indifference. She gathered up Tucker and his things and left Jeff's office.

Meredith knew she was unreasonable, but she couldn't help it, and she didn't even care that she couldn't help it. She felt like she was grasping at the end of a frayed rope. She had pinned her hopes on the second evaluation, which did not help at all, and now she felt backed into a corner. And like a cornered animal she was lashing out.

Jeff went back in and sat down at his desk. He crossed his arms and laid his head down on the desk. If only he hadn't made a financial commitment to Kate without telling Meredith. Two lives depended on his ability to come up with money. Maybe if he told Meredith what he had done, it would ease her down. Or maybe she would go ballistic. He decided against telling her because his actions only complicated the situation. He thought out loud, *If I could pay out the Amicus tuition monthly that would actually be cheaper especially since Meredith would be back at work. But, of course, even that plan hinged on Tuck being willing to go to Amicus.*

He ran the numbers through his head and the time left on Kate's rehab. The numbers wouldn't stay put in his head. He lay down on the sofa in the office and closed his eyes. He had one foot on the floor and one foot on the sofa while he contemplated his next move.

Chapter 38

Jeff drove out to The 4:12 Center, made another installment payment, and met with Jackie

"Kate is doing great. She has been through the worse part physically and is getting stronger. The hard part of an emotional recovery will take months—possibly years."

"When can I see her?"

"In just a few minutes. She is in group right now and she is looking forward to your visit today. I wanted to spend some time with you letting you know what to expect and how you can help her along with the process of recovery."

"Sure, whatever I can do."

"As you have heard in meetings and can probably imagine, recovery is a lot like a roller coaster ride — a person will feel great for a while and then sink back down in an hour. Kate has been on this roller coaster for the past few weeks. She is now working on finding meaning and understanding in the recovery process and learning to accept and let go of her past that lead to her using alcohol as a tool for coping. And in this process she has to make a new life for herself — a life that she can feel good about and that life will look a lot different than before."

"I get that. I know how she feels. My life looks a lot different now than it did a couple of months ago."

"How so?"

"Fighting the school has been somewhat problematic. The crazy part is the school actually made some accommodations for Tuck. They added counseling and therapies. They quickly dealt with a bullying issue. Overall they have a good program."

"So what's the problem?"

"Tuck has decided that Central is a bad place and he won't go. He makes these rules and they are impossible to break and he needs to be in counseling to deal with his rules, but we can't get him there. It's so exhausting. His problem started because of a bully. So we are asking the school to pay for an alternate school where counseling and learning how to be social are top priorities. I want to see him move ahead. But it's beginning to feel like a no-win—no-win situation." Jeff waved his hand in front of his face. "Enough about me. So you think it will be okay for me to see Kate?"

"Yes, it would be good because she feels supported by you. And from my understanding you were not a part of her drinking experiences?"

"No, I wasn't. I knew she drank, but I never thought it was a problem until I saw her downtown and by that time she was in really, really bad shape. Probably seeing me was her rock bottom," Jeff said hoping to lighten the mood. But the counselor continued on talking in a serious tone.

"Certain things and thoughts will trigger her to want to use alcohol. And what we are trying to accomplish is for her to find a new response to those triggers — something that will be positive and allow her to move forward or to eliminate those triggers altogether. Don't expect too much. Be supportive but understand that she has to do her own work to stay sober herself. She will have to reinvent her life."

People started coming out of a room and milling around in the atrium. "I see the group is letting out. I'll get Kate."

Jeff clicked his cell phone off and stuffed it in the pocket of his sport coat. *Be cool*, he told himself. *Don't say anything stupid.* He waited and looked around feeling out of place. A wave of anxiety washed over him when he spotted Kate, but it vanished when he saw her smile.

"Jeff!" Kate squealed and held out her arms.

Jeff had to smile because she used to be so theatrical and this seemed like old times. He took one of her extended arms and twirled her around. She followed his lead effortlessly. "Kate, you look great— so much better than the last time I saw you." *You already messed up. You're not supposed to mention when she was drinking. You might trigger something,* Jeff said to himself.

"Thanks to you. You know you're my hero."

He ignored the compliment. "Well, how is rehab treating you."

"Great," Kate said patting her stomach. She had gained a few much-needed pounds. "Food's good. Therapy's good. They keep us busy here with big book study, group, and then individual therapy. You know what they say — you can only go up from rock bottom." They walked over to a set of chairs and sat down. "Jeff, I want to tell you how sorry I am for all the things I did. I let Russell and my drinking get in the way of my relationship with family. Truth be told, my drinking is probably what drove Russell away and why he broke it off with me. I was using the breakup as an excuse. And I know you and Meredith have been going through some tough times with Tucker, and I wasn't there for you or for her. And I want to change that when I get out of here. I don't know how I can ever pay you back for being there for me and bringing me to this place. I know there are still those steps, but somehow things are clearer now."

"I'm so glad you are doing so well." Jeff leaned down and picked up a bag. "I brought you some clothes. I'm not much on picking out women's clothes, but Jackie told me your size."

"I'm sure they will be fine. I called mom and dad. They were so happy to hear from me." She rolled her eyes and smiled and then she got a serious look on her face. "I want to see Meredith. Have you told her anything about me— about where I'm at?" Kate's voices trailed off as she looked away from Jeff.

"No, she's been dealing with Tucker and the school. Just the other day, she was telling me this strange story about ketchup and Tuck, and I didn't find the humor in it at all, then she said that Kate would get it."

Kate smiled. "I want to see her. Will you tell her I'm here? Do you think she'll come and see me?"

"I'll ask."

He picked up dinner — a salad and a sub — after a short run to clear his head. Dinner at the office helped him to avoid Meredith and play catch-up for a *wasted* afternoon. He was glad he saw Kate, and she was doing so well, but now he had to make up for lost time. Plus, he was starting to feel as crazy as Meredith was acting. It must be contagious. He decided the best way to deal with this issue was with numbers. He had to get this worked out before he told Meredith about Kate. If Meredith went back to work, her income could cover the tuition to the alternate school and the girls' tuition. And if he could pick up another client or some extra work during tax season, Kate's rehab would be paid, he would have his reasonable wife back, and she could hang out with her sister — provided her sister got through rehab and stayed sober. *That could work*, Jeff thought nodding his head as he worked out the positive scenario in his mind. Jeff agreed with Meredith in principle about forcing the school district, but in reality he knew that getting the school district to pay for Tucker's tuition was next to impossible. The school district had made some accommodations after the second evaluation, but now it was Tucker's attitude. We just couldn't get ahead of this. He had to figure this out himself without counting on the school district to come through with the money. And it was doable. The commitment to Kate was short term. She seemed to be doing well and making great progress, even her counselor Jackie said so. Meredith wouldn't be able to be home full-time, but if this Amicus school was anything like Meredith was saying, it was worth every penny. He could tweak his plan.

While eating his sub sandwich, Jeff checked his email. His biggest client, Craig Parker, wanted to meet with him tomorrow at 9:00 am. Mr. Parker owned a dental clinic and several other businesses that served his dental clinic. Jeff started with Parker Dental; then the dental practice started a lab serving Parker Dental for making the fillings, dentures, crowns, other dental appliances. The lab now serves seven other dental clinics besides Parker Dental. Since that went so well, Mr. Parker got into the dental equipment supply selling himself chairs, sterilization equipment, and X-ray machines, just to name a few. Parker Dental, Parker Labs, and Parker Dental Supply each had auditors on-site. Jeff took the information from all the auditors and kept meticulous books for Craig Parker. This was the account that let Jeff dream about Meredith quitting her job and staying home and now that account would be the catalyst for Tucker getting the educational and behavioral support he needed — they all needed.

Chapter 39

The next morning Jeff went to the offices of Parker Dental. Christmas decorations adorned every table and every counter. At exactly 9:00 am Craig Parker came out and introduced Jeff to Dwight Newbury. "He is the owner of American Dental. And he finally made me an offer I can't refuse."

Jeff looked from Craig to Dwight. Both were smiling. Craig put his hand on Dwight's shoulder.

"I have finally agreed to sell him Parker Labs and Parker Dental Supply. We reached an agreement and effective January 1 of next year, Dwight and American Dental will be the proud owner of Parker Labs and Parker Dental Supply. So, Jeff, you need to spend some time with Dwight and soon I'll be spending more time with my grandkids."

Dwight spoke. "Of course, the name will be changed to American Dental Suppliers."

Jeff wasn't sure if he was losing his biggest client or gaining a bigger client. Jeff shook Dwight's hand again, "Congratulations. Parker Labs and Supply are both solid financially. You obviously have seen the balance sheets and I'm looking forward to working with you."

Dwight motioned for Jeff to come with him. "Jeff, this is Betty McElroy. She is the head of the accounting department, and she will be handling the transition. She is getting the process down because, over the last five years, American Dental Suppliers had been buying up smaller dental supply companies. This streamlining to absorb the smaller companies' assets and liabilities allows American Dental Suppliers to offer the lowest prices."

Betty smiled at Dwight and shook Jeff's hand. As Betty was explaining the process to him, the realization hit Jeff that he was losing his biggest client. As this realization started to sink in, he felt faint. He looked at Craig Parker and Dwight Newbury and noticed in a surreal way that they were both in a celebratory mood because this was a step forward for both of them. Jeff had to deliberately focus on what Betty was telling him because his body wanted to escape the room, but he forced his mind to listen. All of this was to take place by January 1. Jeff had a mere 14 days until his income was cut in half. He wanted to run and thought briefly about disappearing, but he would do the decent thing and head home to Meredith.

Meredith was surprised when she saw Jeff's car pull into the driveway. She and Tucker had just finished reading, and their books were stacked on the table. They were sitting down to chicken strips and macaroni and cheese with the books as their centerpiece. She was making a green salad to add to her plate to dress-up the *kid's menu* she served Tucker for lunch. "Just in time for lunch," she said to Jeff even though her back was to him when he came in the door. "And by the way, I have something I need to tell you," Meredith said and turned around and saw Jeff just standing in the doorway holding his briefcase as if it weighed a hundred pounds. Meredith's smile left her face as she held her breath and waited for Jeff to speak.

"I lost Parker Dental," Jeff said.

She breathed out. "What do you mean *lost* them? Where did you lose them? You mean, the file? What happened?"

"Craig sold his companies."

"All of them?" she asked as her heartbeat sped up.

"Yes, all of them. The lab and the supply were sold to American Dental. He is selling Parker Dental to David and Steve, the two practicing dentists."

"You will be keeping the books for American Dental," she said hoping she was right but judging by Jeff's demeanor she knew she was wrong. She just had to hear it for herself.

"American Dental has their own accounting department. A

wonderful lady named Betty McElroy." Jeff added facetiously, "Maybe I can ask her to hire me. David Beck, one of the dentists, has a wife who is an accountant. She's going to be doing Parker Dental's books."

"What does this mean?" Meredith asked even though she could feel herself panicking with Jeff.

"It means," Jeff started calmly and grew louder, "that we have less income that we had just a few months ago. It means that now I'll be doing good to pay the mortgage and put some food on this table," he said placing his hand palm down loudly on the table. Tucker jumped at the sound. "It means you are going to have to go back to work after Christmas break. It means Tucker is going to have to go back to Central—"

Jeff hadn't finished speaking before books and plates plummeted to the floor. Jeff couldn't register what was happening as Tucker started screaming and rocking and hitting himself in the forehead. Adrenaline raced through Jeff as he tried to make sense of the chaos.

Meredith jumped up and ran to Tucker hugging and rocking slowly with him and talking to him quietly. "You don't have to go to Central. You can stay here with me. I'll be your teacher and your mommy." Meredith led Tucker to the couch and sat him down beside her, and his destructive banging and rocking turned into a soothing rock in Meredith's arms.

Jeff stared at Meredith and Tucker with his face weighed down. "What did you want to tell me?" he asked as he picked up the books and placed them on the table.

"It can wait," she said still soothing Tucker.

He left the food on the floor, and his briefcase on the table, and walked out the kitchen door leaving the door open behind him.

Meredith didn't get a chance to tell Jeff that she had talked to Mrs. Riley at Cornerstone School and discussed with her that she needed another two months leave of absence. The Family Medical

Leave Act provided for 12 weeks off. She would be over the 12 weeks off, so Meredith resigned and told Mrs. Riley that she would like to be considered for a teaching position for the next school year.

Mrs. Riley told Meredith that the teacher filling in for Meredith had asked to have the position if, for some reason, Meredith did not return, and the sub would most likely jump at the opportunity since Meredith wouldn't be returning. That was a relief to Meredith. She felt she had abandoned her class at Cornerstone, and she was happy her students wouldn't have another teacher change this year.

After she hung up the phone, Meredith sat down feeling like a weight had been lifted off her shoulders. It was the first time in the last eight years that she was a stay-at-home mom, and the only kids she would be teaching would be her own. It brought her a focus she needed to get Tucker through his academic crisis and onto a stable footing so he could handle the unexpected better. It had just become too difficult to worry about Tucker, the girls, and the students in the classroom. The reprieve had been brief. A new burden replaced an old one.

Meredith knew that Jeff was stressed about money. They had barely managed to get by paying Tucker's evaluation and partial tuition for the girls. She expected a fight with Jeff, but now she felt as lost as he did. The loss of the Parker Dental business came out of the blue, and her job loss could be a topic for another day. She just couldn't burden Jeff with that information just yet. She sat on the couch rocking gently back and forth with Tucker until she felt the panic inside of Tucker ease. She stopped rocking and looked at him and said, "All better?"

He nodded.

She kissed the top of his head.

Tucker's panic has receded, but she still felt a different panic. Jeff's panic had her in its grips now.

173

The house was dark and the kids were quiet when the phone rang. It was Jeff.

"Where are you?" Meredith asked.

"I'm at the office. I've got to figure things out. I can't come home right now. I'm no good. I can't come home."

"That's not true. I need you here. The girls need you and even if you find it hard to believe Tucker needs you too. We can work this out. You'll get another account. We have lived on less when we were younger."

"Yeah," Jeff laughed, "but we didn't have a four-digit house payment and four kids to feed."

Meredith said quietly, "I know. Please come home."

"I can't. I'm too tired. I'll call you tomorrow," Jeff said and hung up.

There was nothing more to say. Meredith held the phone in her hand but didn't hang it up. She heard the recording of the operator to hang up the phone or if there was an emergency to call 911. If only there were 911 for when a family falls apart.

She was tired, too—more like weary — the kind of tired that doesn't go away with a good night's sleep. She hung up the phone and lay awake in the bed. There was no way to tell Jeff she didn't have a job to go back to after Christmas. She lay in bed thinking of ways she could come up with money, and Jeff would never know that she didn't go back to teaching.

Maybe she could babysit someone else's kid? No, Tucker would never be okay with that. He might end up being destructive. She could sell things. There were a lot of girls' clothes that could be sold at a consignment shop and a garage full of rummage sale items.

Meredith was pressed from every side. Jeff needed her to

work. Tucker needed her to be home. Meredith hated deceiving Jeff, but he couldn't take any more bad news. She also knew that she couldn't leave Tucker. He needed her and he needed her to get him educational help. The girls also needed Meredith but in a different way. The girls would grow up and marry and find love with another person. Tucker would only have her to love him. Most likely he would never meet a girl, fall in love, and have someone else to make him the center of their world. The girls all had that possibility. They would fall in love and be loved. Tucker only had Meredith. Meredith would be the love of Tucker's life.

Meredith loved Jeff. He was the love of her life too. It was hard seeing him defeated and disappointed. He had worked so hard for his accounting practice. He had planned everything out so carefully and everything had been going so well. She told herself, *This is a temporary setback.* There had been other unexpected things, but Jeff had always even planned to have unexpected things. He always had it covered. She would tell Jeff about resigning after circumstances improved. Tomorrow she would go through the girls' clothes and take what she could to the consignment shop and hopefully get some needed cash. Thankfully, the Christmas gifts were already bought and wrapped. But there were a couple of gifts that could go back to the stores.

The next day, Meredith unwrapped one each of the kids' gifts. She would have to take the gifts back to the store when Myla or Jeff was home so she could leave Tucker. Holiday shoppers and shopping were way off the sensory overload charts, and there was no way she could go to the store with Tucker right now. She stacked the gifts in the trunk of the car and planned to take them back after all the kids were snoozing in their beds tonight.

"Myla, I'm going out for a bit," Meredith told Myla, who was sitting up reading in bed and listening to music through her headphones. Myla had gotten used to that routine because after bedtime was the only time Meredith could get out and get the grocery shopping done. Jeff was mostly gone at night now.

Gifts for the kids arrived in the mail the next day. She took them to her bedroom and carefully unwrapped each one. Her parents usually overspent on the kids and this year was no exception. Many of the gifts could be replaced by a cheaper alternative. Each year her parents would travel in for a few days for the holidays and bring extravagant gifts. The kids looked forward to the yearly migration of the grandparents. But this year would be different—no visit—because her Dad suffered a small stroke, and although there was minor cognitive impairment, he was still in physical therapy for his leg and arm. The stroke had been on the right side of his brain and even though he had regained most of his cognitive skills, he tended to ignore his left leg and arm and slightly drag them. He wasn't able to make the drive from Florida, and her mother couldn't drive it by herself.

Meredith had thought about asking her parents for some money but didn't want to worry her parents about what was going on with Tucker's behavior and Jeff's job. Meredith's mother had enough to worry about right now. She was trying to take over aspects of their lives that previously had been done by Meredith's dad, such as banking, caring for their pool, and overseeing the details of the house and yard. Everyone had enough worries of their own.

Meredith stashed the unwrapped gifts from her parents in the car for another late night run to the store. The toy store was staying open late this close to the holiday. All total the returned gifts netted Meredith $600. If she were careful with the money, it would be enough to cover groceries for January so she wouldn't have to tell Jeff until after January. After all, this financial downturn wouldn't last long. *Jeff will figure it out,* she said out loud to herself.

Christmas was an oasis. Nothing was thrown and only a few sibling squabbles materialized but no meltdowns. Jeff spent the entire Christmas week at home reconnecting with the kids and Meredith.

Both Jeff and Meredith were holding back. Each had a secret

176

that would devastate the other. Their conversations were nice but too polite for a couple married for 16 years.

Even though Jeff had lost Parker Dental and its related companies, he planned for Meredith to go back to work in January. He could probably string out his hidden financial obligations with a short-term loan. His mind constantly worked the numbers and the angles.

Meredith knew she didn't have a job to go back to. She checked the mail every day for a correspondence from the school hoping that the school wouldn't wait out the entire time period, and by some miracle the hearing would occur before school started. Every time Jeff brought up the subject of her starting back to teaching in a few days, she changed the subject.

On the Saturday after the Christmas week, Jeff went into the office. Meredith was relieved when he left; it had been exhausting avoiding conversation about work and finance. She had never actually said she was going back to work, but she hadn't said she wasn't either. Meredith just let Jeff believe what he thought was true and Meredith had been hoping for a way out. Maybe the school would reconsider and think the cost of a hearing would be more than Tucker's tuition and send a letter saying Tucker's tuition would be covered. She walked to the mailbox and there was a letter from the school district. She took the letter into her bedroom and opened it. The letter acknowledged her request for a hearing with a hearing date set in February.

Meredith sank down on the bed. February was over a month away. Every fiber of her being wanted Central to work out, but Tucker wouldn't allow that—not now. She just didn't have the strength to fight him. Unless Jeff could work this out, Meredith would need to go back to work and where would that leave Tucker? She couldn't even get Tucker to Central.

Meredith took out the money from the returned gifts and counted it again.

Chapter 40

The second week of Christmas break was at an end. Meredith kept trying to sneak in suggestions that Tucker go to Central until she could get him into Amicus. Tucker would not be fooled and Meredith would back off. She still hadn't told Jeff about not going back to work, but with Tucker unable to attend Central she was in an impossible situation. If only she hadn't told Mrs. Riley to go ahead and let the substitute have her class. If only Jeff hadn't lost his client. If only . . . it was a cruel game she kept playing with herself.

Meredith kept reminding herself that this setback was temporary. But Jeff would assume she was going back to work, and the girls would know differently. It was possible that they would never mention it to Jeff since he was still spending most evenings at the office. But Jeff was observant. He noticed little details. It was in his nature. Meredith would have to make sure those little details were in place. She would need to confide in the older two girls. Isabelle generally said anything and everything that was on her mind and actually enjoyed being the first to pass on new information. This situation required delicate handling. She didn't want the girls to become co-conspirators in her lies. However, Myla or Isabelle could easily blow her cover. Clare could inadvertently say something to Jeff, but Meredith thought she could cover any remarks made by Clare rather than take Clare into confidence.

Meredith called both girls into her room. "You both know that I have been staying home with Tucker until I can get him into a new school."

They nodded.

"Well, I thought I would be going back to work after Christmas, but it looks like it's going to be a little bit longer. And you know Daddy has been busy at work, and I don't want him to worry about money, so I need you both to help me."

"Will we have to quit our school if you are not a teacher there?" Myla asked in her usual practical manner.

"No, Daddy and I will just pay your tuition. But right now Daddy is very busy at work, and I don't want him to worry, so I'm asking you not to tell Daddy that I'm not working at Cornerstone," Meredith explained.

"You want us to lie to Daddy!" Isabelle exclaimed with wide eyes as if her mother had changed into a monster.

"Of course not . . . no, I do not want you to lie to Daddy. If he asks you if I'm teaching at Cornerstone, you need to be truthful. But I don't think he will ask. You know how people usually see what they believe to be true? Like when the magician came to school and you believed what he did even though it wasn't real?"

They nodded in unison, remembering the magician.

"Well, that is what I want to do. I want Daddy to see the things that he believes are true. Daddy will believe that I'm going back to work, and he will believe that Tucker is going to Central. Even though neither of which will be happening, but he believes them to be true so he will think they are true. Then I won't have to worry Daddy, and I can still stay home with Tucker until I get him into the Amicus school where they can help him. You girls will still go to school. This will be for a short time, and then I'll go back to work, and I'll tell Daddy about our *little magic trick*. But right now I don't want him to worry. It would be hard for him to do a good job if he's worrying. So can you help me?"

Myla asked, "If he asks what do we say?"

"He won't ask. He never asked me if I went to work. Does he ask you if you go to school? He might ask if you had a good day, and you should tell him the truth. He might ask me about my day, and I will tell him the truth. I'm still teaching. I'm just teaching Tucker at home for right now. So I won't be lying. I don't want you to lie to Daddy. Just don't say I'm not at school. I don't think he will ask you if I went to school. But if he asks you did I go to Cornerstone and teach a class, then tell him I didn't. I'm not asking you to lie. Just don't bring it up that I'm staying home with Tucker. I'll tell Daddy in a few weeks after his job gets better."

"Okay," Myla said wearily, already feeling uncomfortable with the arrangement.

"I'll do it," Isabelle said with more confidence. She took the assignment like she was an undercover cop. But Meredith knew that Isabelle was more likely to blow her cover than Myla.

"Thank you," Meredith said matter-of-factly. "It starts today. Are you ready?"

Chapter 41

On New Year's Day, Jeff got a call from his parents.

"Did the gift cards arrive?" Jeff's mom asked.

"How are the girls?"

"The girls are fine," Jeff said emphasizing girls. He could feel his face getting hot. His parents never asked about Tucker anymore. It was like Tucker disappeared when he was identified as being autistic.

"We had a fabulous Christmas," his mother said. Julia and the kids came over. You should have seen Jordyn's little face when she opened up the little diamond stud earrings we got her. She just got her ears pierced this year. She was so excited. And Jerry —your nephew, who you really should spend some time with, is already eight— spent all afternoon with the remote control cars we bought him. Your dad had to get him two so they both could play."

"That's great, Mom," Jeff said barely listened to the rest of her account of the *fabulous* Christmas she had with his sister and her children. The big things and the little things were both painful. His family was never invited to the Christmas event with the expensive gifts and fabulous stories to tell.

"I know how busy you are," Jeff's mom said repeating the lie she told herself.

"Yeah, I'm busy," Jeff repeated back to his mother in a monotone voice.

"We would love to see Meredith and the girls sometime," his mother said. "Tell them to come by and see me."

Jeff wanted to scream that he also had a son, but instead he just said, "I'll tell them you asked about them."

Jeff clicked off the phone and went outside. He was pacing back and forth running both hands through his hair and talking to himself. "Mom, why can't you accept Tuck? He is not that different. I know you thought we should put him in an institution, and you still think he will end up there after he has worn us out and destroyed our lives. And maybe you're right, but times are different now. Can't you see that? I can't believe my own mother, of all people, would turn her back on her own grandson. And I bet those diamond stud earrings for *precious* Jordyn cost a lot more than a $10 gift card. Just don't call anymore or at least quit bragging about your *precious* favored grandchildren. *Bless their hearts.* Why? I don't understand."

Meredith came outside and brought him a bottled water and sat down on the outdoor bench. "Let me talk to her next time. It's too upsetting for you. It doesn't get to me like it does to you."

"I shouldn't let it bother me, but she's my mother and I never expected this attitude — this rejection."

"Well, you were the one that told her she couldn't only see the girls. You drew the line in the sand, and she is making you pay."

"I had to do something. Tuck was crying that he wanted to go to grandma's too. It broke my heart. You remember. He was only three or something. He was little. Yes, he was a handful, but that was even before this OCD crap. He was busy but manageable then. I saw Tuck watch the girls go out and do things and visit grandma, and he didn't get to go. That *crap* about girl time didn't float with me," he mocked.

"Well, if it makes you feel any better, the kids are delighted with their $10 gift cards. They are looking forward to going out shopping."

"I know, but that makes it almost worse for me. My kids are happy with so little and if Julia's kids ever want any little thing, they just run and ask grandma, AND then she brags about giving them whatever they want."

"Our kids don't know that. It's probably better the girls aren't around her. She might make them feel different about Tucker. And if YOU didn't know it," she said emphasizing you.

"Then you wouldn't be upset which is all the more reason to let me talk to her."

"You're right." He paused and seemed for a second to be over the phone call but then wilted again. "I can still hear her say, *Oh, how tragic,* when I told her about Tuck's label. What is truly tragic is that she is missing out on getting to know her grandkids — well, some of her grandkids."

"I think maybe Tucker is embarrassing to her when he flips his hand or dances on his toes."

"I know people stare when we are out in public. I guess I have gotten used to it, but for her it's too much. It's just —"

"It's just that she used to make you feel special like you were the king of the roost. Before kids, I always thought she overdid your *wonderfulness.*" Meredith rolled her eyes.

"I just wish she had tried to get to know him or had wanted to be a part of my life."

"It's really her loss. Some people just don't have the resilience to embrace life and whatever it throws at them. When things get messy, we have to look through the mess and find out what is really important and what is worth saving. But some people can't even deal with the mess. So they just walk away from it—like your mom did. Her life stayed nice and tidy. And you may have to forgive her for that. Tucker is messy and loud and he sings and flips his hands at strange times."

Chapter 42

The night before school started back after the Christmas break Jeff stopped by the house. "I just wanted to tell my kids good night and give some good luck kisses out before they started back to school." He started with Myla and worked his way down the kids in age. Myla's was a gentle kiss on the forehead. Isabelle's kiss ended with tickling her neck; Tucker's ended with a raspberry on the belly causing him to squeal with delight. Clare couldn't stand the anticipation and ran around the room while Jeff chased her.

"Tucker, I'm sure you will have a great day at Central tomorrow," Jeff said. Myla and Isabelle stopped what they were doing and looked at Meredith and Tucker with their eyes darting back and forth. If Jeff were observant he might have noticed the fear in their eyes.

But Tucker only replied, "No!"

Jeff spoke to Meredith, "Are you ready for tomorrow too, Mrs. Howard?"

The girls both locked eyes with Meredith as she said, "I will be. I'm mostly ready," Meredith sent the girls to their rooms without a word by making eye contact and pointing towards their room. She knew they could blow her cover any moment by the apprehensive look in their eyes; she hated drawing Myla and Isabelle into her deception.

The girls heard Jeff ask Meredith, "Do you think Tucker will do okay tomorrow?"

Meredith only replied, "I hope so."

Jeff kissed Meredith and left to head back to the office. "See you in a bit." The new fiscal year was starting for his remaining clients, and he had been working on proposals for keeping the books for a couple of prospective clients.

Meredith sat down at the table and propped her head up with both hands when he left. Deception was exhausting. "I don't know if I can keep this up," she whispered out loud. She prayed the new clients would come through for Jeff.

Jeff sat in the car a few moments in the dark staring back at the house. He exhaled deeply. Deception was exhausting. He hoped he had pulled it off.

When Meredith went into Myla and Isabelle's room, they were sitting beside each other on the bed. Isabelle had her arm around Myla and Myla was crying. "You lied to Daddy."

Meredith shook her head and spoke with confidence. "Oh, honey. No, I didn't lie— not really. He asked me if I was ready for tomorrow and I said, *I will be.* He didn't ask me about being ready for Cornerstone. He just asked if I was ready so it wasn't a lie."

"But he was talking about Cornerstone and you know it," she scolded Meredith and scooted away from her. "He thinks you are going back to teaching."

"I know he thinks I'm going back to teaching, but I didn't lie. Remember when I said that people believe what they want to believe. This is what I'm talking about. People see what they believe even if it's not true. Besides, Daddy is having a hard time at work right now, and I have to look out for Daddy and Tucker and you girls. This is only for a short time. Daddy will get another client, Tucker will get into his new school, and I'll go back to teaching. But right now Daddy is sad about losing Parker Dental. So I don't want to make him sadder. I'll make it right when the time is right. You have to trust me. I would never do anything to hurt Daddy or you girls or Tucker."

Myla's tight lips showed she was apprehensively reassured. She distrusted this arrangement of vague deception, but logic kept her emotions in check. The girls climbed under their covers. Meredith prayed with them and prayed for Jeff's job and Tucker's school and for each of the girls. Meredith got up and walked to the door and turned around and looked at the girls.

Myla said, "Mom, I want Tucker to be happy too. I want him to have a good school and learn. I'm glad you are taking care of Tucker. I'll pray for Daddy's job too. Mrs. Sawyer said that she prays for us every day. She said being a mom of a child with special needs requires a special person. She said you're one of those special people."

"Tell Mrs. Sawyer, *thank you.* Did you tell Mrs. Sawyer about Tucker's school?"

"I did," Isabelle said. "She said that she wished there had been schools like that for her son because she thinks it would have helped him so much. She said that when her son was young, he couldn't even go to a public school. Some people told her to put her son away and forget about him and have other children. She couldn't do it. Many people don't understand a mother's love. She said you have that love for Tucker."

"I think Mrs. Sawyer is a wise woman. I love you both very much. You know that, don't you?"

The girls smiled and nodded.

"Good-night," Meredith said as she switched off the light.

Tucker was rocking on his bed when Meredith went in to read and pray with him. "I'm not going to Central," Tucker said as he rocked.

"You and I are going to do your schoolwork together at the library. But we are going to go to Central. We will go to Central and wave but we won't go in. You can tell Daddy that you went to Central. How does that sound?"

Tucker smiled and danced around on his toes briefly rubbing his hands together. He echoed, "We'll go to Central and wave good-bye at the school."

Meredith smiled, "Yes, we will go to Central and wave at the school. Do you think it will wave back?"

186

Tucker smiled and joined in the joke. "Maybe."

Meredith prayed and kissed Tucker, switched off his light, and left the room. When she got to Clare's room, Clare was mostly asleep. Meredith kissed Clare and whispered, "I love you," into Clare's ear. Clare rolled over and hugged her doll. Usually Meredith started with Clare, then Tucker, then the older girls, but tonight had been different. She was teaching the girls the act of deception. *A strange lesson to teach your own children*, she thought to herself. Meredith thought about Mrs. Sawyer's comment and she definitely didn't feel like a special mother, considering she was teaching her girls to be deceptive. Meredith crawled into bed. She was tired but couldn't sleep. She was going over the details in her head of how to maintain the façade of going to work. She had to work out all the details. First, she would pay the girls' tuition for the next two months using the 0% interest offer on the credit card that she got in the mail. She would have 12 months to pay it back. In 12 months, stability would have undoubtedly returned to her life. She would need to always intercept that bill from Jeff. That one seemed easy. What if he stopped by Cornerstone, to eat lunch with the girls, which he sometimes did? The plan had its flaws, but Meredith moved forward, putting the trust of her husband on the line.

Chapter 43

Meredith dropped the girls off at Cornerstone. They happily joined their classmates. She and Tucker went into the office and she wrote a check out to cover two months' tuition. It was so simple to write the check. Tucker waved and smiled at a couple of his former classmates. Meredith wished she could go back and undo the fateful day when Tucker shoved the chair in the lunchroom at Cornerstone. *If only,* she thought. Her life was filled with too many *if onlys* lately.

Mrs. Riley spoke to Meredith, "Any news from Central?"

"Not yet."

"Well, I'm hoping they hurry the process up so Tucker can get the opportunities he needs."

"Me too," Meredith replied, but she wanted to beg Mrs. Riley for one more chance for Tucker to attend Cornerstone. Life had been so much simpler then. But Meredith knew it was impossible. Mrs. Riley had to answer to a school board and the other parents. She couldn't risk her job to include Tucker. Meredith knew the policy at Cornerstone. There was a no tolerance policy for aggression. Tucker's chair incident seemed like aggression, but it wasn't. Nevertheless, someone could have gotten hurt. Meredith wasn't willing to risk that. But she had tried to explain that same fact at Central. Aggressive behavior has to have an intent behind it. Tucker was responding impulsively to a sensory issue. He was not acting aggressively. He was having a meltdown. The outcome looked similar and the result would be similar in that another child might be hurt. The key to everyone's success was limiting the sensory overload.

In the car, Meredith said to Tucker, "Let's go to Central and wave at the building."

Tucker brought his shoulders up by his ears and smiled, "Yes, let's go wave good-bye to Central."

They drove to the school and waved as they went by on their

way to the library. Carrying Tucker's backpack full of schoolwork, they signed in for a study room.

Tucker worked steadily and consistently without needing many breaks. He was very task oriented and was working on grade level easily now. With Meredith available to provide individual directions and work a few sample problems with him, Tucker breezed through the work.

Tucker's most difficult area was reading comprehension. His phonic skills were excellent, but when Meredith asked him to retell the stories from the reader, he was lost. He couldn't sequence the events. He had strategies for answering the detail questions. Skimming back through the material to find a word or phrase to answer the workbook question was simple. Tucker's specific challenges were becoming clearer as Meredith worked with him one-on-one each day.

Tucker's reading story was about a pioneer child lost in the wilderness. The parents and families on the wagon train searched and searched for the boy. And just when they had almost given up hope, the boy was found by a stream playing with a raccoon. The boy's mother was crying when she ran to him, fell to the ground, and hugged him. Tucker's answer for why the mother was crying was because she was sad that the boy was playing with a raccoon.

"Tucker, sometimes people cry when they are happy. She was crying because she was so happy and thankful that the boy was found and that he was okay."

"I don't cry when I'm happy. I cry when I'm sad or sorry."

"Sometimes people cry when they are really happy and relieved."

"People are confusing."

Making inferences and reading between the lines was almost impossible. Meredith had to give him hint after hint and have him reread the paragraph that contained the answer. If reading and rereading a conversation posed so many difficulties, Meredith could only imagine how difficult it was for Tucker to follow an actual conversation. This was probably why he relied on his favorite subjects. It gave him a conversation pattern to follow.

The staff at Amicus had discussed at length social stories and role playing to increase social understanding and awareness. The student's schedule involved an hour per day of *social studies* and the class wasn't about history but about understanding people. At first Meredith had thought an hour a day about "social studies" was a lot, but she now understood the importance of "social" classes. The students at Amicus were learning to be successful in navigating society through *social studies.*

While Tucker worked through his math worksheets, Meredith watched some people in the library as they arrived for story time. They were random. It was amazing that typical people could make sense of the randomness. Some preschoolers burst into the library and skipped to the story time area. Some quietly walked beside their parent. Some cried and wanted to be held. One preschooler sucked his thumb and walked beside his mother while holding her leg. All those different reactions to going to story time. If she had asked Tucker about the kids, he probably would have thought the skipping child was happy, the quiet child was scared, the crying child was sad, and the one sucking his thumb was hurt. Meredith watched all the children join the circle. They equally enjoyed the time, but they all approached the situation differently. Tucker was right. People are confusing.

The schoolwork was finished by 11:00. It was amazing how quickly Tucker could complete his work at the library. The classroom had lots of distractions and extra sensory issues. Study rooms as the library were quiet. Tucker loaded up his backpack, and they headed to get tacos to celebrate their first day "back to school" after the winter break. When they turned down the street, Meredith saw Jeff's car in the driveway. He must have come home for lunch. Going to the library to do Tucker's schoolwork had been an excellent decision. If Meredith and Tucker had been home when Jeff stopped by the house, her plan would have fallen apart on its first day. Meredith turned the car around in a neighbor's driveway so she wouldn't drive in front of the house.

"Where are we going?" Tucker asked immediately when they pulled into the neighbor's driveway.

"I want to take a drive and enjoy the lovely weather," Meredith said. "You can eat your tacos in the car, and I'll drive you to the park." It was cool but no wind. The park wasn't a bad idea after all. She backed the car into a parking space near the swing set. Tucker ran around on his toes, flipping his hands, doing his dance. The swings were vacant during this afternoon of the first day back to school. Meredith watched as Tucker effortlessly pumped the swing high into the blue skies closing his eyes and feeling the cool breeze he created. His high swinging eventually turned into twirling and Meredith decided that was enough and called her classroom of one back to the car. He hopped on one foot all the way to the car. She wondered what Tucker would think of himself if he could watch himself.

Meredith picked up dinner groceries quickly with Tucker in tow. She knew there would be fewer people in the store now that school was back in session, so she dared the store with Tucker. Maybe it was the swinging, maybe just luck, but no sensory overload in the store. They returned to the house and Jeff was gone. His plate from where he made a sandwich was on the counter and so was a company file. She hoped he wouldn't come home to retrieve the file before she picked up the girls. She started working on her explanation in case he returned. But Jeff only came home for dinner, and she could tell he was in better spirits thinking she was back at work bringing home income. He hadn't been home for dinner in a while. It seemed like he was always busy at work. But tonight, he seemed like his old self. She knew he was driven to do well at his business, and that was one of the things she loved about him. She also knew that part of his more relaxed demeanor was that he felt like she was sharing the financial burden again. Instead of sharing, she had weighted herself down with deception and a 12-month no interest financial burden.

Chapter 44

By the end of the week, Meredith could barely open her eyes when the alarm rang at 6:00 am. She had been in bed about 2 hours. Tucker had a bad night—again. He hadn't been able to sleep and he paced the house stopping to rock in the living room for a few hours. She was exhausted, but she got up to start the routine for getting the girls to school. She decided not to take a bath and pretend to go to work. If Jeff came home from work like he had been doing all week, she would say that Tucker and she were sick. She certainly felt sick. Lack of sleep will do that to a person. Tucker hadn't slept well for the last three nights. She had tried to figure out what was causing him to be so sleepless, but there was no answer. Tucker and she had read books and watched movies. She had fed him ice cream, hoping the high carbohydrate count would knock him out. But he still paced and rocked.

She speculated that the change in routine was responsible for Tucker's sleeping issues this week. After all, this had been the week school started back after the Christmas break. She and Tucker had gone to the library each day after dropping the girls off at school. Other than Monday, the weather had been threatening and raining all week so instead of eating in the park, they packed their lunches and ate in the car watching the rain. By that time Jeff was gone from the house from his lunch break. He was trying to save money by eating at home. She had offered to pack him a sack lunch so he could eat in the office, but he said a change of scenery helped him be more productive.

Tucker had slept well on Monday night, but Tuesday, Wednesday, and Thursday nights were ruthless. She caught a few minutes of sleep while sitting up in the living room chair. Tucker had tried to go outside on Tuesday night, and now she had to guard the door. From the living room she could see the front door, and Tucker would have to go through the living room to get to the kitchen door. The basement had an outside door and her upstairs bedroom had doors out to a balcony. She asked herself why this house had so many doors. It was a mystery how Tucker was still standing, but he was asleep right now while she was getting the girls ready to go to school. She would have to wake him for the ride to the school.

She woke the girls one by one. They slowly emerged from their beds. The cold front that had pushed its way into the area over the last few days had finally settled in making the bed more difficult to leave on this cool and raining morning. Everyone wanted to sleep. She sat on the couch in her house robe as the girls got themselves ready. Myla had quite a morning routine of washing and straightening her hair. Meredith couldn't understand why she straightened it because her hair was already straight, but Myla thought her hair looked frizzy so she spent 30 minutes each morning straightening her hair.

Isabelle came in the living room and saw Meredith, "Mommy, are you sick?"

"Yes, sort of," Meredith answered, "I didn't get much sleep because I was up with Tucker."

Clare came in and asked Meredith the same question, "Mommy, are you sick?"

Meredith didn't bother to answer because Isabelle gave Clare the full report and then she fixed some cereal for herself and Clare. Meredith smiled and closed her eyes, relieved.

"Mrs. Sawyer said she could take us to school if you ever needed her," Isabelle reported to Meredith.

"Really, I wish I had known that earlier. I might have called her this morning because I hate to wake Tucker up since he finally went to bed at 4 am this morning."

"I'll call her," Isabelle offered, "She goes to the gym by 8 in the mornings and she comes this way. Maybe we can catch her."

Meredith was so tired she didn't refuse.

"Mrs. Sawyer is coming to take us to school." Meredith

startled when Isabelle made her announcement.

Clare clapped her hands together and smiled.

Meredith relaxed back into the couch. What a blessing for someone to drive the girls to school. There was a knock on the door which startled Meredith again and she realized that she had dozed off.

Mrs. Sawyer opened the door and peeked in, "Girls, I'm here. We don't want to be late."

Meredith got up, wrapped her robe around her, and greeted Mrs. Sawyer. "Thank you so much for taking them. I was up most of the night with Tucker. He hasn't been sleeping well."

"I'm happy to do it. I'm on the way to the fitness center. I can take them any morning. If you need to take a nap, I can come by later and sit with Tucker so you can sleep. I know you must be exhausted," Mrs. Sawyer offered.

"Oh my gosh, that would be wonderful. He's asleep now. If he happens to wake up, I might call you. I feel sick because I'm so tired. I'm going to try and get some sleep while he is sleeping," Meredith explained.

"Let me pick up the girls too. That way if you two are napping you won't have to set an alarm or anything."

"Thank you so much."

The girls each kissed her good-bye and Isabelle gave her an extra long hug and told her to get some rest. Meredith needed the hug. She watched the girls climb into Mrs. Sawyer's Suburban, and she waved as they backed out of the driveway. She closed the door and locked it. She tucked a chair under the doorknob hoping this would prevent Tucker from going out or would at least make some noise and alert her. There was no way to block the other doors. She went and got a pillow and a blanket off of her bed, and she laid down on the floor in the hallway in front of Tucker's door and went to sleep.

Jeff came home at lunch and found Meredith sleeping in the hall. He shook her awake. "What's going on here?" he asked. "Are you sick or something?"

She looked at him as if she was trying to place who he was as she climbed up off the floor. "Tucker hasn't slept much at all the last three nights. If you had been home you would have known," Meredith said with anger and fatigue in her voice.

"So you missed work because you didn't get a good night's sleep?" Jeff said in an almost mocking voice.

"Not one night but three nights!" Meredith said starting to raise her voice but lowered it because she knew Tucker was still asleep, and she knew he must be as exhausted as she was. "And besides, I can't believe you woke me up!"

Jeff just looked down at the floor. He had no room to talk. He could barely look Meredith in the eyes anymore. Work was his excuse for escaping home which he found more and more unbearable because he noticed Meredith never looked him in the eyes anymore either. It seemed to be an agreed upon distancing. Arguing was their predictable mode of communication.

"And what is with you coming home at lunch and not at night? Are you seeing someone else? What's wrong with being home with your wife and kids at night?" Meredith fired off one question after another. With Tucker asleep, the girls gone, and Meredith's exhaustion leading her on, she was ready for a showdown with Jeff.

For a few minutes, Jeff didn't say anything. After all these years, he knew better than to argue with Meredith when she was tired. She was meaner when she was tired. He wanted to say, *Let's talk about this later when you're rested*, but he knew that was like adding fuel to the fire. So he decided to be honest—brutally honest. He looked at Meredith who stood there in her housecoat looking like a neglected Barbie doll. Her eyes looked more than tired.

Jeff began, "Honestly, I have a hard time being around Tuck. It seems his behavior is worse when I'm around. The last time I tried to interact with him, I ended up with a mess on my hands. I said one wrong word—Cornerstone." Jeff threw his hands up. "And he threw the dishes to the floor."

"What are you talking about?"

"Remember I was home with Tuck and you went to pick up the girls? He asked me where you were, and I said *Cornerstone* and he knocked the dishes off the table. I had been trying so hard with him, and it seems like everything I do is wrong. I feel like I'm making him worse, and he is better without me," Jeff confessed still hanging his head down.

Meredith's anger melted. She took Jeff's hand and looked him straight in the eyes. "That's not true. Tucker needs you in his life." This time, she was telling the whole truth.

"But don't you see that I caused the problems. Tucker has problems because of me. I look at the girls, and they are like you—especially Clare. I see you in each of the girls. Your gentleness is apparent in each of them. Myla has your teaching side, Isabelle your wild side, and Clare has your love of nature. And then there is Tuck, my son. I must have caused Tuck to be the way he is. I'm to blame for his autism. It's in my genes somehow. I love order and numbers. Balancing the books makes me happy — truly happy. I love Tuck and I want the best for him. But he has problems because of me and . . . the least I can do is not cause any more problems for him or for you or for the girls. When I look at him, I see my failures. Girls are like their mothers. Boys are like their fathers. Look at what I have done. My son — the son who is like me — throws things, hits his mother, and gets expelled from school. He hates me. I didn't want this, and I don't know how to fix it. The best thing I can do for him is stay out of his life."

Meredith stared at Jeff trying to process what he was saying. This definitely wasn't the fight she thought she would get. She repeated, "Tucker needs you. The girls need you and I need you. I need you to be okay. I can't do this on my own. We can only make this work — for all the kids and us — together."

"It just seems too hard being here at night and feeling like I'm messing up his life. At lunch, it's different. I come home, it's quiet, and it makes me feel nearer to you and the girls and Tuck. I look at their drawings on the refrigerator. I eat the leftovers from dinner for lunch. And I think about you, the girls, and Tuck having dinner together. The other night you had spaghetti, Tuck's favorite. He's always so excited when you fix spaghetti. I'd wonder which girl loaded the dishwasher because I doubt if they added detergent to the dishwasher. The dishes seemed a little crusty." Jeff smiled a crooked smile and then continued, "I fixed the hole in Tucker's wall this week. I got some joint compound and filled up the holes he had made in his wall throwing things. I guess you noticed. I still need to put on a second coat."

Meredith diverted her eyes downward and shook her head. She hadn't noticed. She was surprised at herself not noticing, but she had been so tired from lack of sleep.

Jeff spoke softly, "I'm sorry. I wish I was a stronger person like you."

"You are strong. You know it's not your fault, don't you?" Meredith began, "The autism is not your fault. It's nobody's fault. Tucker is not broken. The autism is just part of him. It makes him who he is. I guess I always think about autism like a trait like Isabelle is a chatter-box. It's just part of her. Some think it's good, others bad. I know sometimes she exhausts me with her constant chatter. And Clare—I don't know how to keep her from bringing lizards in the house. I found another poor dried up lizard yesterday. They all have something" —she paused trying to come up with the right word— "unique. Tucker's autism gives him some of the things I love about him. I love how he delights in things that seem simple to us but are joyful to him. He loves his GPS watch. I've never seen a kid love a watch more. He wears it all the time and still keeps track of time for me. And you found that for him. If I say we need to leave at 4:30. He keeps me on time— just like you. He is good with numbers and math comes easily for him—just like you. So he gets good things from you too." She tipped her head and rolled her eyes playfully and said, "I could do without the impulsiveness and the destructiveness." Meredith sat down beside Jeff. "But I think with time and instruction, he will get better. I thought Isabelle would never quit whining, but she hardly does that anymore. Tucker will get better too. We are just in a dark season with him right now. I have to believe that. I couldn't go on if I didn't believe it. There are dark seasons with typical kids too. We're all changing — whether Tucker can embrace that or not—and the change is a constant. It's the one thing we can count on." Meredith paused. "And it's the one thing we can count on to upset Tucker," she said with a smirk at the irony. "We change as we grow and learn." Meredith grew serious. "And I know Tucker needs us to help him right now and to be supportive, and that's why I'm pushing so hard. I'm tired too, but I need to see this through even if it kills me because I know the right education can make all the difference."

"He is doing okay at Central this week, isn't he?" Jeff asked.

Meredith realized that she was about to be caught in her lie. Here she was talking about changing and growing, and she felt like she had changed into a liar and a thief. She felt disgusted with herself. She took both hands and tried to tame her hair down and think of some way to not lie again to Jeff. She looked around and then she heard Tucker come out of his room. "Don't mention Central to Tucker," she mouthed to Jeff and felt relief as she thought to herself, *Saved by Tucker.*

He nodded okay slightly and she noticed the fear in Jeff's eyes as Tucker stumbled into the room after sleeping all morning.

Tucker sat down at the kitchen table still looking sleepy and acted like it was perfectly normal to see Jeff in the kitchen in the afternoon. Tucker said, "Dad, I'll have some cereal with bananas."

Jeff looked at Meredith. Meredith shrugged her shoulders.

"Dad, he'll have some cereal with bananas," Meredith repeated.

Jeff smiled his crooked smile and opened the cabinet and looked at the variety. "Well Tuck, we have several to choose from this afternoon," Jeff said in his best announcer voice and then listed all the choices and Tucker responded although he still seemed sleepy. Jeff poured the cereal with milk and sliced the bananas just right and set the bowl down in front of Tucker like he had just placed a bowl full of raw meat in front of a gray wolf. Jeff stepped back. Tucker picked up the spoon and ate with his cheek propped up with one hand. Jeff relaxed and smiled at Meredith. She smiled back at Jeff. It was a simple connection.

The girls bounded into the house with Mrs. Sawyer after school. Meredith had her hair pulled back out of her eyes with several bobby pins. She was wearing sweat pants and a T-shirt. Tucker was playing with blocks and had an elaborate structure built in the middle of the living room floor. Clare and Isabelle ran to Meredith and gave her a hug.

Myla surveyed Meredith as she gave her a gentle hug with one arm and asked, "Are you okay?"

Meredith answered, "I was able to get some sleep, but I still feel like a zombie. Hopefully tonight will be better."

Mrs. Sawyer knocked on the door but came on in without being asked. "How is everything going? Did you get any rest?"

Meredith was embarrassed at her appearance and smoothed out her sweater. "I'm sorry, I look so terrible," she said apologetically.

"No worries," Mrs. Sawyer said, "I remember a few sleepless nights myself." She sat down at the kitchen table and continued. "When my son, Brian, was young he was sickly, and I stayed up many a night just watching him breathe. He always seemed to get the croup in November. His immune system wasn't the best and I would make a tent out of sheets and lay down with him with vaporizers running under the sheets. It would calm his breathing, but I never was able to catch more than a few hours or minutes of sleep night after night. I was sometimes relieved when he was admitted to the hospital for his croup or bronchitis—whatever the case may be—because I knew the nurses would be checking on him. I would snooze in the recliner and hold his little hand while we slept. Not many people can say they slept better in the hospital, but it was such a relief to know the nurses would check on him too."

Meredith sat down with Mrs. Sawyer.

Mrs. Sawyer declined a beverage. "Is Jeff able to take turns with you on staying up doing night duty?"

Meredith again felt embarrassed. "No, Jeff isn't home most nights. He stays at the office. He is . . . busy." Mrs. Sawyer nodded knowingly. "I'm too tired to complain, and it seems easier when he is not here. It's one less person to worry about."

"I had no idea." Mrs. Sawyer looked away. "Marriage is hard, and when a couple has a special needs kid, it gets even harder. I read once that parents with special needs kids are more likely to divorce. And if the divorce rate is 50%, then parents raising a special needs kid divorce more times than not."

"We used to have — what I thought — was a good marriage. But lately with the challenges Tucker is facing, it seems everything is so —" Meredith searched for the right word but only came up with—"difficult. As his mother, I want to protect him. Jeff thinks Tucker will work out whatever issues he is having at school. I think Jeff is coming around though. Tucker more than doesn't want to go. I can't get him out of the car. It's heartbreaking."

"What about truancy? Is there not a law requiring you to send Tucker to school?"

"Well, since we requested a due process hearing about Tucker's placement and I consider the current educational placement that the school offered to be detrimental for Tucker, I'm keeping him at home. The school is sending out a homebound teacher once a week with his schoolwork. It's easy to be Tucker's teacher. He works very well for me and he is very task oriented. We get all his work done by noon every day at the library where it's nice and quiet — and orderly," she added looking around the room.

"Well, it's good that you are a teacher. Tucker is benefiting greatly from your expertise."

"It does seem like he is moving along with his academics. And behaviorally when it's just him and me at the house, he is fine. Mostly I'm accommodating him. But I know he can't stay home with me forever. Amicus, the school we are asking Central Elementary to place Tucker in, has a program to help students with socialization which is really Tucker's biggest deficit. And even though I can teach him at home, I can't help him function in the real world. Their program seems wonderful. Socialization is as important as academics at the school."

"Well, why doesn't the school district offer Tucker a place there?"

"Money, the tuition at Amicus is expensive. All those professionals and small classrooms don't come cheap. And we are asking the school to pay for it. One of the staff at Amicus said the school district usually ends up paying about half of the tuition. You would think the school would rather pay the tuition than pay the lawyers, but I get the impression the school thinks if they start paying for one child, it will create an avalanche effect — everyone thinking their child needs special accommodation — and they will have to pay for hundreds of kids. But I really don't think there are hundreds of kids like Tucker that would benefit from Amicus. It's a very specific school."

So you think the school will pay half the tuition and your family will pay the other half?" Mrs. Sawyer asked.

"We're waiting to find that out."

"Well, I hope it works out." She patted Meredith's hand. "But today, I still want to help you. I'll be happy to come back at bedtime and sit up with Tucker so you can get some sleep. Tucker and I can watch a movie and I'll wake you if I have a problem. You can get some sleep and tomorrow I can sleep while you're up with Tucker. Tucker is going to get tired at some point."

"That sounds so wonderful."

"I'll be back at bedtime." Mrs. Sawyer patted Meredith's hand and left.

Relief flooded over Meredith at the thought of a decent night's sleep. She was too tired to cook dinner, so she rummaged through the drawers, her purse, and the car until she came up with enough change to order a pizza. She wanted to have the pizza delivered but couldn't come up with enough money, so she ordered carry out because it was cheaper. Three miles to the pizza place and back and the kids would have dinner.

Meredith caught the car coming towards her out of the corner of her eye, and it was only then that she realized that she had pulled out in front of a car. There was a strange sound of scraping and she tried to make sense of what was happening—then nothing.

As the paramedics wheeled her into the emergency room, she tried to open her eyes, but they felt glued shut. Darkness overtook her again. One of the paramedics briefed the doctor. "It appears she pulled out in front of an approaching car. The driver of the car that hit her is in another exam room. He seems to be shaken up but not injured. He said he was traveling about 40 mph and hit his brakes when she pulled out in front of him. His air bags deployed as he hit the woman's car right in the driver's door. She was unconscious when we arrived. Her air bags did deploy, but there were no side air bags, so her head hit and broke the driver's door window. Vitals are stable."

The doctor looked at Meredith and ordered an X-ray and MRI.

Jeff made it to the Friday afternoon briefing with Jackie. "It's time to transition Kate out of rehab and get her set up to start a new life. She has made wonderful progress. She is moving upward and is working to reinvent her life and her attitudes. Coming out of rehab — of course — she won't have a job or a place to live. There are several options that can be set up for her. First, we have a halfway house where she can stay while she looks for work. She will continue to need to go to meetings, and there are meetings at the halfway house. Second, she can move into her own apartment and look for work and come to meetings here at The 4:12 Center. Personally, I think the halfway house is a better option because she will have support. Sometimes being alone with your thoughts and feelings can make it easier to resume the lifestyle that caused the addiction in the first place. Her parents offered for her to stay with them in Florida, but that is over 12 hours away. Although that might be a good option, it means she will have to access the meetings and support herself when she gets there. Here she has already tapped into the resources and has a sponsor. Be thinking about options and if your family can be a support for her if she stays in this area."

"I haven't told Meredith yet that Kate is in rehab."

"What is stopping you?"

"Timing and stress. I went home and found Meredith stayed home from work because she was tired from being up with Tuck all night. Tuck was asleep when I got there but came out and talked to me which has been rare lately — so that was nice. I can tell he is better, and by better I mean fewer meltdowns, but being up against the school — basically the government — feels like a no-win. Meredith keeps holding out hope, but I just want to figure out how to work it out without the school's good graces. And I might have been able to do it except I lost my biggest client right before Christmas." Jeff shifted uncomfortably in his chair. "I don't know your policy, but I hope I can spread the last few payments out a bit more." He clasped his hands together, put them on top of his head, leaned back in the chair, and looked at the ceiling. "The holidays were great except for a call from my parents who act like Tuck doesn't even exist. It breaks my heart. I can't even tolerate talking to my mother anymore because it makes me feel bad. It's physically painful." Jeff grimaced and realized he was tired of his own voice, so he ended his complaint. "Such is life."

"Maybe your parents aren't as strong as you. Maybe they are jerks, but they did raise a very caring and compassionate son." Jackie smiled at Jeff, and he looked down not knowing how to take the compliment. "And although it may be painful, you might need to let them go. It seems like you have enough things going on right now that you have no control over, but you have control over your contact with your parents. Sometimes it's helpful to write a letter to the person but not mail it. You need a way to let go of your anger at them without having to engage with them again. There is no such thing as forgive and forget. Because that implies that we didn't learn. Forgive them, learn from it, and let it make you stronger. Sometimes we have to let go of a painful past to be able to grab on to a future. You have so many good things in your life — a wife, four great kids that you love, and a sister-in-law that basically thinks you and Meredith hung the moon."

Jackie stood up and Jeff followed. He shook her hand and lingered with the handshake, looked into her eyes and said, "Thank you. You're really good at this."

Jackie said in a teasing voice, "That's my job." They walked to the front door, and Jeff realized that he had missed the family support meeting when he saw the other family members filtering out. Several people greeted him.

Wow, one session with Jackie and I feel better already. *No wonder Kate is doing so great,* he thought as he headed back into town.

Jeff got stopped in traffic on the road near home that he called fast-food alley. *There must have been a wreck*, he thought to himself as he noticed the flashing blue lights ahead. He was startled when a tow truck passed him with a car that looked like Meredith's. As it went by, he turned to check the license plate and felt his heart begin to race when the numbers matched those of Meredith's car. He tried Meredith's cell phone. No answer. He called the house and Myla answered the phone.

"Can I talk to your mom?" Jeff asked without any introduction or pleasantries.

"She's not here, but she should be back any minute. She went to get pizza for dinner."

"Did anyone go with her or are you watching all" —he emphasized all—" the younger kids?"

"She went by herself."

Jeff hung up the phone.

Traffic had started slowly moving again. Jeff cupped his hands over his mouth and took several deep breaths trying to calm himself. After all, he didn't really know what happened. Meredith may be fine. The kids are at home and they are fine. The car probably looks worse than the actual wreck. Jeff consciously focused on slowing down his breathing again. The hospital was a couple of miles away and he took the next turn to head to the hospital. If she was hurt they would have transported her to the nearest hospital.

He parked and jogged into the emergency room. He was thankful he didn't recognize the nurse. "I think my wife is here. She may have been brought in after a car wreck."

"Your name?"

"Jeff Howard."

"Yes, she is in exam room 4."

"She is alive," Jeff told himself as he walked down the corridor looking for exam room 4. He entered the room. There were two nurses in the room. One was looking at the monitor beeping out heart rate, blood pressure, and oxygen levels. The other was assisting the doctor who was just finishing stitching up a cut on the right side of Meredith's forehead. *Another scar,* he thought. "How is she?" he blurted out when both the nurses looked up at him.

"And who are you?" one of the nurses asked calmly.

"I'm her husband, Jeff Howard. I saw her wrecked car being towed away and took a chance that she was here. Is she going to be okay?" Jeff felt the panic returning when he realized she was not awake, and he didn't get his question immediately answered.

The doctor spoke to him, "I can tell you that she is stable. She has been to X-ray and had an MRI."

Jeff went to Meredith's side and spoke to her, "Meredith, wake up." Jeff looked at the nurses surprised when Meredith only moaned, *No.*

Jeff stayed with Meredith after the doctor left, and he was standing next to Meredith stroking her head and hair when the doctor returned with the labs results. He spoke quietly to a nurse giving her instructions and details.

"Mr. Howard, it's mostly good news," the doctor started, "she has a concussion and a couple small cuts that are already sutured. We have done an X-ray and an MRI. Her concussion is mild and is not showing up on the MRI, but because she lost consciousness briefly, I'm keeping her at least overnight for observation. We are waiting for a room now. She also has a broken clavicle."

"A broken what?" Jeff asked feeling disoriented by the medical setting.

"Clavicle, her collarbone. I have spoken to her. She was unconscious when the paramedics arrived at the scene, but she wasn't unconscious for more than a few minutes. The paramedics spoke to her and I spoke to her. She was oriented to time and place. She knew she had been in a wreck. She told me she hadn't been able to sleep for the past three days because of her son. She said that she just wanted to go to sleep. And we are going to let her do just that. The nurse will be checking her regularly. Her MRI showed no internal bleeding and we have been able to rouse her. We will get her to a room and get her collarbone set. She will need to wear a sling that will keep the arm immobile while the bone heals.

An orderly walked in with the room assignment.

"I'm going to go home and check on the kids. I'll be back." Jeff asked the orderly for Meredith's room number so he would know where to go when he returned." Thank you, doctor," Jeff said and then headed home to check on the kids.

Jeff arrived at his house with a pizza in his hands for four very hungry kids. Isabelle hugged him tightly like she hadn't seen him in weeks. He tried to recall the last time he had seen Isabelle, but he couldn't. Stabs of guilt shot through him like pieces of shrapnel at the realization that he hadn't seen his kids in a week.

The girls ran up and hugged him. "Daddy!" they said in unison.

Jeff kissed each girl on top of the head. Myla took the pizza to the coffee table. Each girl picked up a slice with their hands. Tucker snatched him a piece and went and sat at the kitchen table and put his pizza on his white plate with the blue circle.

The girls sat on the floor around the coffee table with their pizza. Clare looked up at him and asked accusingly, "Where's Mommy?"

"Well," Jeff began, "Mommy had a wreck. She is in the hospital." All three girls stopped eating and looked at him. Tucker continued eating alone at the table in his usual spot. Jeff continued. "She is going to stay in the hospital at least tonight. She hit her head really hard on the window. I talked to her before I left, and she is very tired and is going to get some rest. I'll take you up to see her tomorrow, and hopefully we can bring her home."

The phone rang. It was Mrs. Sawyer. "Is Meredith available?"

"Mrs. Sawyer, Meredith's had a wreck." There was no sound on the other end for a few moments and Jeff thought the connection had been lost. "Are you there?"

"Yes, is she okay?"

"She is in the hospital with a concussion and a broken collarbone," Jeff stated matter-of-factly.

"Oh no, I knew she was extremely tired from staying up with Tucker the last three nights. I was calling to offer to stay with her tonight so she could get some rest. I guess she will rest in the hospital."

More guilt hit Jeff as he realized he had no idea what was going on with Tucker. "I would like to go up to the hospital and check on her, but I don't want to leave the kids alone at night. If your offer is still available, I would love to see Meredith. They were taking her to her room when I left. I just want to make sure she has everything she needs."

"Sure, I'll come over. Take as long as you need. I can stay up with the kids and I'll call you if I need you."

As soon as Mrs. Sawyer arrived, Jeff grabbed a slice of pizza, gave Mrs. Sawyer a quick hug, and headed back to the hospital.

Jeff looked down at Meredith, who was in a deep sleep resting peacefully. He gently stroked her forehead and ran his finger around the three stitches in her forehead. He ran his finger across the "lucky" scar on her eyebrow. It was barely visible like the doctor said, but he knew right where it was located. Her left arm was in a sling that held the arm tight against her body. She looked so young. The physical scars were obvious, but the unseen emotional scars are the ones that changed an optimistic young woman into an old woman with dark circles under her blank eyes. Jeff felt responsible for many of the emotional scars, but in reality he was just trying to survive too.

The hardest part for Jeff had been the loneliness. The first time he had noticed the loneliness was when he went to a barbecue at a client's house. His client, John, owned a growing and successful landscaping and nursery business. John was about his age with four kids but with two boys and two girls. Jeff had taken the girls with him to the backyard barbecue held around a beautifully landscaped pool while Meredith had stayed home with Tucker. Divide and conquer was his and Meredith's usual strategy. Jeff was surrounded by people, but as he watched John's wife interact with the guests and joke around with the kids, Jeff knew he was an outsider. He would never again have the carefree life like the people at the party.

Later an invitation came for Jeff and Meredith to go out to dinner with John and his family. Jeff accepted because he knew Meredith and John's wife would get along. They had the same upbeat outlook on life. But later the invitation had to be declined because Tucker was having a bad day and couldn't be left under Myla's supervision for even a couple of hours. The dinner was rescheduled a couple of times, but the couples never went out. Something always came up. Jeff's life was too unpredictable and sometimes volatile. There were no more invitations, but John was still a good client. He couldn't remember the last time he and Meredith had been out with friends.

Meredith sleepily opened her eyes and smiled at Jeff. He

stroked her head. "You rest. You've had a rough day."

"Who's with the kids?" Meredith asked.

"Mrs. Sawyer."

That was just like Meredith. Her first thought was about the kids. Meredith smiled sleepily and closed her eyes. Jeff kissed her forehead. He knew she was the only other one who loved Tucker like he did, but Meredith didn't run from it like Jeff did. She embraced it. Jeff lived more in the world of typical people, and when he was home, he noticed the difference in his life and the lives of his clients. But Meredith and the girls never seemed to notice. Tuck was just part of their group—good, bad, or ugly. Meredith was in a unique group of people who loved a disabled child without ever questioning *why did this happen*. He was her son and she loved him, and that was the end of the story. No pity.

Jeff didn't believe Meredith when she first thought something was different about Tuck. He kept telling her that Tuck was just all boy, and she was used to girls. The day he watched Tuck line up his chubby first crayons and then run around them in a circle was the first time he had thought maybe Meredith was right — something was off about Tuck. Tuck didn't respond when Jeff called his name and tried to get him to stop running in the circle. He was wet with sweat and bowed his back as Jeff struggled to pick him up. Meredith kept insisting that knowledge was power and if she knew what to do she would do it, but first she had to know what she was up against. I can't help him if I don't know what's going on. She would always fight for her kids. The hearing test came first and showed normal hearing. And then they completed the questionnaires and Tucker was tested. The results: mild autism.

Jeff watched Meredith sleep for a while and then he dozed off in the chair. The room brightened and Jeff startled. A nurse was taking Meredith's blood pressure. He wiped his eyes awake and went over and looked at Meredith. She was sleeping peacefully. The nurse smiled and told him that the blood pressure reading was normal. He wrote a note and put it on the over bed table. He drove home in the early hours of the morning to find Mrs. Sawyer sitting on the couch reading a book. All the kids were asleep. The kitchen and living room were straightened and cleaned. Jeff hugged Mrs. Sawyer again and thanked her. She said she would stay so he could rest. Jeff collapsed into the bed.

Chapter 45

He squinted at the clock. It was 10 am. He never slept that late. He looked over to the side of the bed where Meredith usually slept, and the realization of the wreck rushed back into his mind. He jumped up when he heard the kids in the kitchen. He ran down the steps and into the kitchen and all sound stopped as all eyes were on him. He stood there breathing hard as his sleeping body was beginning to catch up with his mind. Mrs. Sawyer had fixed pancakes, and all the kids were enjoying them. Jeff's panic retreated, and he went around and kissed each child on the top of his or her head. He felt like he was still dreaming. Everything seemed so normal, but it wasn't. His wife was in the hospital.

The kitchen was clean when Mrs. Sawyer left. "Thank you so much," Jeff said sincerely.

"I'm glad I could help with your precious family," Mrs. Sawyer replied.

Yes, they are precious, Jeff thought.

Myla brought Jeff a plate of pancakes. "These are for you," she said smiling.

Jeff devoured the pancakes. Myla smiled at him as she watched him eat. Jeff wondered if he dared take all the kids to pick up Meredith from the hospital. First, he decided to call Mrs. Riley at Cornerstone and leave a message on the school voice mail to let her know that Meredith wouldn't be in class on Monday. Jeff had the school number stored in his phone and he dialed it. Myla was watching him.

"I need to let Mrs. Riley know that your mom won't be able to teach on Monday," he said as the phone rang. Isabelle and Myla both looked at each other but said nothing. They stared at their Dad and listened as Jeff left a message. "Mrs. Riley, this is Jeff Howard. Meredith has been involved in a minor car accident. She won't be there Monday, but I'll bring the girls. If you have any questions, you can call me at this number. Thanks." He pushed disconnect on his phone and looked at the girls who were still looking at him with wide eyes as they held their breath. "One less thing for Mom to worry about—right?" The girls breathed again and smiled at each other and at Jeff. Myla shrugged her shoulders. Isabelle and Myla maintained the rule that they didn't have to offer any information but not to lie if asked a direct question. Jeff hadn't asked them anything. "Let's go pick up Mommy from the hospital," Jeff said picking up Clare, who clapped her hands together at the statement.

The kids piled into the car without any prodding, and they were on their way to the hospital when Tucker began rocking back in the car seat hard enough that Jeff could feel the car shaking when they stopped at a red light. Jeff looked at the girls, who were not alarmed at Tucker's behavior, and then he decided to ignore the behavior too as if everyone driving down the road had someone rocking their car. Jeff had no cause to be anxious because Tucker walked without incident up to Meredith's hospital room. Jeff kept himself in a prepared for anything stance because he never seemed to know what would set Tucker off on a "meltdown."

When he opened the hospital door, the kids rushed to Meredith's side. Jeff wondered if Tucker was just following the girls or if he was concerned about Meredith too. Now that she was alert and sitting up, she looked older again. And even though she smiled and hugged the kids with her good arm, Jeff felt like he had just brought down the weight of the world on Meredith. But she didn't seem to notice. Clare climbed into Meredith's bed and sat beside her. She gently touched the bandage covering Meredith's stitches.

"Does it hurt?" Clare tenderly asked Meredith.

"A little. I'm so thankful that you all stayed home together, and no one was in the car with me when I had the wreck," Meredith said after she tenderly kissed Clare's head. Clare snuggled in close to Meredith.

Jeff took Tucker with him to get the car. The girls stayed

with Meredith, who was sitting in a wheelchair while being escorted out of the hospital by a nurse. Jeff had already informed the kids that Meredith was to be allowed to rest, but the girls' helpfulness kept her from resting. Isabelle wanted to read a book to Meredith. Clare just wanted to take a nap with her mommy. Myla needed to talk privately with Meredith about something from school on Friday. Jeff began to wish that the doctor would have let Meredith stay in the hospital one more day.

Sandwiches for lunch should be simple enough. Isabelle and Myla made their sandwiches and took them to the table. Tucker and Clare sat at the bar watching Jeff as he fixed their lunch. He felt like a teppanyaki chef as they watched his every move.

"And here's your turkey sandwiches," Jeff said to Tucker and Clare as he slid their sandwiches over to them.

"I don't like that bread," Tucker said.

"Well, just eat it this time."

"I don't like that bread. I'm not going to eat."

"All bread tastes the same. Just eat the bread and next time I'll use the bread you like."

"I don't like that bread. I'm not going to eat it. It tastes bad."

"Please just eat it," Jeff pleaded, but then he decided to remove the plate before it became a projectile.

Myla came to the rescue. "He doesn't like the crust. Cut the crust off the bread."

"Since when doesn't he like the crust?"

Myla just shrugged, "I don't know. He just doesn't like the crust. Neither does Clare," Myla said as she looked at Clare, who hadn't touched her sandwich either. Myla rolled her eyes at Jeff's lack of understanding of common knowledge about who eats the crust and who doesn't.

214

Jeff cut the crust off the bread of both Tuck's and Clare's sandwiches and slid their plates back to them. "There."

"I don't like it," Tucker informed.

Clare began munching her sandwich and watching Jeff, who now felt like a comedy performer at a dinner theater.

"What now . . . Myla? He still won't eat it."

"Did you put mustard on it? On both pieces of bread?"

"Yes."

Myla came over and inspected the sandwich. "Oh I see," Myla said. "You cut it in two triangles. Tucker likes his sandwiches cut into two rectangles. Clare likes the triangles. Also, Tucker doesn't like that plate. He likes the white plate with the blue circle."

Tucker began to whine, "I want Mommy to make my sandwich."

Jeff searched through the cabinets for the white plate with the blue circle. He finally found it in the dishwasher and transferred the sandwich to the desired plate and cut the sandwich into four triangles. "Tuck, how about four triangles? It's pretty cool to have four triangles."

Tucker eyed Jeff suspiciously as Jeff slid the plate in front him. Tucker leaned over towards the plate and studied the sandwich. He even sniffed it and then Tucker looked up. "There are no carrot sticks on the side —four carrot sticks."

Jeff grinned slightly because he was delighted that Tucker communicated some helpful and real information to him. "Four carrot sticks on the side coming up, Tuck." Jeff swung open the refrigerator and said a silent prayer of thanksgiving for a baggy of peeled and washed carrot sticks. He placed the four carrot sticks on Tucker's plate and turned to Clare, "Four carrot sticks on the side for you too?"

"Yes, I take four carrot sticks and a glass of milk," Clare

responded in a matter-of-fact way.

Jeff had already realized that sandwiches for lunch were not a simple task. "Does Tucker take milk with his sandwich too?" he asked Clare.

"Yes he does," she said instructing Jeff like he was a child, "but he likes strawberry milk or strawberry yogurt if we have it."

Jeff smiled and repeated, "If we have it? Okay." Carrots and milk were served as Myla and Isabelle brought their plates to the sink. Jeff flopped down in the overstuffed chair in the living room and thought, *that was just a 'simple' lunch of sandwiches.*

What's next?

Chapter 46

Jeff was scrambling the cage-free eggs when Mrs. Sawyer knocked to see if the girls were ready for church. Isabelle was sticking to her rule that if Tucker wouldn't or couldn't go, she wasn't going. But Clare and Myla ran by.

"Clare, come here," Meredith said and kissed her and straightened her glasses. "Have fun at Sunday school."

Tucker stood at the door and watched Myla and Clare leave. He announced, "Elvis has left the building."

Jeff looked at Meredith, and she shrugged with her one good arm and then winced.

"Thank you for breakfast. You always make good omelets," she said looking at the western omelet. She shifted in her chair and her forehead furrowed showing the pain was creeping back up.

"Let me tighten that sling so that arm won't move around on you," Jeff said working on the sling as Meredith closed her eyes and took several deep breaths.

Meredith made her way to the couch not ready to tackle going up the stairs to her bedroom yet. Tucker came and sat down beside her. He had a book in his hands. "Let's read," Tucker said.

Meredith patted the couch with her good arm so he would sit beside her next to the arm that wasn't in the sling. To Meredith's surprise, Tucker read the story to her. He even pointed to the picture when the sentence he was reading was about the picture. He had seen Meredith do this a million times.

After Tucker had finished reading, he held the book so only he could see the pages and began to ask Meredith questions. "Who was the story about?"

This made Meredith smile because she had always read the story and questioned him, but this time the tables were turned. Meredith answered correctly.

Tucker said, "Good job" and then he continued. "What

happened to the dog in the story?"

Meredith decided to answer this one incorrectly to see Tucker's reaction.

Tucker knew she was incorrect and said, "Think again. What happened to the dog in the story?"

Meredith made another wild guess.

Tucker told her the answer.

Meredith looked at her son who had been struggling so much with the social aspects of school. Academically, he had some low areas, but their question-and-answer session revealed to Meredith how much progress Tucker had made in the time she had been working one-on-one with him. If only others could see Tucker like she did. He was smart and loving. She was very proud of him. Socially, he was a little bit lost.

Meredith smiled as she watched Tucker, but the pain was creeping up on her. She shifted uncomfortably on the couch. She called out for Jeff who appeared almost instantly with dish washing bubbles on his hands.

Meredith was pale. "I just can't seem to take my mind off of this pain. My arm is throbbing."

"Let's get you upstairs in your bed. You'll be able to rest better, and you should probably take one of those pain pills that the hospital sent you home with," Jeff suggested. He was surprised when she agreed and downed the pill with some orange juice. He walked her up the stairs and got her positioned in the bed. She wanted the sling off. Then she wanted it back on. She wasn't comfortable either way. She whined a little and then Jeff could tell the pill was taking effect. Then he propped her up with pillows, and she dozed off which was a relief for Meredith and for him. He rummaged through Clare's closet and found the old baby monitor and put it beside Meredith's bed so he could hear her if she got up

Chapter 47

Jeff had slept on the couch but felt like he just rolled over and over all night. At 6 am, he went upstairs and checked on Meredith, and since she was sleeping soundly, he closed the door to Meredith's bedroom. He woke the kids whispering to them to be "vewy qwiet" so Mommy could keep sleeping. All the kids complied and whispered and walked quietly getting ready.

Jeff dropped off the girls first. They waved good-bye and Myla took Clare's hand as they walked into the building.

Jeff drove to Central Elementary. "Come on, Tuck."

Tucker got out of the car and followed Jeff into Central.

"Where is your class?" Jeff asked.

Tucker just looked at him, confused.

"Show me the way to your class. I think it's down this hall, but it has been awhile." Jeff started walking towards Mrs. Canon's room.

Tucker didn't follow Jeff, so Jeff took his hand and pulled Tucker behind him.

"Hi, Mrs. Canon," Jeff said trying to set a good example for Tucker.

"Hi, Mr. Howard," Mrs. Canon said and then directed her attention to Tucker. "Hi, Tucker. It's good to see you again. Will you be joining our class today?"

Tucker stood behind Jeff and had Jeff's arm gripped with both hands.

Mrs. Canon ignored Tucker and spoke to Jeff. "I hadn't heard the outcome of the hearing. But I'm glad to see you have decided to let Tucker come to my class. When was the decision made?"

Jeff asked, "What are you talking about? Is Tucker not in your class?"

Now Mrs. Canon was confused. She looked at Jeff like he had a head injury. "No, Tucker only came for a few days. He hasn't been in my class since before Christmas."

Jeff's face flushed. He felt foolish. He didn't understand what was going on. "Well, whose class is he in? I thought Tuck was supposed to stay in the same placement while we were waiting for the hearing." Jeff made a statement that sounded more like a question.

"Yes, he had that option. But Mrs. Howard said that his placement was detrimental for him, and she had the option of not sending him to current placement until the hearing was complete. She chose not to send him. He is or was on homebound instruction last time I heard. He hasn't been back in my class."

"Well . . . where has he been going to school?" Jeff asked stammering.

"I don't know that. I only know that he has not been in my class. You might check in the office."

Jeff looked at Mrs. Canon. Then he looked at Tucker, who still had a grip on Jeff's arm, and then back to Mrs. Canon. "Okay, thank you. I will." Jeff headed to the office.

In the office, the receptionist took him to see Dr. Fisher. Jeff sat down in the chair and Tucker insisting on sitting on Jeff's lap even though Tucker's head was level with Jeff's. Jeff just looked around Tucker.

Dr. Fisher began, "Mr. Howard, I think you need to speak with your wife." The receptionist brought in a file and handed it to Dr. Fisher. He took out a page." Here are the letters we received from you and Mrs. Howard. This is the form your wife signed saying she couldn't leave Tucker in his current placement because she disagreed with the placement, and she indicated if Tucker stayed in the placement it would be detrimental to him. Tucker was placed on homebound instruction. Has a teacher not been coming to your house once a week?"

Jeff looked at the paper. It was Meredith's signature. He looked at the date. It was the same date he lost Parker Dental and Parker Dental Supply. That was a date etched in his mind. *No wonder she didn't tell me,* Jeff thought. He flashed back to Meredith saying, *I have something I need to tell you.* He then turned and looked at Dr. Fisher. "If Tucker hasn't been going to Mrs. Canon's class, where has he been going to school? Is he taking any classes or any therapy? Meredith has told me about how much progress he has made. Where is he going?"

Dr. Fisher said, "Again, Mr. Howard, I think you need to speak to your wife. All I know is Tucker is not attending any classes or therapy at Central Elementary. He is receiving homebound instruction. Here are the notes from the teacher."

Jeff turned Tucker's face so he could see him head on. "Tucker, where have you been going to school?"

"The library."

Jeff was more confused now. He took Tucker and went home. Meredith was still sleeping. Jeff paced, waiting for Meredith to wake up. He started making noises partly because he wanted to wake Meredith and partly because he wanted to throw something. Finally, he heard Meredith calling his name through the baby monitor. He walked stiffly into the bedroom trying not to jump to conclusions.

"What time is it?" Meredith asked groggily. "Did you already take the kids to school?"

"Yes, but a strange thing happened when I tried to take Tucker to school," Jeff said in a mocking voice.

"I can explain." Meredith's eyes widened.

"I hope so!" Jeff escalated.

Meredith struggled to sit up. "I just couldn't leave Tucker in that classroom. I couldn't even take him. He wouldn't go." She changed her tone from defiant to optimistic. "His behavior has been so much better since I have been teaching him."

221

Jeff shook his head in disbelief. It was like he couldn't understand the words she was saying to him. "You . . .you've been teaching him? Then who has been teaching your class at Cornerstone?"

"I resigned. I had to. The Family Medical Leave Act only allowed for 12 weeks, and I needed to be off longer than 12 weeks. I wanted to tell you, but you lost Parker Dental, and I didn't want to upset you and then I don't know. It just seemed easier not to tell you." Meredith was talking as fast as she could.

Jeff covered his mouth with his hand as he stood shaking his head *no* and slowly backing out of the bedroom looking at Meredith like he didn't recognize her.

Meredith struggled out of bed. When she stood up, the room turned around slowly and then stopped. She got her focus on Jeff and headed toward him trying to reach and take his hand. He kept backing up and staying out of her reach. She had never so blatantly lied to Jeff before. "I couldn't get him to school, and you said that you wouldn't do it. Besides, the social demands at school and the bullying are too much for him. He's my son! I couldn't do it," she said even though it sounded more like pleading. Then softly she said, "He's our son. I couldn't let the situation destroy him. Don't you see? Don't you see? Don't you see how much better he has been? He hasn't been so overwhelmed. He's so smart, and the sensory issues and social difficulties overwhelm him at school so much that he isn't able to learn. He just acts out."

Jeff went downstairs. Meredith followed him taking one step at a time. Jeff sat down at the kitchen table and propped his head up with his hands. "You lied to me. So everything since Christmas has been a lie. I thought we agreed Tuck would go to Central. I thought everything was going fine."

"You," she emphasized, "You thought he would go to Central. But you're not the one who had to take him. You stayed gone almost all the time - sleeping at your office." Meredith was on the offensive now because Jeff's solution was to disengage.

"I've been here. I've been in the trenches with my son. I have to protect him. Don't you see? There is no one else. There is only me and you looking out for Tucker. He could so easily get lost. His beauty could get lost and destroyed."

Jeff was hunched over now with his elbows on his knees. "I guess the girls knew. They were in on the lie, the cover-up, making a fool out of dear old Dad."

"The girls know I'm not working at Cornerstone. But I told them not to lie to you. If you asked them a direct question, they were to tell you the truth. But you never asked. You've been gone. *Working your plan, planning your work,*" Meredith said. Her voice escalated as she quoted one of Jeff's favorite sayings.

"That's low. That's not why I haven't been here. I'm been trying to earn a living. Who do you think makes the house payment and keeps the lights on? Do you think that is done by magic?" Jeff raised his voice but then exhaled as he changed his train of thought. "If you haven't been working, you aren't bringing in any money. My income is half what it was!" This realization made Jeff almost hyperventilate, "Oh no, oh no, how are we going to keep the house, keep the kids in Cornerstone, feed the kids? He stopped and put his hand over his mouth like he was stifling a scream. Our insurance was through the school. We are getting ready to be hit with a truckload of medical bills." Jeff's mind was racing through the numbers.

Meredith just said, "I'm sorry. I didn't know what else to do."

Jeff just stared at Meredith like she was an intruder standing before him. Neither said anything. "You lied to me. All this time, you have been lying."

Meredith was in pain because of the look on Jeff's face. She knew she had betrayed him, but she had no choice. She had to protect Tucker. They each knew they were miles apart.

Meredith tried to win Jeff over to her side. "Being in a

classroom to Tucker is like you and I sitting in a rock concert for eight hours. We enjoy it for a little while, but then it becomes overwhelming, and we will do anything to get the sound to stop. That is how a class is for Tucker. It's overload. He starts acting out. It's too much. I can't have him suffer and be bullied."

"There is more than Tucker to think about," Jeff said and instantly regretted it.

"How can you say that?" Meredith cried out, "We are a family. "

"I can't talk about this anymore. You . . . you . . . you are a liar." Jeff spat out the words as he backed into the table and scooted it slightly. He watched Meredith as he backed his way to the door keeping his eye on his opponent so he wouldn't get hit unexpectedly.

"Jeff, don't . . . please . . . please, don't leave . . . I never meant to hurt you." Meredith tried to soothe Jeff, but his eyes looked at her like he was looking at a stranger.

Jeff backed his way to the door and then went out and sat in the car. He tried to make sense of the situation, but nothing made sense. He turned on the car automatically and slowly backed out of the driveway without any particular destination in mind.

Jeff thought about going to the office, but he knew Meredith could reach him there. It wasn't that he just wanted to avoid her calls. He wanted to be in a place where she couldn't call. He needed some time to think. It seemed like everything he had believed to be true was false. His mind refused to process that information, but his intellect could find no way around the lie. Without Meredith's accident, he would still be a pawn in her games of lies.

Jeff drove around for a while and finally decided to get a hotel room. He checked in without a word to the hotel clerk other than saying a single room. He lay on the bed with his clothes on and began to list the things that he knew to be true. But all he could do was come back to the lie. Was his life nothing but a lie? If she would lie to him about work and money, what else was she lying about to him? Was his whole life with Meredith a lie? This woman that he thought he knew seemed like a stranger to him as he reviewed his life over the last year. He kept playing the scene in his mind from the school where the principal said, *you need to speak with your wife*. He was such a fool. How could he go home and pretend nothing ever happened? Meredith had said it wasn't a lie; she just hadn't told him the truth. He believed what he thought to be true. The realization hit him. He couldn't throw stones. He was guilty too. Jeff knew that Meredith believed something to be true that wasn't also. He hadn't lied either, just did not tell the events. He kept thinking what Meredith did was different, but in his heart he knew he was doing the same thing. His omission about Kate seemed harmless, and he was helping someone which made it better he thought.

Jeff was coming to his senses, but the grief of all the circumstances over the last few months pressed down on his shoulders like a weight that was too heavy to lift. He could feel his knees buckling but knew he had to shoulder the weight. If he buckled and fell, he would never get back up.

Jeff gave in to the weight of it all, and he found himself down on his knees sobbing. His tears flowed freely. He covered his mouth to keep his sobs from echoing around the empty hotel room. His tears were for the loss of dreams and what could have been and now he knew would never be. He remembered the first time he held Clare and how wonderful it felt with Meredith beside him looking at their newborn and Myla, Isabelle, and Tucker gathered around for a peek. It was a perfect moment in time that he held secure in his memory.

And then shortly after, a label was on Tuck. The label of autism might as well have been dream stealer. The diagnosis was a mild blow. It had hurt, but it didn't even knock him to his knees.

He and Meredith just said nothing has changed. He is still our son, and we will do whatever we can to help him just like we will the girls. And as luck would have it, Tucker's disability was mild and Jeff's dream continued but on a slightly different course. They would make the deals and be one of the success stories. All they had to do was find the right therapies and Tucker would be held up as beating the odds. He managed to be successful in school. His memory skills scooted him along in the early years of academia. But when the application phase began, it was impossible for Tucker to memorize every scenario. The world became confusing, and Tucker tried to control his world with rules.

The bruises, black eyes, stitches, holes in the wall, broken toys, and flinching at Tucker's raised voice all flashed through his mind. The dream was battered. Business was good. The OCD reared its ugly head and school was no longer an option. The strain of expulsion from two schools, the abuse of Meredith at the hand of their growing soon-to-be teenage son, Kate's reappearance, the loss of his big account, and now Meredith's wreck. He wiped his tear-stained cheeks and thought about how Meredith had aged in the last few years. It wasn't so much the wrinkles and a stray gray hair here and there, but the weariness in her eyes that made her look old. Jeff tried to stop, but the tears rolled silently down his cheeks now, and he didn't bother to wipe them away.

He knew it was cliché, but he asked "Why" aloud. They were good people. They had done the right things at the right times. The girls deserved better. Tucker deserved better. Meredith deserved better. He lay back on the bed with his feet still on the floor and another wave of tears hit, but this time they were tears of bitterness. He knew he had grown bitter even though he tried to deny it, but bitterness was his new normal. He stayed away even when he could have gone home. It was just too much for him. He let Meredith bear the burden he should have helped shoulder. He justified his absence by saying making money was the most important thing he could do for his family. But he could have gone home. Meredith never asked him why. They were better off without him was his great justification. He thought he triggered Tucker's outbursts or was that just another excuse for staying away? Why wasn't he a better person? The will to get up and make a difference and be a stand-up guy was gone. He had no strength left for his work, his children, his wife, or to fight against the disability. He curled up on the bed and fell asleep.

Meredith sat down at the table after Jeff's car pulled out of the driveway. The look of betrayal in his eyes was burned into Meredith's mind. She called him on his cell phone, and she heard it ringing. His phone was on the counter in the kitchen. She tried the office phone but only got his cheerful voice on the voicemail. Jeff's absence at the home was a matter of routine, but this time it was different. He was gone not because he was escaping the drama of the house but because she hurt him. She didn't mean to hurt anyone. She was actually trying not to hurt him — she was trying to protect him. She was going to tell him when the time was right— when he picked up some new accounts or when the school hearing was settled or when Tucker was going to Amicus. When—she didn't know. But there were no new accounts, the hearing was dragging out, and Tucker and she were going to school at the library—not Amicus. She tried calling the office again. This time, she left a voice mail hoping he would hear it and pick up. "Jeff, I'm so sorry. I thought it was a temporary setback and everything would work itself out in a few months. This wasn't my plan — to hurt you. You have got to believe that. Please call me. I want to know you're alright. Please . . . I'm sorry."

Meredith got up from the table cradling her sore arm. Her whole body ached not just her arm.

Tucker walked into the kitchen, "Is it time to go to the library for school?"

"We are going to do school at home today. Get your backpack so we can get your books." Meredith's pain was mounting, and she needed to rest, but if she varied the routine too much, Tucker would become upset, and that would be harder to deal with than the pain from the accident. So she sat down at the table to help Tucker with his schoolwork.

Tucker read his reader oblivious to Meredith's pain. He systematically worked through his lessons as usual. Meredith sat by watching him and feeling a little proud of his independence in his work. She wasn't able to be of much help, and he worked through using the strategies they had practiced for comprehension.

Tucker spoke the words out loud that Meredith usually said and talked about himself in the third person. "You can do this, Tucker. Take your time and let's think about the question. What question word does the sentence use?"

Then Tucker switched to his own voice. "It says when."

Then back to Meredith's voice. "*When* questions are asking about the time something took place."

Then back to his own voice. "I see it, Mommy. It says yesterday at 10:00 AM."

Then back to Meredith's voice. "Very good, Tucker."

When Tucker had finished all his work, he said, "Time for lunch." Meredith got up and struggled through fixing him a sandwich and cutting the crust off. She gave him his milk and carrots. When he finished, he looked at her and asked, "Can I play now?"

"Yes, Tucker, you can play in the basement or in your room."

"My room."

It was impossible to make sure Tucker didn't leave the house if Meredith was in her bedroom. So she pulled a few pillows off Myla's bed, slid down the wall, and laid down in the hallway to rest. She fell asleep to the sound of Tucker reciting a Disney movie word for word. Meredith knew, if he started the movie, he would finish it, so this gave her about an hour to rest. She was asleep in no time, and she woke up to the phone ringing that she had laid down beside her in the hall hoping that Jeff would call.

"Mom, Dad forgot to pick us up," Myla said through the phone.

"I'll be there in a few minutes," Meredith said, "I fell asleep, honey. I'm sorry. Do you have Isabelle and Clare with you?"

"We're in the office. There are no other kids here," Myla reported.

"I'll be there as soon as I can."

Meredith accidentally put pressure on her arm in the sling and winced out loud in pain. Every muscle in her body screamed as she stiffly rose to her feet. She realized Tucker must be finished with his movie and looked at his open bedroom door. A wave of panic went through her as she called Tucker's name.

There was no answer. She checked the front door. It was locked from the inside. She hurried to the back door, wincing with every step.

It was unlocked. The door Jeff had left out of this morning. The chain at the top of the door hung straight down the frame. She knew Tucker had been through the door when she pulled on it and it wasn't latched. She stepped outside and looked around and called Tucker's name. No reply. She had the cell phone in her hand and called Jeff's office. All she got was the friendly voice mail again. This time, she dialed Mrs. Sawyer and asked if she could pick up the girls from school. Fortunately, she said, *yes*. Meredith called the school office to let them know that Mrs. Sawyer was on her way. Meredith searched the backyard as she talked on the phone. There was no sign of Tucker.

She went back into his room searching for him. She looked under the bed and in the closets. She picked up his GPS watch from the floor. If only she had taken him to the library, he would have been wearing it. She steadied her breathing as she stared at the GPS watch. She looked at the phone and dialed 911. Her voice was shaky. Her hands were shaking. "My son is missing. He has autism. Please hurry. I need help finding him." As she said the words, she began to feel light-headed.

"Ma'am, what's your name?" asked a calm voice through the receiver.

"Meredith . . . um . . . um . . . Howard." She barely remembered her own name.

"Ma'am, officers have been dispatched to your location. Do you think he ran away or do you think he was abducted?"

The words sent a chill through Meredith's body. Tucker would be an easy target. She had to shake her head to rid the thought from her mind. "No, he probably simply wandered away. But I have no idea which way he might have gone or for how long he's been gone." Meredith had been asleep for several hours. If he finished reciting his movie, that meant he could have been gone for about an hour. Meredith was walking down the street when the first police car arrived.

The officer wanted a current photograph, something with DNA, and a description of what he was last seen wearing.

"I have this picture of him on my phone. It's from yesterday at the park."

"Send it to me and I'll distribute it," the officer said.

Meredith felt her legs weakening and she went inside the house to sit down on the couch when the officer told her that Tucker did not qualify for an Amber Alert. Amber Alerts are for possible stranger abductions. The second police car arrived when Mrs. Sawyer pulled up with the girls from school.

The girls ran to their mother. "What happened?" Mrs. Sawyer and the girls asked almost at the same time.

"Tucker is missing," Meredith stated without emotion even though her cheeks were stained with tears.

The police were searching the house and yard. Mrs. Sawyer led the girls inside. Meredith was still wobbly on her feet, and her muscles now screamed in protest to her movements, but she continued looking.

A police officer came up to Meredith. "You need to stay inside and let the officers do their job. Even though this situation does not qualify for an Amber Alert, we do have a protocol to help us locate your son. We have officers and volunteers on their way. We have a dog trained to locate people. But you need to let us look. Tucker might come home and you need to be there."

"You don't understand. He's autistic. He is not going to answer you even if he hears you call his name. The only person he will answer is me, my husband, or —"

The officer interrupted. "Where is your husband?"

Meredith looked down. "I don't know. We had a fight and he left."

"Could he have taken the boy with him?"

"No, he left — alone. I fell asleep and Tucker. . . I slept right through him stepping over me." Tears streamed down Meredith's face. "So, you see, I have to look. He will come to me. He might hide from the commotion. Someone would just have to see him. He won't respond to his name except when Jeff or I or the girls call him."

Meredith started yelling. "Tucker! Tucker!"

"Mrs. Howard, can I speak to you privately?" The officer led her away from the girls. "Is there anything else you remember or can think of? What kind of car does your husband drive?"

"He wouldn't take him — not without telling me."

"We need to consider all possibilities. What kind of car does your husband drive?"

Meredith shook her head no as she answered the officer's questions.

Police cars started arriving. Another officer arrived with a dog. Meredith, Mrs. Sawyer, and the girls stood huddled together like an island in a raging sea. People hurried around them purposefully. Meredith stood motionless with no purpose other than to breathe and survive as the girls and Mrs. Sawyer kept her from falling over.

Finally, an officer came over to them. "Just to update you, we have volunteers here to help search. They have been told not to call his name but to move quietly and just look for him. We are going to move these police cars out of the area in case he comes back to the house. We don't want him to be frightened. The local television station will air his photo. We will be positioning the volunteers, and we'll let you know of any developments. Is there any place he might try to go? Have you heard from his father?"

Meredith shook her head no to both questions.

"We are trying to locate Jeff also in case he has Tucker or knows his whereabouts. Tucker's picture has already been aired on the local station. Our canine officer is ready. Can you get something that Tucker recently wore for the dog to smell?"

"Yes." Meredith led the officer and his dog to the house. The girls stood by Mrs. Sawyer wide-eyed afraid they might get lost in the sea of activity. Inside the house, Meredith saw the news report about Tucker being missing. His smiling face flashed on the screen describing him. Then it said Jeff was being sought for questioning. Meredith had to do a double take on hearing this. Jeff had left without Tucker; maybe Jeff did come back and take Tucker. It would serve her right. She didn't know for sure. The thought of her sleeping while Tucker wandered off brought the throbbing of her arm to her consciousness, and the throbbing demanded attention. Meredith decided sitting on the couch waiting might be the best thing since the officer kept suggesting she sit back down. But it felt like another failure. She slept while Tucker left and now she just sat on the couch while he was lost.

Meredith began to pace. The kids stayed nearby her afraid they would be snatched away too, just like Tucker. Each time she had questioned the detective in charge he just said that they would let her know if anything changed. Now she watched as the officer walked towards her. "Mrs. Howard, we need you to come with us. We may have located Tucker."

Meredith turned to Mrs. Sawyer. Both Meredith and Mrs. Sawyer had tears brimming in their eyes."I'm here . . . with the girls," Mrs. Sawyer said. "Go."

Meredith asked the question she knew she couldn't bear if the answer were no. "Is he okay?"

"We have located a boy matching Tucker's description. He is fine. A clerk at a convenience store detained him when she realized he was alone, and something wasn't quite right. She saw his photo on the news and called in."

"A convenience store?" Meredith laughed although there were tears on her cheeks.

The officer relayed the story as he had heard it as he drove Meredith to the convenience store. "Apparently, Tucker wanted an Icee and made himself one, but he didn't try to pay for it. The clerk stopped him because he was alone, and she knew something was up because he usually comes into the store with you. She was waiting for you to come looking for him, and she had a television on in the store and saw his photo."

Meredith was laughing thinking of Tucker and his Icee. She put her good hand over her mouth and pressed her elbow on her injured arm close to her side to keep it from moving. They arrived at the store, and Meredith was out of the car in one easy motion. She saw Tucker, and she got down on her knees and hugged him. Tucker loosely hugged her back. Meredith realized she was still in her drawstring pajamas from the hospital when the camera lit up her and Tucker. Meredith composed herself and spoke to Tucker. "I was worried about you. You didn't tell me where you were going. You shouldn't leave the house without letting me know."

"I was thirsty. I told you."

"But I was asleep. Wake me up to tell me next time . . . okay? I can't hear you when I'm sleeping." *A new rule to teach Tucker,* she thought.

"Okay, Mommy. You're crying. Are you sad?

"No, I'm happy."

Meredith hugged the clerk who was smiling. All Meredith could say was, "You saved his life. Thank you."

The officer said, "Tucker, do you want to ride in a police car?"

Tucker responded, "Yes." Then he turned to Meredith and said, "Elvis has left the building."

Chapter 48

Jeff woke up and it was dark outside. He had slept nearly six hours. His head hurt from the crying, and he wondered why people even cried. His stomach growled, and Jeff realized he hadn't eaten all day. But he still wasn't hungry. He should go home, but instead he just started to drive. Without much thought, he ended up sitting in front of The 4:12 Center. He could see inside the atrium through the large glass windows. The nightly meetings were ending, and he watched as people lingered and chatted. Some walked to their car. He was startled when someone knocked on the passenger side of the car. It was Kate. He flipped the key on and rolled down the passenger window.

"Did you miss the meeting?"

"Yeah, I did," Jeff lied.

Kate got in the passenger side of the car. "It was a good meeting. Jackie is so insightful."

Jeff continued to look forward and said nothing.

Kate leaned sideways in the seat and looked at Jeff. "Are you okay? You look terrible. What happened?"

Jackie walked out and looked in the rolled down passenger window. "Kate, it's time for big group evening sharing. They are waiting on you."

Kate got out of the car and whispered to Jackie, "Something is wrong with Jeff."

Jackie looked in the window at Jeff whose hands were still on the steering wheel. "Jeff, come on in. Let's visit in my office," Jackie said nonchalantly not giving away her concern.

Jeff obediently got out of the car and followed Jackie. His clothes were wrinkled, his affect flat. He plopped down in the wingback chair in Jackie's office.

"What happened, Jeff?"

"Meredith had a wreck. When I left here last time, I saw a tow truck go by with Meredith's smashed car. She broke her collarbone and got tossed around pretty badly. But that's not even the worse part. I found out she has been lying to me and getting the girls to *lie* too," he said as he used his hand to indicate quotes around the word lie. "I feel so betrayed and like my whole life with her has been a lie. I started driving around and ended up here because I don't know what to say when I go home. I don't know if I want to go home. You think you know someone and then they—" Jeff put his head in his hands and leaned over with his elbows on his knees and looked at the floor."

"People lie to the people they love sometimes. But there is forgiveness."

Jeff leaned back and started feeling agitated. "You don't get it. Maybe I can forgive, but I'll never forget — like you said. And if I can't forget it then I can't face her. I'll never trust her again." His voice was getting forceful. "Everything I thought was true turned out to be false." He looked at Jackie with his eyes red from tears. "She had been pretending to go to work. She doesn't even have a job anymore. She put us thousands of dollars in debt. My business is struggling. I've got financial commitments — here — with Kate." Jeff got up and started pacing in the small office. "And all this with Meredith started because Tuck had problems with school. He couldn't make it anymore in school. And that basic core problem still exists. Meredith hasn't solved anything. She's just made it worse, and it may never be resolved. Tuck's education" —he started alternating between holding his head and holding up his hands while he paced— "is out of control. I'll never get him the help now. He's not going to be okay. It's hopeless. I can't fix him. I can't fix this." He stopped, put his arms around himself, and shifted his weight from side to side. "I've got nothing and nowhere to turn." Jeff sat down in the chair and put his head in his hands rubbing his temples trying to keep the tears he felt from appearing.

Jackie didn't speak for several moments. The silence hung in the air. Finally she said, "Welcome to rock bottom."

Jeff looked up at her. "I'm not an addict," he said defiantly and put his head back down in his hands.

"It doesn't matter. Rock bottom is when you come to the end of yourself and your own efforts. And you have had a real loss — the loss of your dream. Parents who have a disabled child grieve the loss of the child of their dreams. Many times they spend time denying the disability and trying to make the child typical until it's obvious no amount of effort can fix the disability."

Jeff was staring at Jackie now, but his eyes lacked any emotion. "I love my son."

"I know you do. But if you're honest with yourself, autism wasn't in your plans. And then many times — to make matters worse — parents feel guilty about their feeling towards the child with a disability. I can tell you this. There is no answer to the question *why* in these situations. You can't fix Tucker, but you can love him. You have got to let go of the son of your dreams to grab hold and love the son you have. Quit trying to fix him."

"I can't," Jeff said slumped over in the chair as tears started down his cheeks. "I can't."

"You have to. You can't make him into what you want him to be. But you do have a son who needs you." Jackie handed Jeff a box of tissues. She had his full attention now. "Rock bottom is not a bad place. It's a place to begin again, to leave behind all the things that aren't working, and reinvent your life — a life that works and makes sense for your situation, not what works for other families."

Jeff leaned back and was slightly nodding his head, but his face still looked pulled down by some invisible force.

"You have been working so hard to keep things together, and they are still falling apart in your hands. Let them go. You are powerless, and it seems to me that your life — for you — has become unmanageable."

Jeff looked at Jackie and smiled ever so slightly as he heard the familiar principles discussed in the family support meetings.

"It's not going to be a simple or easy process. But let go of what is not working. Let your parents go and others who aren't supportive. Grieve the child of your dreams. Free yourself of what society says is the American Dream. Leave it all behind. And embrace your life as you define it. Embrace your life and the children you do have." She stopped and gave Jeff a chance to speak. She could tell his breaths were steady and not ragged as before. "Rock bottom is a gift. As you climb out without any chains, you will be able to be happy in a way you never imagined."

Jeff nodded. "I need to go home." He paused and neither he nor Jackie spoke for a full minute. Jeff broke the silence. "Don't I?"

"Yes, and you need to forgive yourself and forgive Meredith. She was just doing what she needed to survive too. I'm sure this hasn't been easy on her either."

"You're right." He stood to leave. "Thank you."

"You're welcome. And one more thing — be gentle with yourself. This is a process. You will have good days and bad days. It's enough to move in the right direction. Keep coming to the meetings—"

"Sorry to interrupt, but you need to see this," Kate announced at Jackie's office door in a voice that made them both jump up and follow her. Kate grabbed the remote control for the television in the atrium and turned up the volume.

"This was the scene earlier today when a young boy with autism who wandered away from home was reunited with his mother." Jeff stood motionless as he saw the picture of Meredith kneeling down hugging Tucker outside of a convenience store. He used his hands to smooth back his hair as his mind tried to make sense of the events he just saw on the news. He reached into his pocket to check his cell phone and realized he didn't have the phone.

"I gotta go home," he said to Jackie and Kate and ran out of The 4:12 Center.

He drove down his street and noticed two police cruisers. Otherwise, the street was quiet. Mrs. Sawyer's car was parked at the curb in front of the house.

"Dad's home," Isabelle ran upstairs and announced to Meredith.

Meredith looked down and was surprised at her feelings. She wanted to run to him and find comfort in his arms, but when he left, he was so angry. She didn't know if he would forgive her. So much had transpired since he left that she felt like a different person. But when she saw him, she walked up to him, and he opened up his arms. She walked into his embrace and buried her face in his chest. They stood there two weary souls battered leaning on each other for support but not defeated. Jeff finally spoke, "I saw the news report."

Meredith, who didn't have any words to begin to tell the events of the afternoon, only said, "It was the worst day of my life."

"It's over. Everyone is safe," then Jeff added quietly, "for today. Where are the kids?"

"Downstairs—as if nothing happened. Kids are so resilient."

Mrs. Sawyer came up the stairs. She patted Jeff on the arm. "I'm going to go on home, now.

"Thank you so much for being here," Meredith and Jeff both managed to say. There was no way to pay Mrs. Sawyer back. How can you pay someone back who was there when you were not? He had to shake the negative thoughts from his head and think on the present and the fact that everyone was safe and at home. Everything was okay at this moment — one moment at a time. Then he thought of Kate.

Jeff looked at Meredith and saw her puffy eyes. He placed his palm on her cheek and she leaned into it. He tipped her face up towards him and looked into her eyes and searched for his young bride. He wondered if she was gone forever. Her shoulder slumped toward the arm in the sling. Her face had yellowing bruises from the wreck. "I'm home now. You can rest. I'll watch the kids. Go on to bed," he said.

She smiled. "Thank you. Is it okay if I take a bath first?" she asked. "I've got to wash this day away plus I haven't had a bath in a few days and—" She smiled weakly.

"So that's what that smell was?" Jeff teased and smiled.

Meredith grinned and shook her head.

"Sure, take your bath. I'm going to be here. I'm not going anywhere." The bedroom door closed and in a moment he heard the water running. He headed downstairs to the playroom and was greeted with shouts of "Daddy!"

He breathed in the scent of each of his children as he hugged them. This was what was important. He was to be their protector, and he had been lost himself. But in this moment, he felt found. Isabelle reported the details of the day to him, and he enjoyed every minute detail she remembered. Clare, always the nature and animal lover, added the details about the dog that came to find Tucker. Jeff drank in the words of his children. Debts, bills, and lies faded from importance in his mind.

After baths and checking in to make sure each one was asleep, Jeff headed to check in on Meredith. But before he did, he removed the chain lock from the back door and the front door and secured both of them to the outside of Tucker's door. If Tucker tried to go out, maybe he would hear him pulling against the chains. Jeff went into the bedroom he shared with Meredith. She was already asleep, and she looked relaxed and peaceful in her sleep. No worry lines etched her face. Jeff paced awhile and double-checked the doors and double-checked to see if Tucker was still in his room. He wasn't going to let Tucker get lost—not on his watch—and he planned to be there watching from now on. He sat in the chair in the bedroom listening for the rattling of the chain locks on Tucker's door, and then he moved to the couch to be closer to Tucker's room. Jeff kept trying to listen for Tucker. He slept in spurts.

Chapter 49

The next day after Jeff took the girls to school, he brought home his computer from the office. He set up a desk and printer in the upstairs room off of their bedroom. Clare was moving downstairs with the girls. He used his cell for work, so he was ready to take calls if needed. No one called. So he spent his day settling into his home office. He ended up driving up to his old office and getting his work chair and lugging it home. With his comfortable work chair, he was ready. He called several accounting friends to see if they had any business to send his way as a subcontractor. It felt like begging, but he tried to keep his spirits up. He went through the new tax changes. He balanced the bank statement from home and paid the bills. So far nothing was encouraging. The home account was drained. His commitment to Kate, the loss of income, Meredith's medical bills, and a house payment he could no longer afford loomed in his mind. Numbers ran around in his mind automatically calculating profit and loss. It was the loss that he couldn't get out of his mind. Then his phone rang.

"I would like to invite you to a *power lunch* in the downstair's cafeteria otherwise known as the kitchen. We will be serving sandwiches with no crust and sides of apples and carrots."

"I would be honored to attend this *power lunch*."

The lunch had to be an effort for Meredith with one arm in a sling. Tucker sat with them at the table, and Jeff and Tucker had a conversation — a real conversation. Of course, the topic was one of Tucker's choice, but there was actual information exchanged and Jeff was surprised. When lunch was over, Tucker took the plates to the counter and set them beside the sink. Meredith smiled. "That's home economics for the day."

Now if Jeff could just have a real conversation with Meredith. She looked so much better today. His phone rang again. He looked down at his phone and saw Kate pop up on the caller ID. He grabbed the phone and pointed at it. "I need to take this."

Jeff headed upstairs and closed his home office door behind him.

"I want to like to speak to Meredith," Kate said through the phone.

"Kate, please I haven't told her anything about what has gone on with you yet. I'm not sure she is ready for another *stressor.*"

"So that's what I am—a *stressor?*"

"Kate, you know what I mean."

"It's okay," she said softly. "Just let me tell her. Please. I want to talk to my sister."

"What are you going to say?"

"First, I'm going to ask her to forgive me." Kate paused for several seconds. "I don't exactly know what I'm going to say other than that. It will come to me." Jeff could hear Kate's sassiness returning. She turned serious when she said, "Jeff, you do know I've got to do this? I've got to make things right."

"I know. Okay," he said and walked downstairs and handed the phone to Meredith.

"Who is it?" Meredith mouthed to him as she took the phone. He waved her off without an answer.

Jeff heard Meredith exclaim Kate as he walked upstairs to work on the few tasks he had for his small clients. He spent most of the day pacing around the house, alternating between his new home office and the backyard, trying to stay out of Meredith's way, and still making sure Tucker hadn't escaped. His biggest accomplishment was comparing and scheduling installation of a security system. Most people bought security systems to keep people out. He wanted one to keep someone in.

He walked to the mailbox and found a letter from the school district. It seemed like eons had passed since the hearing process had been started with the school. He thought about how just a few months ago, his life was relatively normal, and this seemed so important. He opened the letter and read that prehearing interviews had been scheduled. Dates and times were listed. He felt a feeling of weariness and helplessness creep into his mind. It surprised him that he didn't feel like the system would work.

Jeff thought of the words that Meredith had yelled at him, *I'm not going to sacrifice Tucker to the system.* She was right. He wondered if the events of the last few days would change the school district's decision. Was the local school district equipped to deal with a student who was a flight risk? Jeff made a mental note to do some research and then contact the district. He hung his head down and shook it. I'm not sure I have the will to fight the school anymore.

Meredith came up to Jeff and put her good arm around his waist. "Kate's okay. But I guess you already knew that." Meredith couldn't suppress her smile. "Kate said she is moving to a halfway house. She chose the closest one to us, and Mom and Dad are going to help her. Her move date is next Monday. I want to see her.

"I've been going on Fridays to see her and her counselor and attend a family meeting. Let's go together this Friday."

Chapter 50

The girls came into Meredith's bedroom. "When do we get to go see Aunt Kate?" Myla asked.

"Soon. When she gets out of rehab, I hope we get to see her all the time."

"We made these for Aunt Kate." Isabelle handed Meredith three homemade cards.

Meredith read the sentiments and said, "These are beautiful." She hugged each girl. "Mrs. Sawyer will be here in a few minutes. Be sure and put the chains on the door when I leave and help Mrs. Sawyer keep an eye on Tucker."

Myla nodded.

Meredith looked around at the surroundings as they entered the driveway up to the rehab center. "This looks like a resort. I think I'll take up drinking if I can come here and relax," Meredith said to Jeff as he parked the car. He just shook his head at Meredith. They parked the car and headed into the center. Meredith looked around and realized she was walking way ahead of Jeff. She turned around and waited for him to catch up. As soon as they entered the atrium, she saw her prize — her baby sister. She was thin but looked healthy. Kate had a worried look on her face as she stood and faced Meredith. Meredith smiled and went to Kate, and they wrapped their arms around each other and swayed back and forth in an extended hug.

"Oh, your arm. I'm sor—"

"No, it's fine." Meredith pulled back and said, "You look great." They walked over to a table and sat down to talk.

Jackie had joined Jeff as he watched Meredith and Kate.

"That went well." They watched the pair for a few minutes. "You know she has a long and treacherous road ahead."

"I know she does. They both do. But they are going to make it".

Jackie looked up at Jeff, who was continuing to watch his wife and sister-in-law. "And what about you?"

"I'm going to make it too. I'm learning to let go. I'm not going to be a workaholic anymore and miss my life. I'm letting go of my son — the one I planned for— so that I can love the son that I do have. It was so hard trying to fix him and put him into some type of box of what is typical. It was exhausting." Jeff looked down, and his shoulders slumped forward as he remembered the past few weeks. But now," he said and rolled his shoulders back and took a deep breath, "I feel freer — lighter and more focused than I have been in a long time. I'm going to do what works for us and not worry about how I thought things should be." He looked at Jackie. "I moved my office home. It never occurred to me how much money I spent maintaining a separate office. I can meet clients at their offices. It's better customer service and saves me a bundle. It's going to make that bottom line look great." He smiled at Jackie.

She looked at him in his jeans, running shoes, t-shirt and unzipped *hoodie* that hung loosely on his shoulders, and she realized this was the first time she had seen him not wearing a suit. "You know. Be gentle with yourself. And you know what they say, *You can only go up from rock bottom.*"

"I think I might have heard that somewhere before," Jeff said teasingly.

"Here's one you might not have heard, *Don't get back on the highway that was taking you nowhere.*"

Jeff nodded. They both started watching Kate and Meredith again who seemed to alternate between laughing and crying. They both were fragile. The reasons were different. Jackie said, "It's about time for the meeting. This will be Meredith's first meeting and one of Kate's last meetings here." They headed into the large classroom.

Chapter 51

It had been a week since Tucker wandered off and for the first time, Meredith woke up and realized she had slept through the night without waking up to check on Tucker. She felt refreshed for the first time in weeks. Her first thought was *where's Tucker?* She heard Jeff talking to Tucker in the kitchen and she relaxed. She stretched her arms—both her arms—and there was only the slightest twinge in the arm with the healing collarbone. She looked at the clock, and it was 10:30 am on a blue sky day. She could feel the events of the past few weeks fading behind her. She walked into the kitchen and found Tucker sitting at the table working on his math and Jeff sitting behind his laptop opposite of Tucker. The kitchen was clean.

Jeff got up and kissed her and said, "Look who's up, Tuck."

Tucker turned around and said, "Hi, Mom." Meredith went over and kissed Tucker on the head and then kissed Jeff too.

"I think I might have picked up another client. It's a small business that just needs payroll services. My buddy, Harry—from Accountants for the Community—passed them along to me. He's too busy and doesn't want to mess with a small business, but I'm loving it."

"Great news." Meredith looked at the table with Jeff's papers scattered about and Tucker working on his math. "I missed the girls this morning. I guess they got off to school okay?"

"They did. Tucker and I took them to Cornerstone and waved good-bye. Didn't we, Tuck?"

"Yes, we did," Tucker stated matter-of-factly and then said, "Elvis is in the building."

Jeff smiled at Tucker and got up and gave Meredith a kiss. "Coffee's on. And since you're up, I'm going to the office."

Jeff stopped on the steps and turned around, "It's supposed to be a beautiful weekend. I think we should go to the lake," Jeff started.

"It's January." Meredith looked at him.

"So, your point is?" Jeff asked.

"It's unseasonably warm this weekend," Tucker said obviously repeating something he heard on the television.

"Yes, unseasonably warm," Jeff repeated. "Only if you're up to it. But I'll row and you can float."

"Unseasonably warm, you say."

Chapter 52

Friday evening by the campfire was chilly. The kids kept piling logs on the fire until it bordered on being a bonfire. The girls discussed sleeping in the car to try and stay warm. Jeff convinced everyone that if they huddled together in the tent, they would be okay and stay warm.

Morning came, and Jeff and Meredith wormed their way out of the pile of kids huddled together. Jeff added logs to the embers from the night, and the fire quickly blazed up. Camping always seemed to center both Jeff and Meredith. Whatever the stresses were, when they were in the woods, it all didn't seem to matter. Leaving civilization behind also meant leaving their worries behind. Meredith turned on the camp stove and started some water boiling for the coffee percolator that they used on camping trips. She sat by the fire and huddled with a blanket trying to capture some warmth from the fire. The sun was rising, and it promised to warm the ground and air.

Jeff brought out his laptop and sat it on his lap. "This would be a great time to go over our finances." Meredith only gave him a look, and he knew they wouldn't be going over finances this morning. Jeff began the speech he had been preparing in his mind. "Meredith I have something I need to say to you."

She raised one eyebrow and looked warily at Jeff as she huddled by the fire. "Okay," she said.

"Meredith, I'm sorry for the hurt I caused you. I was so wrapped up in being a success and making money that I failed to see what was happening to you and Tuck and the girls. I guess I used to think about Tuck as a weak link that I needed to strengthen to make him stronger. I always wanted him to learn to manage so he could be as strong as typical boys. But now I see our life more like a team sport. When I played basketball, I knew the other teammates' weaknesses." Jeff's voice took on a playful tone. "But of course, I didn't have any weaknesses on the court."

Meredith rolled just her eyes and Jeff continued talking.

"Seriously, on the court the team protected each other's weaknesses and drew on each other's strengths. If John, our 6'9" rebounder had to shoot from the three-point line, it was air ball. So he was the inside man. I don't care how much John practiced at the three-point line. It never was his strength. We did have a great three-point shooter, and we set him up whenever we could. I could weave around taller guys and take an inside shot. It's a poor analogy, but the point I hopefully am making is that we know each other's strengths and weaknesses. We have to work like a team, not links in a chain where every link is equally as strong."

"It's a good analogy, and I'm glad you are on my team. I wouldn't . . . I couldn't do this life without you. I have always felt safe with you. You always have a plan." She smiled, and their eyes lingered as they looked at each other. "And I'm sorry for hurting you and lying to you. I never meant for you to get hurt. I was only trying to protect Tucker."

The tent zipper opened, and the kids started filing out heading straight to the campfire. Clare came up to Jeff, and he put his laptop down and she climbed up in his lap and put her head on his shoulder. He wrapped his jacket around her to keep her warm. Tucker and the girls stared into the fire as the sun brightened the campground. Meredith looked at Jeff and said, "So, we are okay?"

"We are more than okay. We are lucky."

Chapter 53

Jeff and Meredith were setting up a double bed in the one of the basement bedrooms. Isabelle popped her head in the door and looked at them. Tucker came in and said, "It's 10:30. It's time to go pick up Aunt Kate." They heard Isabelle whispering to Tucker, "Good job."

Meredith walked through the doorway that Jeff had made between the two basement bedrooms. The walls had lines of joint compound. The first room had windows that brightened the area and the second room was stashed away in the corner. "You did a great job. I picked up some paint samples, and I'll show them to Kate."

Isabelle came in. "When is Aunt Kate going to move in?"

"She is going to the halfway house, first. Then when she is ready — hopefully — we'll have this area ready for Kate if — and that's a big if — she wants to move in here."

"I want her to."

"We'll see what she wants."

Isabelle left and Tucker came in, "It's 10:40. It's time to go pick up Aunt Kate."

"Okay, Isabelle, let's go."

"I'm going to take my shin guards since we are going to the park after, right?"

"Yes, yes, yes."

Isabelle ran upstairs and went outside to put on her shin guards. The mailman drove up, and she went out to get the mail from him.

She came bouncing in the house and announced, "The mailman came. I got the mail."

Meredith took it and said, "Thank you." She stared at the letters in her hand. She looked solemnly at Jeff as she held up two

251

unopened letters, one from the public school district and another from the State Board of Education.

He looked back at her and said as he took the mail from her hand and sat the envelopes in the windowsill, "We are on our way to the park."

Meredith kept her eyes on the mail in the windowsill but said to Jeff. "Yes, we are but —"

"We are on our way to get Kate and go to the park."

Kate was ready. The kids gathered around Kate like she had hit the final shot in a tie game. Hugs were distributed to everyone.

Jeff went into the office to talk to the receptionist. "I need to work out a payment arrangement for the balance on my account.

The reception turned to the computer and worked her way through the accounting program. "The account is paid in full."

"I sure thought I had a balance," Jeff said

"There was a large payment last week from Harper check #4389. Does that sound familiar or maybe it's been posted to the wrong account."

"No, that right. That's Kate's parents." Jeff stepped back and rubbed his hand across his mouth. *They are part of our team*, he thought to himself.

The Bermuda grass was still brown in most places but had a hint of green announcing spring was near. Jeff, Meredith, Kate, Tucker and the girls arrived at the park on a beautiful morning. The kids ran around kicking a soccer ball across the field. Aunt Kate, a natural born athlete, joined them in their game making it more fun. Kate, Tucker, and Clare were on one team, and Myla and Isabelle were on the other.

Jeff sat down by Meredith on the bench to watch the kids play. "Your parents paid off Kate's balance."

Meredith smiled and nodded. "Aren't you curious about what's in the letters from the state and the school?" Meredith asked. "It could fix everything if the hearing is in favor of Amicus."

"Not really." He paused. "Because it doesn't matter. We are going to be okay regardless of what the school district decides. It's not about fixing something that's broken. It's about learning how what we have works." He paused and leaned back and put both arms across the back of the bench. "And what works for us is our decision, not anyone else's. The school may think they get to decide, but they don't. We might decide that fighting the school for his educational placement is what works for us, but maybe it isn't. We are not broken, maybe beat up a little, but not broken. We are going to do something. I don't know what that something is right now, but I do know we are going to make it—all of us." Jeff pumped both fist in the air as if he just completed a race and said, "And we are going to pay off those bills . . . one day and one payment at a time."

Meredith sat on the bench and studied Jeff. "We have just always had a plan," Meredith said looking at Jeff uneasily.

"I know, but plans sometimes don't work out. Look at it this way. It's like when we would go hiking, and it would drive me crazy because you wanted to explore off of the path. You never wanted to follow the map. You always wanted to get off the path and— "

". . . take the road less traveled," Meredith said reciting a line from their favorite poem.

"Exactly," Jeff said pointing at Meredith.

"But when we hiked, it was when we made our own way that we found the most beautiful places. Remember coming out onto the bluff where we could see forever. It was beautiful, and there was no path to the bluff.

"Yeah, it was beautiful," Jeff said looking off in the distance. Then he turned to look at Meredith and scolded. "But it was hard getting up to the bluff, and we didn't make it back on time after your little detour."

"Yeah, but…it was so worth it," Meredith said nodding yes.

"You always do things differently. I guess Tuck is like you in that way. He is definitely different, and he has given us a different direction. It's not bad—just different. It's different than what I thought it would be. But that's okay. Tucker has taught me that. I'm going to find out how this works."

Meredith considered Jeff's words and finally spoke. He has taught me so many things too. I always think about how much the girls have taught him, but he is teaching them too. They are lucky to have each other."

"There's that word again," Jeff said.

"What word?"

"Lucky"

Meredith nodded, acknowledging her understanding of Jeff's reference.

And I have some good news," Jeff said with a wide grin on his face.

" I could use some good news," Meredith said brightly

"Remember John, the landscaper?"

Meredith nodded.

"Well, he just purchased a nursery supply facility and is expanding it." Jeff pulled out a newspaper that he had stuffed in the back pocket of his jeans. It was open to a page with a photo of Jeff and John with a group of smiling people at a Chamber of Commerce ribbon cutting ceremony to celebrate John's purchase and groundbreaking of the new facility. "And guess who is going to be his accountant for all that expansion?"

"You!" Meredith said beaming.

Jeff got up and started dancing.

"What are you doing?" Meredith asked chuckling.

"A dance of joy."

The kids and Kate stopped and looked over at Jeff. Tucker knew exactly what Jeff was doing and began his own dance of joy.

Meredith watched Jeff and remembered why she fell in love with him. She didn't get up and dance. Her arm was still achy, but she smiled at him and in her heart she danced.

Bibliography

"Considerations for Specific Groups." Considerations for Specific
    Groups. Accessed July 8, 2015.

Erhmman, Max. Desiderata. 1927.

Frost, Robert, and Louis Untermeyer. Robert Frost's Poems. New
    York: Washington Square Press, 1971. 223.

Kipling, Rudyard. The Best Fiction of Rudyard Kipling;
    Introduction by John Beecroft. New York: Anchor Books,
    1989.

"The Impact of Childhood Disability: The Parent's Struggle."
    Childhood Disability: A Parent's Struggle. Accessed June
    19, 2015.

"Welcome to Al-Anon Family Groups." Home Slide Show RSS.
    Accessed June 19, 2015. http://www.al-anon.org/.

Dance of Joy

Desiderata

Go placidly amid the noise and haste, and remember what peace
there may be in silence.
As far as possible without surrender be on good terms with all
persons.

Speak your truth quietly and clearly, and listen to others,
even the dull and ignorant; they too have their story.
Avoid loud and aggressive persons, they are vexations to the spirit.

If you compare yourself with others, you may become vain and
bitter;
for always there will be greater and lesser persons than yourself.

Enjoy your achievements as well as your plans.
Keep interested in your career, however, humble;
it is a real possession in the changing fortunes of time.

Exercise caution in your business affairs; for the world is full of
trickery.
But let this not blind you to what virtue there is; many persons
strive for high ideals;
and everywhere life is full of heroism.

Be yourself.
Especially, do not feign affection.
Neither be critical about love; for in the face of all aridity and
disenchantment
it is as perennial as the grass.
Take kindly the counsel of the years,
gracefully surrendering the things of youth.

Nurture strength of spirit to shield you in sudden misfortune.
 But do not distress yourself with imaginings.
Many fears are born of fatigue and loneliness.

Beyond a wholesome discipline, be gentle with yourself.
You are a child of the universe, no less than the trees and the stars;
you have a right to be here.
And whether or not it is clear to you, no doubt the universe is
unfolding as it should.

Therefore be at peace with God, whatever you conceive Him to be,
and whatever your labors and aspirations, in the noisy confusion of
life keep peace with your soul.
With all its sham, drudgery, and broken dreams, it is still a
beautiful world.

 Be careful. Strive to be happy.
© Max Ehrmann 1927

Dance of Joy

Readers,

Thank you for reading my book about acceptance and finding joy.

In the story of Howard, I hope I brought to light some specific thoughts about living in a special needs family.

First, a child with special needs impacts the entire family. Special needs do not occur in isolation. They affect the entire family, and that family becomes a special needs family.

Second, one person can make a difference. If you know someone who has a child with special needs, be that one person. It doesn't take a lot to help. Watching a movie with a special needs kid, taking dinner over, giving the parents a night out, or offering to include the typical kids in your life are all simple ways to bless a special needs family.

Third, special needs families want to attend church and many times can't. The whole family misses out because there is no place in the church for their kid with special needs.

Fourth, all kids—not just kids with special needs— can be challenging, and even our "typical" kids challenge our hopes and dreams for them. Regardless of whether a child has special needs or not, parents have to embrace who their child is as a person. It's in our acceptance of our children and ourselves that we find joy.

Fifth, if you have a special needs child in your family, give yourself the freedom to make a happy life for your family even if that life looks very different than the lives of the people around you.

The stories of Tucker and his family are fictional.

In my heart, this is a story of love and joy. And I hope that came through when you read it, and I hope this story helps special needs families to embrace the freedom to enjoy the uniqueness of their life. It will be an interesting journey.

Find Joy,
Melissa Campbell Rowe

www.melissacampbellrowe.com

A percentage of the sale of this book will go toward programming for adults with physical and mental challenges. Check out www.theartswithgrace.org—a nonprofit in Western Arkansas.

51619018R00143

Made in the USA
Charleston, SC
27 January 2016